The Colors of Blue

By

Lance McCulloch

The Colors of Blue

The Colors of Blue

Chapter 1

Long before their engagement, one of Greg's colleagues asked Sarah if she had any interest in seeing the Hudson Valley, via his small airplane. Greg assured her that his friend was a competent pilot and there was no reason to worry.

Stepping onto the rain-drenched street, Sarah recalled her trepidation, climbing into the single engine plane and finding the windshield at arm's length. The plane was smaller than she had imagined and a little research let her know she would feel every shift, drop, and bump of the ride. However, this anxiety proved to be the worst part of the adventure. Shortly after climbing into the New York sky, she unexpectedly felt safe and found herself consumed by the splendor of the Hudson Valley and the river within. She flew two other times in the small aircraft, each covering more of the valley and both trips as enjoyable as the first.

Greg never understood the beauty of the river, which reached the city as a wide mass with a reputation for carrying a variety of pollutants and other unspeakable items. He felt it just another unremarkable part of the landscape, like many, overlooked by those who made New York home. However, this was not Sarah's Hudson, not since accepting the first invitation and then flying over the Catskills, Adirondack, Shawangunk, and Taconic mountain ranges. The river she knew began in the small streams that cut through the thick white pine and sugar maple forests around Tannersville. It held the water that brought rich green grass to the horse farms around Millbrook and other small towns upstate. Where Greg saw the face of an old man in the brackish waters reaching the city, Sarah recalled the youth of its source.

Since moving in with Greg, one of Sarah's favorite walks took her from their apartment down to the water's edge. On a direct path, it would only take about thirty minutes to reach a place where she could sit and watch the large ships pass. However, Sarah preferred a different course, weaving her way through the concrete and brick maze of the city, choosing streets lined with trees and buildings with a bit more flavor in their architecture.

This morning was black, wet, and cold. Thick clouds toyed with the moon, occasionally allowing its magnificent beams to reflect off the dark, wet streets. Sarah was on the same walk she had taken the last two nights. It was two-thirty in the morning and the city appeared unusually quiet.

"What is it?" she asked herself, as if speaking to a trusted companion. However, as she expected, the reason behind her insomnia did not present itself. Folding her arms, she pulled her coat tight before stepping off the sidewalk and hurrying across the street. Stopping briefly in the dark shadow of an awning, Sarah peered farther down the street. A gust of wind played with the light reflecting off a line of winter bare trees. She took this in, briefly anticipating the beauty of the coming spring. The wind was cold, biting at the exposed skin of her face; it was also refreshing. Again, she weaved through the tightly packed row of cars that were lucky enough to secure the rare real estate lining the city's streets. In the open again, the low growl of an engine caught Sarah just as the headlights illuminated her small frame. She stepped to the side, and a long moment passed as the cab edged by methodically. The driver searched for any sign that he might find a fare. She thought briefly about her sister. "You'll hate the city," Rachael had warned. "It's bare, cold, and dangerous." Despite the warnings, Sarah had come, finding a job she loved and a comfortable, exciting life. Most of all, she had found Greg.

A heavy rain broke from the clouds as the red lights of the cab disappeared into the black morning. The moisture was drenching, sending her against a red brick building for shelter. Glancing toward the sky, the darkness told her the rain would not pass quickly. She was not ready to return to their apartment. Not yet—not when the option was to sit awake and watch the clock march through the morning.

Tucking her head toward her chest, she dashed toward a small pizza-by-the-slice shop two blocks down on Delaney Street. It was open twenty-four hours; at least that is what she remembered. Pressing against the door, she was relieved to feel it open and hear the small bell overhead. Pausing as the door closed, she surveyed the place. The room was long and narrow, faded white linoleum covering every square inch of the floor. Ovens occupied half of the room, separated by a counter that only left enough space for patrons to order. A man behind the counter glanced over his shoulder only long enough for her to understand he was disinterested in her arrival. He returned to whatever had been occupying him this early hour.

To Sarah's right and left were two small, round tables. She was briefly surprised to find a man bundled in the corner at one of the tables. Tattered old gloves, offering no cover for his fingers, wrapped each hand. At his feet lay a heap of belongings, unceremoniously shoved into a black plastic bag. She studied this for a moment before lifting her eyes to his face.

He stared back at her with stunning, large green eyes. The man appeared withered — somewhere in his sixties, she guessed. However, his eyes told a different story. They grabbed her and did not let go until she realized the time that elapsed had surpassed acceptable etiquette. She blinked twice, turned her head, and approached the counter.

"Do you have any hot coffee?" The worker again looked over his shoulder toward Sarah. Motioning with his chin, he directed Sarah toward a half-full pot on his side of the counter. Not expecting to be purchasing anything at this hour, Sarah quickly dug through her coat pockets, finding a wad of six one-dollar bills. "I'll take a cup, please."

Seemingly burdened by the request, the worker brushed off his hands, straightened his white apron, and made his way over to the counter. Spurred into service, he now barked toward the corner: "Hey old man, no freeloading; buy something or get out of here." He returned to the transaction at hand. "Two bucks."

Sarah glanced toward the homeless man. As if he had been waiting for the command, he was already standing and readying to leave.

"Give me another cup, please."

The clerk looked toward the corner, rolling his eyes before turning to fill the second cup. "Four bucks." As he extended his right arm, Sarah quickly tried to make out the tattoo that began at his wrist and extended to the short sleeve of his shirt. The series of Japanese characters was impossible to decipher. She untangled and straightened five dollars, handing him four and stuffing one into the empty tip jar. In turn, he lifted his chin, glancing back toward the homeless man before returning to his corner.

As Sarah approached, the man was lifting the plastic bag from under the table. "Sit down, please." She placed the coffee on the table and watched as he briefly studied the offering.

"Thank you. It's a cold night," he said, glancing toward the counter to make sure there was no problem.

"You're welcome. May I sit down?"

Again, the man studied Sarah's face, curiously digesting everything before shoving a chair out from the table. She wrapped both hands around her warm cup as she landed on the small, wooden chair.

"People are kind to me because of my eyes. Is that why you brought me the coffee?"

"I don't think so, but I did notice your eyes."

He considered this for a moment. "I've seen you before. It's not safe to be walking by the river at night."

Sarah suddenly felt vulnerable. "When?"

"Two nights ago. You were lost, watching the water's black mirror." They both took this in, the old man searching for a question as Sarah quietly sipped her coffee. "Why do you walk at night?"

Sarah set her coffee on the table as she considered the logic of opening up to a homeless stranger. "Something is wrong. So I can't sleep."

"Take a pill. It's not good to be out here so late."

Sarah only smiled, returning to the hot coffee for another drink. He studied her as the rim of his cup sorted its way through the thick, grey tangle of his beard. Taking a long sip, he swallowed, closing his eyes briefly as the fluid warmed his throat. Again, his eyes caught hers, "What's wrong?"

She assessed her companion; he appeared lucid and completely sober. "That's just it, I don't know."

He took another long drag of coffee as his magnificent eyes searched hers. "Yes, I can see that something is not right." This was the first hint of an oddity, she thought. She had expected to find that he was an alcoholic.

Sarah's head tilted with curiosity. "You can see it? What do you mean?"

"Nothing more than that. I just see it."

"Ok." Sarah simply accepted his explanation, knowing that digging into such an answer might challenge her own sanity. Perhaps the time had come to end this ridiculous two dollar therapy session. For the first time, she saw that the man's right thumb was missing. She returned to his eyes, the penetrating green coming from the shadows between his beard and the hood that covered his head. As she studied his face, he seemed to drift within himself. His beautiful eyes glazed over, and he appeared to leave the present for a moment. As quickly as he left, he came back. "Do you still have colors?"

Sarah's chin dropped; she was shocked but certain she had heard him wrong. "Excuse me?"

"You have colors, don't you?"

The question was perfectly clear, and she knew precisely what he was asking. However, there must be some confusion in his question or a twisted meaning in the words. There were people she had told about her colors, when she was young, when the colors were in everything.

Nevertheless, no one had ever guessed, or somehow known of her colors so quickly. "I'm sorry. Colors?"

"Your eyes can't hide your gift." He studied her intently until she blinked. "Are the colors still with you?"

Dazed, Sarah digested the question two minutes before she responded. "I can only see them in children now," she confessed. "But...please, I don't understand. How do you know about them? Do you see...?"

"No. I only know them because of your eyes; I once knew a woman who saw the colors. She died long ago." At this, the man sank back within himself, reflecting on a time long gone. "Her eyes were the same as yours."

He suddenly stood, simultaneously lifting the black plastic bag containing his life. "Where are you going?" Sarah asked instinctively, quickly realizing she did not want to know the answer.

He did not reply, moving toward the door and stepping out into a light drizzle. Sarah followed, the door closing just behind her. "What is your name?" he asked.

"I'm Sarah."

He did not offer his own name. "Time will find your problem, Sarah."

She looked at him curiously, the last few minutes allowing her to forget why she was out on this night. "Yes. I suppose it will." The rain had matted her hair, and now a small stream of water trickled down her cheek. "I need to know about my colors."

"I'm sorry. I can only see that you have them. Until tonight, I have only met one other…the woman I mentioned. I don't have any answers for you." At this, he turned and started into the cold nowhere.

"Wait."

He stopped briefly, looking over his shoulder. "I'm sorry, Sarah. I have nothing for you."

Chapter 2

Easing the door closed behind her, Sarah made her way to the large living room windows overlooking the city.   Leaving the apartment hours ago, she had hoped the walk would clear her head and perhaps even lead to a few hours of restful sleep. Instead, she now peered out over the rain soaked city, confused by a homeless stranger who somehow knew about her colors.

Cracking the bedroom door, Sarah confirmed that Greg was still sleeping; she was happy that her insomnia had not disturbed him. After hanging her coat in the front closet, she made her way to the couch, where she tucked her knees to her chest and pulled a blanket over her damp clothing. Adjusting her vision to the low light, she found the stainless steel clock perched on the mantel; three twenty-five am. She could get by on three hours of sleep, she told herself.

How could he know about the colors? Surprisingly, the problem that took her on the walk this morning was now obscured by the provocative questions raised by the old man. As she berated herself for letting him slip away so easily, she realized that something had suddenly changed; she was tired and ready to fall asleep. His eyes were beautiful; the thought of the old man and her colors put her at ease. Focused, Sarah drifted into a deep sleep and dreams of her childhood.

~~~

Sarah Field lived in a world of colors. She had lived in this place as long as she and those closest to her could remember. Her father first noticed the colors and mentioned them to her mother and even to Sarah.   Most children show some affinity or attraction to the beautiful tones that flood into their understanding but, by the time she was seven, it was clear his little girl had a unique sense of color. He first noticed it because of her stubborn insistence about the color of socks she would wear on Sundays — one of the few variables adorning her knee-length white dress. The decision about which socks she would wear was Sarah's from an early age, just as her sister Rachael had a similar freedom.

The family made it a point to attend church every Sunday — one of many things done together. Her parents were not God-fearing people, but they thought perspective was healthy, so they always attended and listened to the sermon together. For Sarah and Rachael, it was the promise of chocolate chip pancakes after the service that tipped the scales of compliance and made the day special.

Leaving the house in the morning always proved to be a hectic, last-minute dash. The reason for this turmoil was that socks, Sarah's socks, simply took time. Eventually, it was the decision about socks that split the ten-block walk to church. Rachael, who picked her socks from the top of the drawer, would leave with her mother when ready. Sarah and her father would follow when, and only when, the perfect color had been determined.

Most fathers would press along such a trivial decision, even if tears were the result, but Sarah's father was different. He was a thoughtful man and recognized that decisions of color were something more than an opinion for his little girl, so he was tolerant.

Shortly after his wife and daughter would begin the walk to church, Sarah's father moved to the kitchen window with a warm cup of coffee in his hand. There, he patiently waited for the ceremony to begin. Sarah would fly through the back screen door in her bare feet, holding several colored socks in each hand to begin the search. One by one, she lifted the socks, seeking an opinion against the day's sky, slowly twirling in circles as her white dress lifted and her curls swirled around her face. Next, she brought them lower, the color set against the trees in their season. Finally, she held them against the ground so the grass her feet danced on could have a say. She would stop briefly, closing her eyes to feel the color before starting again with a different sock. The decision came when the color told Sarah it was right.

When it first began, the decision of the socks was a nuisance to her parents, adding pressure to meet the church's schedule, but in time, the little ritual became the very moment that Sarah's father waited for each Sunday. Certain it was God who had brought him this gift; he took his time to watch every last turn.

After choosing the socks, Sarah and her father would begin their leisurely walk toward Mass. She found security by tucking her hand inside her father's, her eyes wandering in every direction, looking for the colors of a butterfly.

Pancakes and other delicious things were found three blocks from the church. Sarah's family and other parishioners slowly drifted toward Dot's Diner soon after Mass ended. Routine always seated the Fields family at the same table and in front of the same window. Everyone helped at Dot's, initially to keep things flowing, but over time, it became a pleasant ritual. Customers would help themselves to coffee, wipe their table, and set silverware so that things ran smoothly. This was the way things worked, and it only added to the charm and familiarity of the restaurant.

The menu had not changed in years and only loosely followed the construction of breakfast. The ingredients, size, and combination of most meals could be altered by a request to Dot's son, Jimmy. He had been cooking breakfast for his mother's diner for more than fifteen years and was an integral, if somewhat reluctant, part of the routine.

It wasn't just Sarah's concern about socks that hinted at the importance of color in her world, at least not for her father, though the sock ritual definitely added to the case. Ultimately, it was what she told him during breakfast one rainy Sunday morning. Their family had seated themselves before Sarah excused herself to use the rest room. On her way back, Gretchen Rhess, who had also come from the church, stopped her. She was an elderly lady, and she and her husband had been in the community for longer than most could remember. They were both overly friendly to anyone who might give them a moment of their time, but it was Mrs. Rhess who most savored the conversations with children. She had stopped Sarah just outside the rest room and in full sight of her father. Mrs. Rhess took care to ask silly questions so that Sarah would surely have an opinion. Her father watched but could not hear them talking. In the end, Mrs. Rhess smiled and laughed as Sarah reached up to hug her before returning to the table. Sarah said nothing as she climbed into the same wooden chair she picked each week. Two forks and a knife found her attention for an interesting game of balance over the glass of water. Her father waited before he asked, "How is Mrs. Rhess today?"

Sarah looked at her father for a moment. "She's fine…like a light blue."

A smile crept across his face. "Light blue?"

"Yes…light blue. She's happy; can't you see, Daddy?" Scratching his head, he glanced at his wife. With equal confusion, she shrugged her shoulders and lifted her eyebrows.

"How about Jimmy? What color is he?"

Certain her father was teasing, Sarah lifted her head as she answered. "Daddy, he's gray; you know that."

Sarah's father looked at Jimmy, who, generally, was not an outgoing man. He was working by himself in the kitchen and had the scowl of someone who did not want to be where he was. In fact, more often than that, he was just cranky. Her father thought to himself, *Definitely not light blue.* Then he replied, "Yes, yes, I guess I do…he is gray."

"Of course he is, Daddy." Sarah returned to the same game that had just landed the fork in the water. Her parents exchanged glances and, without saying a word, told each other that their daughter was indeed different from the rest. They smiled and moved on to the business of enjoying breakfast.

Though her father was well aware that colors played a role in Sarah's world, at this breakfast he began to understand the depth of her sense. He also began to realize that her colors influenced how she perceived the world in which she lived.

Sarah's mother was not as certain that the world of colors her husband described actually existed, but by the time junior high school was over, her mother also knew that Sarah felt things differently because of the colors few ever experienced. It was also around this time when Sarah brought the questions about her gift directly to her parents. The satisfaction of understanding she sought never came — her parents, doctors, and medical journals did not offer much more than opinions.

Ultimately, her father decided the best way to approach things. "You've been given a gift...a beautiful, fantastic, and exciting gift, but it's so special that only you can decide what to do with it. Your mother and I only ask that you share it with us whenever you would like. It is a part of you and so wonderful that we would almost feel lost without hearing about your colors."

However, by the time she reached college, the colors had begun to fade until they occupied only a small place somewhere deep within Sarah; it was a safe place for a sense no one else could understand. Buried like this, the colors that filled her childhood rarely made an appearance. The exception was with children. For reasons she never understood, the colors and feelings would flow in at first sight. This brought her an abundance of energy and a satisfaction she felt necessary in a career.

Sarah was persistent and enthusiastic in her pursuit to teach, rewarded with both a certificate and a job in an overcrowded public school in New York. Here, the uniqueness of each child brought her different colors. There was nothing to remembering the names that easily rolled off her tongue at first sight. And, there was something more. As with Gretchen Rhess, her special sense let Sarah understand how each child felt. In all, this was the feeling that they brought her — a warm, gentle, comfort amidst life's pressures.

Soon, most every parent was requesting the first grade class of Ms. Sarah Field. Her class was warm and known to everyone. Children wanted her when they didn't feel good and when they did feel good. Most of all, they wanted her because she wanted them. Sarah had found her passion.

It was halfway through her first year of teaching before the colors were right in her classroom. Reorganized in the most unorganized way, the once systematically aligned desks now made sense. Large circular carpets replaced the open spaces where the stale matrix of desks had previously resided. The children would never sit in the large rocking chair at the front of the room, leaving it an open invitation for their teacher and a book.

During the first summer break, a large claw-foot tub magically appeared in Sarah's classroom. A multitude of colored pillows filled the tub, and a sign-up list eventually was required to manage the demand for it during reading hour. Pictures of flowers, letters, and numbers surrounded the classroom in a common theme — once again, color.

Chapter 3

The smell of fresh coffee pulled Sarah out of sleep, turning her on the couch and searching until her feet found the floor. The best few hours of sleep she had had in days, she considered. She stood, turned toward the kitchen and the wonderful smell of freshly ground coffee. Rounding the corner, she found Greg on the other side of the island, wrapped in a white towel. Admiring his wide, muscular back for a moment, Sarah quietly crept over the travertine floor, wrapping her arms around his waist as she reached him. "Good morning."

"Good morning baby," he replied. Turning, he pulled her in tight. "Did I wake you?

"More like the coffee," she said. Her arms stretched toward the expansive ceiling as she yawned.

"Sorry. You were so far out-I tried to be quiet, but a man needs his coffee."

"I forgive you," she said, thrilled to finally feel rested. Again, she wrapped her arms around him.

"How'd you do?"

"Great. Slept like a baby, as always." Greg was suddenly aware of her damp clothing. His hand found her wet hair. "Did you go out again last night?"

Sarah moved toward the coffee, facing the pot as she replied. "No."

"Yeah, right! It's not safe at night; I told you! Tell me you didn't walk to the river."

"I didn't walk to the river," she quickly replied, turning with a full cup in her hand and a guilty look on her face. Greg rolled his eyes.

"Please, Sarah. If you need to go, wake me up. I'd rather lose a little sleep than have you out there by yourself."

"It was fine; most hardened criminals don't work in the rain."

His eyes narrowed, delivering a stern look. "Funny! Wake me up, okay?"

"Okay. I promise!"

"Good. Now drink your coffee, night owl."

Sarah took a small sip, focused on Greg and debated if she should bring the next subject to their morning. She needed to talk. "I met someone last night."

"You met someone last night." He repeated her words, confirming what he had heard. "Great! Tell me it was a police officer."

"Not so much a policeman as a homeless man."

"Sarah!"

"He was harmless, just sitting in a pizza place and about to be kicked out."

"Let me guess; you bought him dinner?"

Sarah smiled. "A cup of coffee." Greg said nothing, folding his arms and letting out a long, deep breath. She considered exactly how to present the next words, then jumped in. "He knew about my colors."

Time moved slowly as Greg searched for the next words. "You mean you talked to him about that?"

"No! I didn't say anything about them until he asked."

"Sarah…"

She started again before Greg could finish his thought. "I know you don't believe me…but they are real…and somehow he knew I had them. I thought I had heard him wrong too, but he knew."

"I believe…" His face contained a familiar pose of skepticism. "Okay, what did the vagrant say?"

Sarah's expression changed. "Homeless…okay?"

"Yeah. What did the homeless man say?"

"Just that he could see I had colors. He had known someone long ago who had them and he could see them in my eyes."

"Another homeless person?"

"Huh?"

"The person he knew…they were homeless too?"

Sarah hesitated for a moment. "I don't know…I didn't ask." Sarah's tone indicated that bringing the subject to their morning might have been a mistake.

Greg was unsure of exactly where to take the conversation of colors. "I want to hit the gym before work. Interested?"

Sarah realized that the sudden change of topic would benefit their relationship. "No. Not this morning. I need to get in a little early and grade some papers. Can I fix you something?"

"Toast," Greg responded.

"Got it," she replied, moving toward the walk-in pantry.

"Sarah. I'm glad you met the man."

Smiling, Sarah returned to his arms for a hug. "Thanks."

"I gotta get dressed."

"I know," she said, shifting back toward the pantry. Greg's hand swung forward, shocking Sarah as he made contact." "That's a great ass!"

"Go get dressed, you goof."

~~~~~

Sarah's right hand held the knot in his tie as her left tugged at the bottom. "There. That's better," she said, reviewing his jacket before her arms wrapped around his neck. "I love you. Have a good day, okay?"

"I will," he replied, meeting her lips with his own. What's your plan today?"

"Nothing special." She checked the clock. "If I shower fast, I can walk if the rain isn't too bad."

"Take a cab, would ya?" She answered him with a smile. Moving down the hall, Greg had one final question, turning to find her standing in the door. "Are you coming home for lunch today?"

"When was the last time I came home for lunch?"

"Right," Greg replied, lifting a finger toward his fiancé. "Have a good day, baby."

"Love you."

~~~~~

The closet was just off the shower's entrance. It was the size of a small bedroom, uncommon for the precious square footage in New York City. Like the rest of the apartment, it had been gutted and rebuilt to Greg's satisfaction. Each pair of his shoes, coats, slacks, and shirts had their place. He liked organization. Although the remodel had preceded their meeting, Sarah had heard the story told at more than one happy hour. He was proud of the fine work but down right ecstatic over how he had pried it from the group of skilled immigrants for such short money.

After turning on the shower, Sarah undressed in the closet, placing her wet clothes properly into the solid oak retractable hamper. As she reached for a towel in one of the oversized cabinets, something on the floor caught her eye. Buried in the lush carpet, she did not recognize the bobby pin until holding it in her hand. "Unacceptable," she said aloud, considering Greg's response to anything dotting the uninterrupted landscape of his closet floor.

Chapter 4

Jason Holms always sat in the front of the bus because he wanted to be the first into her arms. He bounded down the steps as the door opened, simultaneously straightening his oversized New York Yankees hat and backpack as he hit the ground. He found her immediately.

His was a color of green uniquely distinguishable from hundreds of other such shades. It rushed into Sarah's being in the fraction of time it took to close and open her eyes. It was a green known and felt to be his alone. Not the green of a crayon in a box, nor of paint in a can, but a color unknown to most—one that moved, changed, and flowed with feelings and emotion. She felt the excitement and energy of the young boy before he ever reached her. "Good morning, Ms. Sarah," he said as her arms pulled him in.

"Good morning, Jason. You're feeling good today."

"My frog jumped into the toilet last night."

"Wow! Why would he do something like that?"

"Frogs like water, Ms. Sarah."

"That's true. Frogs do like water. I hope you didn't flush?"

"I didn't. My dad got him out. He wasn't very happy."

"I bet not."

Two teachers, standing a few feet behind, appeared unaware of the little conversation that brought a fleeting smile to the start of Sarah's day. A moment later, the rest of the children reached her, swarming with hugs, feelings, and colors. In recent days, this had become her last sanctuary. She welcomed each of them, making a note about those she would pull aside later to make sure everything was okay. After the greeting, each hurried past to ready for the first bell.

As she had done many times during the last few days, Sarah reached into her pocket and felt for the object. It was tiny, and the pocket around it appeared vast, hiding it only briefly. Finally grasping it between her thumb and forefinger, she rolled the coated metal while considering what it might mean. Could it have fallen during a party? Logic said no; it wouldn't have been in their closet. She again did the math. I cleaned last Wednesday; that's three days before finding it. Is it possible I just missed it? Her stomach knotted as she answered her own question. No, it wasn't there. Three days and we haven't had any guests at least none I knew of, she thought. Nausea accompanied the conclusion. Again, she rolled the object before bringing it from her pocket. As she looked it over, it appeared simple and pretty; then something inlaid in its construction brought a glimmer of purple to her eye. Cheap, tiny, and holding almost no physical weight, it contained an enormous contrast. The bobby pin held the potential of an incredible burden — one that could change her entire life.

Yet, if it were only the pin, it might have easily been dismissed — something curiously discarded or perhaps added to the drawer that contained other such mismatched things but last week, and again this morning, Greg had asked something odd. "Are you coming home for lunch?" Sarah could not remember whether she had ever come home for lunch.

As if pulling herself from the trance of a magician, Sarah shook off the thoughts that had taken her again. She promised herself that the pin would not affect her here. The children were too important.

The last bus pulled up, and the door flung open. The children piled off and headed straight for their favorite teacher. She closed her eyes as they approached, but this time there was nothing but black. Again, Sarah tried, but there was nothing. Feeling the warmth, she angled her head to hide the single tear that rolled down her cheek — a heavy tear that would take her home for lunch today.

Chapter 5

Shortly after Sarah moved in with Greg, a friendly neighbor had shown her the trick to using the service elevator: insert her door key and turn it twice to the left. She arrived at eight minutes past twelve and entered the building through the side entrance, avoiding the door attendant. In the elevator, her eyes fixed on the panel of buttons. Going to their eighth-floor apartment meant all trust was lost; but so too did the fact that she had asked to leave the school and come to this point. Still, she could not help but hedge her trip, pressing the button leading down to the parking garage.

An eerie silence met her as the door opened. The majority of spaces were still full — most cars in the city were used for weekend trips rather than daily transportation. However, Greg's BMW was different. He spent an exorbitant amount of money each month on parking spaces here and at his work just to avoid crowds.

Taking a long gasp of air, she made her way toward the large concrete pillar that would expose his parking space. Each step brought an echo from the cold, hardened structure. You fool. See the open space and return to work, she told herself. Go back, trust, and never doubt again. There is no need to go to the apartment. You will ruin things; the wedding and your life with him will be over. Go back and trust; tell him you doubted him, apologize, and beg him to forgive you. Repeatedly, she tried to convince herself not to doubt, but her legs carried her forward, giving her no option but to look.

Reaching the corner, she leaned her back against the bare pillar and took one final breath. "Trust," she said loud enough for someone to hear. Taking another deep breath, Sarah rounded the corner. Greg's BMW — polished brighter than the first day it was delivered — pointed out of the parking space, as if ready to make a quick escape. Her gaze fixed on the car, Sarah felt her stomach turn, her heart pounding through her thin linen shirt.

~~~~

Stepping onto the eighth floor, the smell of fresh paint and new carpet permeated the air — the results of an effort lobbied for by the owners association since she moved in with Greg two years earlier. A child-like joy had accompanied this same walk the day they had completed the work, a little more than a two weeks ago. However, the walk from the elevator had not been the same since discovering the pin, and now it felt ominous. The end of the hallway was distant, small, and dark.

Turn around and trust him. There's a reason he's home, and he'll explain it tonight over dinner. He's forgotten some papers or has come home sick. *Go back to school,* she told herself. Each step now labored, her legs heavy and the pounding in her chest demanded that she just turn and go. Go and think this over, she reasoned. Nevertheless, the consequence of being wrong yielded to doubt, propelling her body forward until she was standing at their door.

Placing her hand on the knob, she rotated it slowly until the lock caused it to stop. She moved to the side of the door and stood with her back and palms against the wall, telling herself to just think. Her legs felt weak, and she slowly slid down the wall and rested against the new carpet. There's no reason for him to be home, or for me to be here for that matter. If I enter and he's alone, I need to tell him why I'm here; I didn't trust or believe in him. Three heaving breaths exposed the realization that she did not trust her fiancé. Bringing her hands to her face, she covered her eyes. Love can't exist without trust. She wanted to run away and pretend she had never come, never doubted. But she was here, and now doubted him more than ever. There's no way to pretend you have trust. You must open the door and find him alone. Tell him what you've done and ask him to forgive you. Delay the wedding until he can forgive you, she concluded. "Will he?" she whispered.

Standing, Sarah found the keys in the bottom of her purse. Sorting through the ring, she located the long silver key that would more than just open the door. It was now so much more than that—the key to her future.

Sliding the metal into the jagged slot, she suddenly stopped cold. An unmistakable sound came from within the room — a laugh, a woman's laugh. "No," Sarah said aloud, removing the key and returning to her place on the floor. "Shit." Her worst fears were now tangible.

She tried to make sense of it all. There is a good reason he is with someone inside. Some sort of surprise for me, or perhaps something to do with the wedding. Her mind raced, significant and trivial matters taking equal space in her thoughts. Sarah arrived at the inevitable. I can't afford to live in this city by myself, not on a teacher's salary. What will I do? Where could I go? The tangled web of two lives — two that had become one — would not separate easily.

Standing again, Sarah's mind drifted away from the immediate pain, and she scolded herself for being so careless with money and relying on Greg for everything, even friends. Key in hand again, she knew the consequence of walking through the door: the life she had been living and her certainty of the future may end. Then another sound came from the room. This one, too, was unmistakable; this time it was not a joyful laugh, but the passionate resonance from feeling. Sarah's hand stopped suddenly, shaking uncontrollably as she withdrew the key once again. Retracting her arm, she took two steps backward before retreating down the hallway.

Chapter 6

Sarah glanced at the clock on the wall; her last meeting would begin any minute. This had occupied her thoughts since it appeared on her schedule the previous day. This principal had replaced the man who had hired her and rumors had been circulating for weeks that he had a singular purpose; the tax revenue supporting the district had reached a breaking point and cuts had to be made.

Principal Henry Carter was a thick, intimidating presence; he stood just over six feet tall. The formality of his dark suit added to Sarah's anxiety. He entered the room exactly on time. "Good afternoon, Ms. Field." She had hoped he would have called her Sarah; his formality was another sign that things would not end well.

"Good afternoon, Principal Carter," she replied, motioning for him to take the only adult-sized chair in the room. Sarah sat in one of the small student chairs. Both now seated, the contrast in their size was even more exaggerated. She sat with her arms folded and elbows tucked tight against her sides, trying desperately to find some protection.

"I'll need to get right to the point, as you are not the only one I need to speak with today." A long, shuddering breath struggled out of Sarah's lungs. The principal opened a folder containing a number of Sarah's employment documents, his eyes using them as a crutch for the news he would now deliver. "The district has lost substantial funding over the last two years. This has forced us to make some tough decisions, and unfortunately we will be eliminating your class next year."

Sarah knew this meant her job, but it was not her first question. "What will happen with all my kids?"

"Each grade is losing a room, so we will be dividing the count across the remaining classes."

She thought the children had never been just a count. "That will mean over forty children in each class."

He was hard and unwilling to engage in anything more than this task. "Yes, well, we're in better shape than some other districts." He stood, leaving Sarah sitting meekly as his eyes narrowed. "Your contract will be terminated at the end of this school year, in about six weeks. Your final paycheck will be mailed to you."

With his task completed, he headed for the door. Turning back toward Sarah, he felt it necessary to make eye contact. "Look. Ms. Field," he swallowed and took a deep breath. "Sarah. This has not been easy on anyone, especially those losing their jobs. I want you to know that this is not about your performance. If that were our measure, I would not be speaking to you. Although I've not had a chance to get to know you or observe your class, you have many supporters, both parents and administrators. I'm sorry."

Sarah had bent forward in her small chair, trying to ease the gnawing in her stomach. Looking up with glassy green eyes, she nodded. "Thank you."

Henry Carter took another deep breath, looking back at the folded figure in the chair. It was easier when they were angry.

Sarah sat alone and in thought for the next hour, her eyes looking forward but focused on nothing. What devastated her had little to do with money, but that is what would take her from the children. Months ago, when life with Greg felt certain, she would have reacted to this news by simply asking to volunteer at the school. However, now alone, she struggled to make the rent on her small apartment. Her paycheck, once absorbed into an account flooded by Greg's income, had become a necessity.

There are always problems with teaching; some sort of love is required to address the inadequate pay, facilities, and periodic encounters with an impossible parent. Sarah always tolerated these, knowing the reward bore so much fruit. Nevertheless, it was impossible to ignore the economic pressure that now tugged at every part of her life. Her home had undergone a radical transformation; she had accepted a cramped apartment, complete with a built-in roommate, as one price for remaining in the city. The periodic side jobs would be important even if she somehow landed another position. As she sat, she considered all this, wondering if the time had come to leave the city, or, perhaps, finally yield to the reality and let the children go. This, of course, would mean letting her colors go, too.

Chapter 7

Sarah's job would officially end in two weeks, but even that did not relieve her of the more potent headaches of teaching. The parents of her most troubled student had decided to check a box that they felt qualified them as good parents, finally showing up for their first conference with Sarah. A frustrating hour let Sarah know there were clear problems at home, yet the parents had no idea why their little angel was struggling. She welcomed the long walk home.

With the end looming, Sarah considered the next two weeks. First grade classrooms have a way of collecting things; hers was exceptional only in that it contained more than most. She wondered what she would do with it all. A mild spring had delivered the perfect evening for her walk. An erratic yet comfortable breeze played with her hair as she weaved her way home. Normally, the sight of flowering trees would have brought Sarah great joy; but today, the thought of leaving the school and the children consumed her.

On her front step, she unlocked the box and removed a short stack of mail. She was surprised by a small pink envelope in the mix. It was not completely square, slightly longer than it was tall, and chosen for its look rather than the capacity necessary for the message within. Fancy designs pressed into each edge told the reader that the contents were both special and important. The address informed Sarah that, whatever was inside, it concerned the wedding of her only sister.

She hurriedly opened it as she climbed the stairs, feeling the excitement of the wedding that would not take place for months. A delicate paper, reserved to hold all things precious, wrapped a perfectly cut white card. The message was simple and intended to provoke interest, speculation, and, eventually phone calls to the sender:

Ms. Rachael Field & Mr. Andrew Strickland respectfully request your presence during the week of July 13 to celebrate their forthcoming union.

They ask that you make this week available for travel and time away from work to join them in the valley of the Tres Piedras Ranch in southwestern Colorado. This is an intimate setting where everyone will get to know each other under the backdrop of the spectacular San Juan Mountains. The days will be as active or as lazy as you want, but get ready for the nights.

Your tickets will arrive soon.

We are a phone call away.

Thank you, and go Wildcats!

Sarah recognized the Wildcats reference as Andrew's touch, which both lightened the message and demonstrated his loyalty to the often-maligned sports teams of Northwestern University, from which generations of his family had graduated.

Two sheets included in the letter held several color pictures. The first contained a beautiful river with its clear waters rushing past an old lodge, the sun shimmering off the surface. Large pine trees grew along the shore, casting their long afternoon shadows onto the water. The next picture showed the inside of the lodge, capturing the magnificent beams that were the backbone of the structure. A small fire in the stone fireplace, along with two filled wine glasses, beckoned everyone to come and relax. The third and forth pictures were meant to show all of the things possible. The first, dedicated to fly-fishing and boasting of wild trout in the five miles of untouched waters, caught Sarah's interest. The caption informed the reader that the river continued another twenty miles before it split into the headwaters. Presented as a simple fact, the five miles of river alone could occupy the best angler for more than a week. Sliced into quadrants, the final picture showed three people in inner tubes, hikers, men on horseback, and others riding mountain bikes. The pictures and descriptions created more questions, returning Sarah to the itinerary. She found the destination was Durango, Colorado — at least that was the closest airport.

Rachael and Andrew's phone had started ringing the previous day when their friends began opening identical pink envelopes. Rachael answered Sarah's call, the fourth of the day, fifteen minutes after opening the envelope. "This is Rachael."

"Rachael, this is Sarah ... yeah ... a funny little envelope came in the mail today."

Rachael intended to enjoy every call. "Really? What did it have to say?"

"Well, it was strange, really. It asked me to set aside some of my extremely valuable time." Rachael tempered her laugh, knowing the normal summer flexibility that teachers enjoyed also carried an edge because of the job loss.

"Okay, are you serious?" Sarah continued.

"Heck, yeah, Sarah. What do you think?"

"Average," she replied.

"Average?"

"Yeah. I mean, it seems a bit underdone. Don't you think, Rachael?" They both laughed, enjoying each other's excitement.

"Where's Durango?"

"The best I can tell you is that it's near where Utah, New Mexico, Arizona, and Colorado meet. It sounds like the Wild West, right?"

"Have you been there?"

"No. This will be a first for me too. Andrew and his dad have taken trips there skiing and fishing, but I've never been along. They both think it's one of the greatest places in the world, and Ted's standards are pretty high."

"The invitation really made my day. I'm so excited. I know this is about you guys, but man do I need a trip like this! Great call on Colorado."

"This trip is for all of us! That's why it's going to be so much fun."

A moment of silence filled the line. Both girls knew what the other was thinking. Sarah spoke first, "Mom and Dad would have loved it."

"I know. It's the one huge void in all of this. It really sucks."

"They'd be proud of you, Rachael."

"Both of us, sis," Rachael responded.

Sarah heard a beep on Rachael's phone, and her voice briefly skipped.

"Sarah, Andrew is calling in, and I need to speak with him."

"No problem. Go. I'll call you back later."

"Thanks, Sarah. Love you."

Chapter 8

As she approached her apartment, Sarah quickly recognized the black BMW parked on the street. Only he had the persistence to find a parking place here, she thought. She saw Greg step out and straighten his suit, brushing off his jacket and briefly playing with the lowest button of his coat.

Instinct told her to be defiant, to keep moving until she reached the cover of her home. However, the draw of intimacy and seeming rejection was oddly powerful. Her heart pounding, she still wanted something from him.

"How are you, Sarah?"

"I'm fine." Her eyes narrowed. "Why are you here?"

He had hoped for a warmer welcome. "I was in the neighborhood and thought I'd stop and say hello."

Friday evenings had always started with several hours in a bar near the office. The fraternity of money-chasing brothers would be missing its leader. Something was up.

"So this is the apartment?"

Glancing toward the upstairs window, Sarah crossed her arms and shifted her weight onto one leg. "This is it."

"Want to invite me up?"

That's not going to happen, she thought. The tiny space, a roommate, and the other contrasts to the flat they had shared together were too much ammunition for him. "Not today," she said.

Greg's chest heaved and his breath exited through his nostrils; he was irritated that she was so stubborn. "How about dinner, then?"

"Shouldn't you be planning something with *her* tonight?"

"I've told you," his eyes rolled toward the sky before catching himself and trying a softer approach. "That's been over for a while."

"Why are you here, Greg?"

"You haven't been returning my calls," he blurted. "I'm trying. I just want to sit down and talk things over with you."

"Did you want to talk things over when you were with her in our bed?"

His temper was quick. "Okay, I fucked up! It was a mistake. How many times do I need to tell you that?" He drew a deep breath, slowly releasing it as he looked up the street. "Listen, I heard you were fired. Wouldn't it make more sense to move back in? I mean, it won't be easy."

He was right, and they both knew it. Sarah's frugal nature had evaporated in the wake of the excesses Greg brought to their relationship. Now she was reinventing her life, but the departure had meant a down payment on the apartment and other unanticipated expenses. There was no room before she lost her job. "Greg, that's not your business." She took a deep breath and continued. "And another thing: I didn't live with you to save rent. I lived with you because…"

"Exactly. You loved me. That can't just go away, Sarah."

Sarah wanted to run away, to hide behind her apartment door and fall on her bed in a heap of tears. She felt the emotion in her throat as she turned toward Greg and weakly pounded both fists on his chest. "Why?" she asked as the tears rolled down her face.

"I'm so sorry, baby. I screwed up!"

"No," she replied suddenly, pushing away and wiping her face with the cuff of her shirt.

In turn, Greg recoiled, unsure of his next action but careful with his persistence. He reached into his coat pocket and extracted a familiar pink envelope for Sarah to see. "We'll be together soon. Can we talk about everything then?"

His question was lost in Sarah's surprise. "Why do you have that?"

"Didn't you know I was invited?" The dazed look on her face quickly answered his question. Considering this, he tapped the envelope with the palm of his hand. "Let's talk in Colorado." He continued tapping the envelope as the next thought arrived. "Look, if you need anything, just let me know, okay?"

The combination of his subdued demeanor and Sarah's instinct drew the last words out of her mouth before she could pull them back. "Thank you."

~~~~~

In her apartment, Sarah pulled the light blue shoebox from the top shelf in her closet. After the accident, this had begun collecting her family's memories and other things she considered precious. She would open the box and fumble through the contents on slow days, or like now, when loneliness tugged at her memories. She removed the invitation and carefully opened it before reading it once again. Why hadn't I thought that he might be invited? Sarah scolded herself; I should have considered his ties to Andrew's father. This would be a difficult situation for Rachael, she also realized.

Sarah was thankful she was alone. To make ends meet, she had a roommate she had only known since answering the advertisement for the apartment. Taking a seat on an old couch in the front room, Sarah considered calling Rachael. The fact Rachael did not tell her about Greg meant she was uncomfortable. Sarah hated the thought of her problems affecting Rachael; she would be careful with the subject and the mood.

~~~~~~~~

Both students and teachers always anticipate the end of any school year. Now, Sarah had conflicting feelings as she left her class for the final time. During the walk home, Sarah's phone rang. Stopping, she moved to the edge of the sidewalk to take the call. "Hey, Rachael."

"Last day, right?"

"Bingo. Just on my way home as we speak."

Rachael knew Sarah would be thinking of the kids. "How are you doing?"

"Conflicted, I guess. I'm happy to have a break, but it's bittersweet, you know."

"I figured; that's why I'm calling. They'll be okay, Sarah, and there will be another class."

"I know, but I'll miss each one of them."

"The good news is that Colorado is just around the corner. We're going to have a blast!"

"Oh, don't think that's slipped my mind," Sarah replied as her mood lifted.

"I couldn't imagine it had. While we are on the subject, there is one thing you need to know. Sorry that I'm bringing this up with you now, but I wasn't exactly sure how to tell you." During the long moment of silence that followed, Sarah felt her sister's anxiety. "Greg's been invited to come to Colorado."

Sarah swallowed. She had anticipated this conversation, even practiced her reply, yet was not quite ready when it finally arrived. The words caught in her throat, "That's not a problem, Rachael."

"I'm sorry. Is it okay?"

"Of course, Rachael. It's perfectly fine." Sarah had practiced the tone of her answer too, wanting nothing to affect the trip.

"It was just one of those things, you know, being a friend of Andrew's family too, and we started planning way back…" She considered everything Sarah had gone through, "Of course that was before, well…before he did his thing…"

"Please don't worry about it, sis."

"I know. He's just such an asshole, and I don't want him to ruin your trip. The good news is that he's coming a couple days after the rest of us."

"Rachael, please don't give it a second thought. We're in a good place, and it'll be no big deal. Besides, it looks like a big place. If there's a problem, I'll just run away into the woods."

"You're funny." Rachael became more serious. "Thanks for understanding. We had more than one heated discussion on the topic with Andrew's dad, Ted. He pretty much insisted on it and pointed out that he was paying for the trip."

"Don't give it a second thought." A moment later, the call ended. Sarah did not immediately resume her course home. Instead, she stood and watched the movement of cars and people around her, wondering how she would handle Greg. She wanted to hide from him, pound her fists in anger, and then, too, wrap her arms around him and cry. The impossible array of emotions needed to be resolved.

Chapter 9

The days leading up to the week of July 13 moved considerably slower as Sarah anticipated the trip. Warmer weather naturally brought the excitement of the outdoors, even in the city. However, the knowledge of spending a week with her sister in Colorado made the wait almost painful. Sarah occupied herself with the necessity of searching for a teaching opportunity and finding some part-time work, neither of which were proving very fruitful.

~~~~~

At the top of the escalator in the Denver airport, Sarah punched R-A-C into her cell phone. The name Rachael Field appeared just before she pushed Send. "Hey, you in?" Rachael answered. Sarah recognized the slightly intoxicated voice of her sister.

"Just arrived. Sounds as if you've been here for a while."

"We're in a bar between …" Sarah could tell her sister was now moving into the jet way. "Between gates 61 and 63."

"Okay, I'll be there in a minute." She hung up, swallowed twice, and headed for her first drink of the trip.

The scene in the bar was predictable: members of the wedding party shoehorned into a rear corner while a waitress worked feverishly to deliver drinks to the shifting crowd. Rachael and Andrew had staged themselves central to the others. Those who had arrived first had greased up on shots of tequila and toasted each new arrival.

Rachael spotted her sister turning the corner. "Sarah!" she shouted, making her way out to meet her. They hugged and exchanged a few words. Sarah was ushered back to the exuberant group. Her entrance brought introductions to several people she recognized and others she had never met before. Andrew stepped forward and delivered a generous hug. "Thanks for coming," he whispered into her ear. Rachael's fiancé stood six feet tall and carried a set of broad shoulders, a trait not understandable by looking at either of his parents. He wrapped his arms around her, and Sarah disappeared briefly as she sank into his chest. It was a comfortable and much needed welcome.

"Are you kidding me? Thanks for asking," she responded. The group appeared to be a good mix of personalities, all from the same collection of young professionals. Looking around, Sarah guessed most to be in their late twenties. The waitress, whose slow afternoon had suddenly turned into a hair-pulling scramble, delivered Sarah's Corona minutes after her arrival. The small airport bar in Denver hosted the week's kick-off.

Settling in, Sarah noticed Kelly Rogers and offered a friendly smile over the noise. In return, Kelly lifted her beer and other arm in unison. "Yes!" she shouted. Of Rachael's friends, Sarah had looked forward to seeing Kelly the most. This had less to do with any commonalities they shared, but rather that they had spent some quality time together visiting

Rachael in college and a subsequent girls' trip to Fire Island. That fall, Kelly had spent Thanksgiving with them at their parents' house.

Moments after Sarah's arrival, everyone had folded back into conversation. Andrew and his father, Ted, carried the undivided attention of the men as they described the ranch. It was clear that much of the interest in Tres Piedras had to do with fishing. Sarah watched this interaction as she sipped her beer. Ted was about two inches shorter than his son, thinly built, and by no measure a large man. He wore a perfectly hemmed and wrinkle-free pair of tan pants. A loud but neat button-down pink shirt helped him to stand out. A full head of white hair framed his orange tinted, tan face. Sarah guessed the pink shirt was about as close to "letting go" as Ted ever allowed.

Nancy, Ted's wife, easily blended into the group of women and seemed perfectly at home despite her age difference. She was also dressed beyond the T-shirts, flip-flops, and vacation shorts worn by many of the others. Unlike her husband, it did not appear that she was reaching for anything. Like the men, the girls were also excited, making plans for hiking and just sitting in the sun to catch up. They all talked, laughed, drank, and just anticipated the next hour.

As the group moved to the gate for the last leg of their flight, Ted did not flinch at picking up the tab for the overpriced drinks. Ted Strickland had been showing off his money for so long that Andrew's friends almost forgot to thank him. He liked people to know he had money and took lavish trips, put on big dinners, and took advantage of other occasions where he could pick up a large bill to the amazement of others. This outing was no exception; the guests would not spend a dime on travel or little else for the entire week.

At the gate, they entered a long hallway leading to a set of stairs. The last door opened up and they were outside on the concrete. A walkway defined by painted lines directed them to a small plane. Kelly caught up to Sarah as she was admiring the beautiful blue painting of the Colorado sky. "Hey, Sarah. How are you?"

"Great, Kelly. Nice to see you again. How have you been?"

"Who cares? We have this in front of us." Her arms opened as if grasping some tangible part of the world.

"Yeah. Who cares?" Sarah replied as her smile grew. It was not hard to share Kelly's enthusiasm.

"I have some news," Kelly added.

"Do tell. Wait. Don't tell me you're engaged, too?"

"Hell no! Nothing like that. I'm moving to New York."

"No way. Really?" Sarah's face brightened. When?"

"Soon. After we get back and I work a few things out. I've been looking for jobs for a few months and think I have something. It will finally get me out of Indianapolis. God, I'm ready!"

"Wow, that's great. Let me know how I can help."

"Will do," Kelly responded as they reached the retractable stairs leading into the small airplane. Sarah briefly thought about waiting at the bottom; it would be a comedy show watching this group navigate the narrow steps and low entrance.

The wedding party occupied the entire cabin, allowing conversations started in the bar to continue, only briefly interrupted. Mild turbulence began bouncing the plane as they reached the Rocky Mountains, but it bothered no one today; drinks were flowing again shortly after reaching altitude. The flight attendant would feel more like a waiter over the next hour.

Sarah had been west, to California, on two occasions in her life but always at an altitude and speed where she could not appreciate the landscape. Their small plane flew southwest from Denver, cutting diagonally across the state. Mountains, trees, and valleys took over as Denver fell behind. Sarah could not pull herself away from the window and the spectacular wilderness below, her eyes finding their way in, around, and out of one deep valley before dropping into the next. In the background, conversations were taking place throughout the cabin, but Colorado's scenery was increasingly compelling and difficult to ignore.

Rachael made her way down the aisle, relying on the top of each seat to straighten out the last two hours in the bar. She gingerly lowered herself into the seat beside Sarah. "Hey, sis."

"Howdy, Rachael. How are the margs treating you?"

"Pretty damn good. I've never been this relaxed flying before."

"It looks that way."

Rachael leaned in close. "Sorry about the whole Greg thing. Ted's got a man-crush on him and insisted he be invited."

Sarah laughed. "It's no big deal. I figured there would be a little pressure there anyway. I'm just excited to spend the week with you and Andrew. Thanks again for the invite."

A break in conversation caused Sarah to study her sister's face. Rachael was about to be sick or working on exactly how to ask something. "Can I ask you something?" she finally said.

Sarah was relieved. "Go for it."

"How are you doing after the whole breakup? I mean…I know, I know, but…now that we're not on the phone…"

Even being intoxicated, Rachael would not swallow the best spin on Sarah's obvious problems. Recognizing this, Sarah tried an honest delivery, "I'm getting by. Losing my job did put a cramp on my style, but all my bills are current."

"I'm sorry. I know that must suck. I can't promise you when, but things will get better." Rachael rubbed the back of Sarah's hand. "I was actually referring to Greg. I mean..." She searched for the right words. "How are you feeling about him?"

"I don't know. I should hate him, right?

"Yes! You should hate him." Rachael's cheek settled on the side of her seat, her eyes glaring at Sarah as the alcohol dug in. "Do you know who he was with?"

Sarah met her sister's eyes. "The woman?"

"Yes. Do you know her?"

"No. I never asked. Why would I?"

"I don't know. Maybe to kick her ass?"

For a moment, Sarah appeared astonished, breaking into laughter seconds later. "I would have opened up a can of whoop-ass on her." The thought of Sarah fighting with anyone joined the two sisters in laughter.

Settling, Rachael's message was more serious, "Ah, well, don't beat yourself up, Sarah. He's the one who fucked up!"

"I wish my mind could be logical about it. It's easy to feel like the ugly duckling. I never thought it would be such a blow to my confidence."

"That's a fragile thing," Rachael observed. The alcohol created a pause. "But it will come back. It will, but some time needs to pass."

"He wants to talk this week."

Rachael shifted in her seat, reaching out to grab Sarah's arm. "You wouldn't give him another chance, would you?" Sarah looked at Rachael's hand on her arm but said nothing. "Sarah, you can't … not after what he did."

"I'm not planning anything. I've just given it a lot of thought and wonder if I have been completely fair."

The four salted sedatives, consumed in the Denver airport, were pushing Rachael's temper. "I don't want to come across wrong," she searched for words, "but what did you ever see in him?"

"I guess it's natural to ask that question after finding out what he did. I certainly don't want to sound as if I'm defending him…but he obviously must have some good in him." The plane suddenly bounced and Sarah stopped for a moment. As the engines regained their monotonous hum, she continued, "God knows, I've wasted some quality time thinking about this. Look, it comes down to this: Greg is not a bad person. I've seen him be as loving, caring, and thoughtful as any man, but he has one horrible characteristic: he's selfish. Over time, that is what has crept to the surface and is the root of everything that has happened. When there is something he wants, it benefits from all that is good in him. The opposite is true, too; when it doesn't serve him, he is hard to tolerate."

"Dad thought you were with him because of your colors…as if they had failed you or you stopped trusting them."

"Rachael. I don't like thinking that Mom or Dad weren't happy with me."

"Sarah, no! I didn't mean it that way. Look at me," Rachael implored. Sarah turned toward her sister, who now sat alert. "Do you remember playing soccer when we were little…how the other kids would be moving up and down the field chasing the ball? You would just sit down in the middle of them, transfixed by the dandelions."

Sarah smiled. "The prettiest of all weeds."

"All of the other parents thought there was something wrong, but Dad knew it was your colors. He loved your colors. When they faded away…when you stopped talking about them, I think he worried. That's all it was with Greg; he was always searching for anything that might take you away from yourself."

Sarah took a deep breath, shifting away from Rachael toward the front of the plane. "I miss them."

"Me too," Rachael replied after a deep breath. Both were quiet for the next several minutes, the other conversations in the background blending into the engine's sedative hum. "Do you still have the shoe box?"

"Of course."

"Did you put our invitation to the Tres Piedras in it?"

"Yes. And everything else that's special to me," Sarah said, taking Rachael's hand and squeezing it tightly.

The plane began its descent just ahead of the pilot announcing they would be on the ground in about ten minutes. Both girls knew the conversation was finished and watched in silence as the ground drew closer. There was not much to the landing; it was a small airport without a control tower or much other traffic. Minutes later, they turned off the only runway toward a small, single-level building.

The town of Durango never came into view from the air. It was twenty minutes northwest of the airport and tucked into the bowl of surrounding mountains. When they stepped out, Sarah noticed the air felt warm and noticeably drier than in New York. A slight breeze came out of the south and teased her hair as she walked toward the terminal.

The excitement of the group lifted again as they congregated and waited for their bags to arrive. They were close now and all could feel it. Kelly took the opportunity to move nearer to Sarah. "I'm sorry about you and Greg. If there's anything I can do..." Sarah turned and offered only a crooked smile. "I heard he'll be here in a couple days." Sarah was not sure how to respond and did not want to begin a conversation on the subject.

"Thanks." She spotted her bag and a way out of an uncomfortable situation.

Ted had arranged for a string of SUVs to take them from the airport to the ranch. Bags located, they all piled into the closest available car without particular arrangement. Everyone was upbeat and anticipating a week without care.

Sarah found herself in the backseat of the lead vehicle next to Andrew's mother. Ted, sitting in the front passenger seat, would guide the caravan to its destination. The driver was in his fifties, his ponytail containing a significant amount of gray hair. He was a pleasant host, chatting with Ted about Durango as they drove. According to him, the weather patterns coming up from the monsoons in Mexico had begun early this year; the afternoon rains were hit or miss but welcomed by this year's dry earth.

Knowing Nancy and Ted had paid for the entire trip, Sarah had been looking for an opportunity to express her thanks. "Thank you so much for all you've done to make this possible. I've been looking forward to it since the invitation arrived," she offered to Nancy.

"You're welcome, honey. We're so glad that you could make it. I have to say, I'm excited to get there."

"Have you been before?"

"No. Ted and Andrew came on a couple father–son trips, but I've never made it. I've heard enough about it to think it's my second home, though." Nancy shot Sarah a smile before continuing. "They absolutely love it, and I can't wait to finally see the place myself."

Sarah thought for a moment before her next question. "What are you anticipating the most?"

"Just relaxing. Letting the boys go fishing so they will get it out of their systems." They both laughed before Nancy answered more seriously. "I really am looking forward to getting to know everyone better. I've met most of Andrew's friends but don't know many of Rachael's. Well...look at this...I'm sitting next to her beautiful sister, who'll be in the family too, and I hardly know you. So that's what will be so good for me, Sarah." Nancy grew on Sarah quickly—she was genuine and easy to talk with. "This is not an easy time for you and Rachael; parents are supposed to be part of things like this. When I heard about the accident, I was so thankful that the two of you made it. It's impossible to replace your parents...and I don't mean to sound that way; Rachael knows she can come to me for anything. I'd be very happy if you felt that way too."

"Mrs. Strickland..."

"Nancy.always! Please."

"That's very kind of you. It's been almost two years since they passed. However, you're right, times when they should be around are not easy. I know Rachael feels a great deal of comfort from you and Ted."

Nancy rubbed the back of Sarah's hand, feeling the mood demanded a change of subject. "Do you have any particular interest at the ranch?"

"It's a long list," Sarah said, pausing a second before continuing. "I also want to learn about everyone. I'm a bit removed from the people who are important in my sister's life, so I look forward to the same thing you mentioned." She thought for a moment. "It's silly, but the thought of just wading shoeless in the river strikes me as so much fun."

"That's not crazy at all, honey. Let's have fun," Nancy added as she patted Sarah's knee. Sarah smiled at the little bond they had just formed.

Near the airport, the landscape was flat and defined by small farms and fields of hay. A small school made of weathered red brick sat between two farms. Tall weeds growing in the cracks of the asphalt told Sarah's trained eye that school was out for the summer. Horses and cows looked for shade in their fenced pasture, their tails working hard trying to interrupt the bothersome flies.

Sarah now appreciated the full size and beauty of the mountains that had looked so distant from the airport. Sporadic pine trees had become full forests thirty minutes into their drive. The road could no longer twist and turn in an effort to find the flattest ground and instead rolled up and down or simply cut its way through unavoidable terrain. Wide edges of the road had been cleared away to catch the rocks that periodically escaped down the encroaching mountain.

In an area no more distinct than any other on the car ride, Ted tired of his conversation with the driver and turned back to Sarah. "How are you and Greg doing?"

Sarah knew the question would come on this trip; even predicting that Ted's association with Greg's father would make him the likely source. However, this surprised her — first Kelly, and now Ted bringing it to her doorstep much earlier than she had anticipated. "He's fine, Ted." She used Ted's name to stiffen her response without appearing rude, making sure her answer was short and vague. She was sure he had heard that they were no longer together and the engagement was over. Nevertheless, Ted would pry, feeling his association with Greg's father, his business partner, made it his right.

Ted knew that Sarah would be reluctant to talk about Greg in the car. He decided to press forward anyway. "He's coming here a couple days late, you know? Too bad he couldn't come with us today, but business comes first. People rely on him; I can appreciate that." Ted wanted to make sure his point was very clear. "He's a winner." His endorsement of Greg was almost too much for Sarah.

She chose to answer briefly again, attempting to pull back on a topic that was trying to spread its roots. "I did hear he was coming."

Their car slowed, its blinker now signaling the coming departure from the pavement. The anticipation of the ranch moved Ted off the subject. Nancy exchanged a glance with Sarah, without words apologizing for the persistence of the "loving ass" she called her husband.

Sarah replied quietly, "Don't worry about it."

Sarah and Nancy's curiosity about the ranch brought their two heads close together as both struggled for a view through the front windshield. The scene was confusing at first, appearing as if the road dipped and disappeared into the side of a mountain. Even more than that, it looked as if there was no place for the car to go except directly into a rugged canyon with impossibly steep walls. Ted was aware of this too. "It looks like there's nothing here, right?"

Nancy and Sarah answered at the same time. "Yes. Where are we going?"

Ted enjoyed knowing the answer. "Just wait."

The driver, who had remained silent for several minutes, came to life. "It plays with your eyes, doesn't it? I have been here before but have never gotten used to it."

The road continued for a third of a mile until the river paralleled its path. The first sight of the clear water brought a glimpse into the exquisite colors and shapes of the different stones that lined the bottom. However, the enjoyment lasted only a moment; as the wheels began climbing along the side of a solid rock wall, just above the river, everyone's nerves engaged. The road, carved out of the solid stone slope, was only slightly wider than the vehicles. To the right, the river appeared unobstructed and right below them, with no margin beyond the car door. It was nerve-racking, but safer than the view suggested because the road tapered slightly toward the wall.

Nevertheless, the drivers were cautious, the vehicles moving slowly and safely.

The caravan proceeded around the mountain until the wall moved away from the river; the road came off the solid rock and back onto the hard ground. Tires had pressed down the vegetation to define the road, leaving tall, wild grass growing in the center and along each side. Further, two old logs were implanted vertically in the earth on each side of the road with a third connecting horizontally across their tops. In the center of this pine beam, a message greeted the guests:

THE TRES PIEDRAS RANCH

To the right, a large field flattened out from the mountain; the river now cut across the eastern valley. Three distinctive large boulders sat in the middle. On top of each of these, someone had stacked piles of increasingly smaller rocks. Sarah was considering this effort when Ted broke the silence. "Was I right?"

Nancy responded. "It's amazing — even your description didn't do it justice."

The previous night's rain still held the dust to the road. Soon, every window opened and the smells of pine and summer grass filled the cars. The caravan continued up the road, passing a small log cabin. The once-perfect squares of the surrounding fence now hung rusted and distorted by the pressure of time. Just inside the fence was an old picnic table that occupied more than its fair share of the front lawn. Along the fence and around the table's legs, long grass escaped the yard's otherwise adequate maintenance. Shade from an old cottonwood tree cooled the yard, creating a lazy spot for an afternoon lunch.

Further down, a canopy of trees, systematically planted years ago, lined both sides of the lane. These escorted the guests to the front steps of the lodge. Just before the engines shut off, three men came out to greet their group.

The opening of doors exposed a new energy, built by everything that entered the passengers' sights and smells since turning off the main road. Sarah drifted a few feet into an open field and turned slowly with her eyes pinned to the top of the valley, her palms brushing the long grass that now surrounded her. She observed how the field slowly transitioned into a forest as it climbed away from the river. Then, up the mountain further, it became too steep for the forests so that only a few trees had found places to take hold.

Near the top of the mountain were massive cliffs. The rain and snowmelt had leached out the minerals, leaving black stains against the white exterior of the rock. Large slides had been set loose periodically for a run to the valley floor, leaving long swaths cut through the trees.

Everyone was taking in the beauty of Tres Piedras, seemingly in awe about their home for the next week. Some of the guests were intrigued by the river, some the mountains, and still others by the beautiful construction of the lodge.

"Welcome to Tres Piedras," said the oldest of the three men that greeted them. The guests all turned toward his gentle face, etched by time and experience. Tilting the brim of his cowboy hat up as they turned, the energy in his eyes pleasantly greeted the guests. "I'm Huff, and I will be your host during your stay at the ranch."

Ted stepped forward and introduced himself, reminding Huff about their conversations leading up to this moment. They had met during his previous trips with Andrew. Huff continued. "Well, this is the Tres Piedras Ranch. Everything you see is part of the ranch. The land stretches for several miles upriver, and beyond that, we're surrounded by public lands. So go anywhere you'd like — just don't get lost." Everyone laughed, but Huff's message was somewhat serious.

As he spoke, Sarah noticed their host's weight shift several times to take the pressure off his right leg. Almost immediately, he made everyone feel comfortable, allowing each to consider the possibilities rather than the restrictions of their plans. "This is a large group for the ranch, so it should be quite a time. Inside the lodge, you will find some papers that have room assignments. I understand it was the groom, Andrew, who worked these out, so talk to him about any complaints you might have."

To this, Andrew bowed and raised his hand. "Ah, now I remember you from your last trip," Huff added. Andrew stepped forward from the back and shook hands with Huff. "How are you, Huff?"

"Well, I'm just fine, but my life has been slower than yours, I see." Huff picked out his fiancée standing next to him. "So you're Rachael, then?"

"Yes. Hi, Huff." She held her ground, waving with one hand.

"You'll test the lodge capacity, but I think everyone will fit. And as I said, any complaints should go to Andrew."

"Thanks, Huff," Andrew said, still enjoying the attention.

"There are three meals a day; the time of each can be adjusted to your schedule by letting me know. Now, please remember, this place is yours for the week. Feel free to dig through the kitchen anytime you're feeling hungry."

Huff saw Ted shift and remembered another message. "Oh, yes, and Ted has made sure you'll all have an adequate supply of drinks, too." Huff lifted only his right eyebrow as he said this, suggesting the alcohol had been greatly over-ordered per Ted's instruction. Ted shrugged, proudly accepting the guilt.

Huff continued outlining the week, questions were asked and answered, and the guests soon understood the basics. "Guides are staying on the property to help with anything you need. Schedules for guided fishing, hiking, rafting, horseback trips, and other activities can be arranged by simply having a conversation with any one of them. They are here to help, so ask."

"One last thing," Huff added. "The ranch has another surprise this week. A masseuse will be here each day, thanks again to Ted."

As he said this, Huff looked at Ted. In turn, Ted quickly defaulted to his wife. "Actually, Nancy gets the credit for this one."

A boisterous "Way to go, Nancy!" came from one of the girls in the back.

Ted had insisted that there be more than enough guides available for their stay. He had a selfish concern: ensuring his wife would not interfere with the competing interests of fishing and drinking. Months earlier, Huff had received Ted's down payment of $30,000, triggering the phone calls to guarantee the guides' time. Each was a member of the traditionally unregimented profession. They came from the surrounding communities of Durango, Pagosa Springs, and as far away as Ouray. All could find fish in the lakes and rivers of the area and knew the mountains well enough to offer a safe outing. Two were good with horses, and at least one could provide the basics of roped climbing.

When Huff finished speaking, the party shuffled through the open pine doors. Inside the lodge, they all hesitated, in awe of the structure. On a long wooden table, just past the magnificent fireplace, the room assignments were laid out. Everyone agreed to meet on the back deck after settling in — for the next kickoff to the weekend.

Sarah returned to the SUV, picked up her bag, and climbed the stairs to her second-story room. Each step brought new perspective of the beams, stone, and structure of the fireplace that followed her up. Placing her bag on the bed, she took in the small, cool, and cozy room.

Chapter 10

Sarah had not yet bothered to look at the clock, but she was certain it was after 6:00 AM, content to just lay awake and listen to the river. Most things in the room, and the lodge for that matter, were dated but functional. Her bed was simple but surprisingly comfortable. *That was a great night's sleep*, she thought to herself.

An hour had passed as she lay listening for a pattern to the tranquil sounds of rushing water. It was an easy, beautiful place even in the darkness. Just lying in bed and enjoying the sound of the river was a pleasant surprise she had not considered before leaving New York.

On most days, Sarah's internal clock did not let her sleep past six. Rolling over, she found the dim yellow glow of an old clock. It read 5:48 AM. Even with the time difference from New York, she knew there was little hope of falling back asleep.

She sat up and turned so her feet touched the floor, feeling for the slippers she had removed before bed. Conscious of the others sleeping, Sarah left the lights off on her trip to the bathroom. Then again, it was a good bet the others were still intoxicated and a passing train would not rattle them. Her decision to curb drinking last night now felt brilliant.

Creeping toward her memory of the door's position, her hands extended, searching for anything to help expose the dark room. Reaching the bathroom, she closed the door before sweeping her hands over the wall, feeling for the light switch. Sarah's eyes narrowed as the bathroom illuminated, opening them slowly to see a mess of curly, black hair in the mirror. With a heavy sigh, the fingers on both hands combed the tangles back into an indefinable acceptance.

Coffee entered Sarah's mind next, and she knew she needed to make it to the kitchen. During their introduction to the lodge, Huff had told them all to make themselves at home, removing any reservation about a haphazard search that might follow.

Making her way down the long hallway, she eased down the stairs toward the kitchen. Each step taken was cautious too, as the old boards produced their own unique sound of age. A small light in the corner of the room revealed the first floor. Reaching the bottom, Sarah now relaxed because her movements were no longer likely to wake the others.

The floor was made of dark wooden planks, sanded multiple times over the years and worn into a smooth, beautiful surface. Large pine beams in the ceiling, striking in the dim light, caused Sarah to stop as she entered the room. The furniture was jumbled because of the different uses the room provided. This space held breakfast, lunch, and some dinners. This was also a place to settle into a cozy, quiet spot and just open a book. Long tables, comfortable leather chairs, and other mismatched furniture somehow defined comfort. Pictures adorned every wall and even the supporting posts.

The morning was cool, adding a second purpose for the coffee she sought. Her oversized shirt and pajama bottoms kept her just warm enough to make the morning's chill tolerable.

A voice from the corner of the room startled Sarah. "Good morning." She hesitated for a moment, gathering herself while searching for the source. She found the figure of a man in the corner, near the small lamp that was providing the only illumination. "Good morning," she said in his direction.

Sarah had not noticed him at first because he sat motionless. His chair angled toward the river, allowing him to listen through the wooden framed screen door. "Coffee?" he asked.

"Please," squeaked from Sarah's lips, the word testing her voice before fully awake. She cleared her throat and tried again. "Please." His only response came by standing and walking toward a small red light in the opposite side of the room. Only then did the smell of fresh coffee reach her nose, another confirmation of morning.

The man that moved in front of her was tall and lean, and even in the low light she could see they had not met the previous day. He wore a long t-shirt that dropped off his broad shoulders, resting just below his hips. The shirt hung straight down from his chest, unencumbered by the possibility of an uncontrolled stomach. A pair of knee-length shorts and some flip-flops completed his early morning ensemble.

"How do you take your coffee?" he asked.

"Black is fine. Thanks."

Returning, he presented an oversized mug with steam drifting from the top. "Please, have a seat," he said. Sarah found a large, relaxed leather chair across from the one he had occupied. She folded both legs underneath her, sipping the coffee at the same time. It was rich and warm, and provided another unexpected pleasure against the cool air and the sounds of the river.

Neither one of them jumped into conversation right away. It seemed natural to just sit and listen to the water. She cupped the coffee with both hands, taking full advantage of the small bit of heat it yielded. He sat quietly, resting the bottom of his cup on the chair's arm.

Sarah considered how odd it was that she was completely relaxed. She was unaffected by the pressure of silence that might otherwise ruin the unfamiliar circumstance of sitting with a complete stranger.

"I'm Rick."

"Sarah," she said. "Thanks again for the coffee."

He nodded but said nothing. She stole a look when he turned toward two birds flirting just beyond the door; he was a little older than the workers she had met yesterday. He was handsome, with dark, curly hair tightly cut to emphasize an already strong chin. His face was unshaven, the natural growth producing a dark shadow covering much of his face.

"We didn't meet yesterday, right?" Sarah asked, already knowing the answer.

"No, I came in late last night." He thought for a moment before continuing. "Are you here with a group?"

"Yes, there are about twelve of us. We're part of a wedding party."

He was quiet, then curious. "Are you getting married?"

Sarah considered the question and wanted to reply, "Not unless you're asking." She decided to save the answer for someone she knew a bit longer. She replied. "No, it's my sister."

"Is the wedding here?"

We are the only guests. Why doesn't he know more? she wondered. "No. Five weeks from now, in Atlanta. This is a get-to-know-everyone trip, arranged by the groom's father. He and his son both love to fly fish and thought the mountains would be a great place for everyone to bond before the big event."

Seemingly fixated on something outside, Rick appeared to have lost interest in their conversation. Pulling himself back, he replied. "Do you want to get-to-know everyone?"

Looking directly at him as the question arrived, she needed a moment to ponder his angle. Rick's face hinted at nothing. She considered saying no, but she was uncertain that he was kidding and remained silent. A moment later, he helped with the question's intent, turning his head and offering a slight laugh. She now saw he was kidding. At that, Sarah received the next surprise of her morning. His grin created an intoxicating smile, exposing a set of beautifully white teeth.

"You just arrived yesterday, then?" he asked.

"Yes, in the afternoon. We all came in on the same plane from Denver," she answered just before taking a long drink of coffee.

"Do you know much about the ranch?"

"A little — mostly what I have heard from two in our group who have been here before. I'm excited to be in the outdoors, do some hiking, and just take it easy with a good book." Then she gave more thought about what she had learned yesterday. "Oh, yeah, and apparently there is a masseuse here all week. I'd be lying if I told you that wasn't on my mind."

"Do you make a habit of lying?"

Sarah was feeling the coffee, immediately realizing he was toying with her. "I do. It's one of the things I'm really good at." She laughed, returning the banter he had started.

Naturally shy, Sarah usually let things happen around her, at least until very sure and comfortable with the situation. However, here, she continued with one of the boldest things to come out of her mouth. It came automatically and without thought, perhaps because Rick was strangely comfortable. "Yeah, I'm a good liar. For example, did I tell you how handsome I thought you were?"

The second she said it, she was immediately embarrassed and wanted to apologize. Nevertheless, in the spirit of their last several minutes, she held firm, simply looking directly into his eyes and hoping the low light was hiding her blush.

At first, he did nothing, giving Sarah's words a chance to sink in. Then he shifted slightly, leaving no doubt the two of them were looking directly at one another. "Oh, shit," Sarah thought, with only stillness between them. Then something wonderful happened; as if in slow motion, the sides of each of his eyes wrinkled and a beautiful smile crept across his face.

A sound near the stairs caused both to turn from the moment, finding the unmistakable figure of Kelly Rogers landing in the room. Seemingly aware she was not alone, Kelly's head dipped slightly and her eyes narrowed, straining to distinguish the surroundings. A moment later she straightened, her confident demeanor returning.

"Do you want to introduce me to your friend, Sarah?" Kelly's focus did not leave Rick, crossing the room and extending her hand as she reached his chair.

"Kelly Rogers, meet Rick."

"Wheeler. I'm Rick Wheeler. It's nice to meet you," he said, lifting himself from the cozy chair.

"It's very nice to meet you too, Rick," she offered, glancing toward Sarah and lifting her eyebrows. "Do the two of you know each other?"

"We do now," he said.

Sarah could see that Kelly was slightly confused, wondering how she had worked this out with Rick. "I see you've located the coffee?"

"Yes. Let me get you a cup," Rick responded, starting toward the coffee maker.

Placing her hand on his shoulder, Kelly answered "No. No, please sit down." Then she looked at Sarah. "Would you mind?"

Sarah sat for a second, shocked at Kelly's audacity. Rick offered again, "Really, let me get it."

"No, it's okay," Sarah said, standing as she looked at Kelly with a slight tilt to her head. "How do you like it?"

"Cream and sugar would be awesome," she instructed, her eyes never leaving her new interest.

It took Sarah no more than three minutes to get the coffee. When she returned, she saw that Kelly had pulled the boldest move yet. She was now sitting in her chair without the benefit of the white cotton jacket she had arrived in, and the thin, braless t-shirt she was wearing was obviously no match for the cool morning. Incredible, Sarah thought as she handed over the steaming cup. What would happen if the hot coffee somehow spilled onto her nipples? Perhaps they would melt. The simple thought produced a slight smile.

Before Sarah could find a seat, the sound of a closing door caused all three to turn. Huff entered the room carrying the same energetic look he had left with the previous evening. "Huff," Rick said, now standing and moving toward him. They shook hands and briefly embraced.

"I thought I heard your car last night," Huff said.

Sarah listened as Rick explained that he had come in around 2:00 in the morning. She thought that she must have been asleep, remembering nothing but the sound of the river shortly after her head hit her pillow.

"How's the water?" Rick asked Huff.

Kelly was disinterested in their conversation. "Quite a find you made this morning, Sarah. If they really knew how to market this place they would have had him meet us yesterday, instead of that old goat."

Sarah had picked up her coffee and peered out toward the river. She simply turned her head toward Kelly and lifted her eyebrows. Returning to the sound of the water, Sarah let her mind drift back to the morning, only now showing signs of finding its way out of the night's grasp. Kelly is not the only one who would find Rick interesting she thought. "He'll create some fireworks," she whispered to herself, concluding the girls' positioning should be an enjoyable study of human nature.

In the background, Rick and Huff continued to talk about fishing, the winter's snow pack, and other things related to the ranch. During this, Sarah noticed his fishing gear on the floor next to where he had been sitting. An open box of flies and several other items led her to guess that she had interrupted him as he prepared for fishing.

Kelly was fidgeting in her seat, clearly irritated that Huff was occupying an inordinate amount of Rick's time. She finally stood. "I'm going back to bed. Any idea where I can find some aspirin?"

"I saw some in the bathroom by my room; on the table to the right of the sink."

"Thanks." Kelly stood, picking a path across the room that took her by the two men. Sarah watched her ignore Huff, catching Rick as she passed. "I'll see you later."

Rick and Huff's conversation slowed just before Huff addressed Sarah. "Sarah, Sarah, how was your night?"

"Great, Huff. Thanks for asking," she replied, astonished he even remembered her name. Huff had met her, and all the others, late on the previous afternoon. Now he was already so certain of her name that he said it twice, and so boldly.

Huff is perfect for this job, she thought; his happiness did not appear fabricated, and he seemed genuinely pleased to meet and learn about everyone. Yesterday she had watched as he put their group at ease, skillfully setting the stage for their visit while making sure to add light strokes to Ted's personality. He spoke in such an upbeat manner about all the available things to do and things to see that it all but assured that even the most timid would seek out adventure.

"Were you one of the party crew last night?" Huff asked.

"I'm afraid I didn't have it in me last night, Huff. I wasn't the first in bed but didn't watch the sun come up, either. I think the trip took it out of me." Sarah reflected further on his question and admitted to herself that a point had come last night when she felt outside of the core group of friends, being a little older and not around when most of her sister's friendships had developed.

"So you're an early riser?"

"Usually, but I hope to break that habit this week."

Huff had noticed Sarah yesterday when he welcomed their group to the lodge. She sat quietly in the back, next to Ted's wife, curiously different from the others, he thought.

Sarah heard a door close and realized that Rick had slipped outside as she and Huff spoke. His fishing gear was missing, along with the most enjoyable few moments she had had in months. She returned to the ranch's host, whom she would enjoy speaking with until the others woke, and began the same search for some of the caffeine that had resulted in a beautiful beginning to her first full day.

Chapter 11

Sarah spent the day with the girls, on the deck overlooking the river; after the morning dew was wiped from the chairs and they were arranged into a socially functional pattern. This was not her ideal vacation, but, nonetheless, she had found it to be a great day. It was set when her sister donned a bathing suit shortly after the morning sun snuck onto the valley floor. Soon, the other girls followed Rachael's lead, and Sarah felt compelled to join. The escape to other activities that she had contemplated in the morning became lost in the unbreakable unity on the deck. As the sun climbed, books appeared and disappeared from oversized bags that also held cameras, headphones, lotion, and a host of other carefully packed items. Conversations about the wedding were the day's theme — the guest list, color of the invitations, hotel problems, and other conversations all took their turn. Sarah eased into just being one of the girls. The warming sun and drinks removed the apprehension built by knowing so few of Rachael's friends.

Surprisingly, the topic of men did not arrive until midday. This perked the girls back to life after having settled into reading or working hard on already perfect tans. The unattached groomsmen were the first to face the deck review, standards dictating that those who were single, and without present company's history, were subject to the most scrutiny. The groom himself, of course, was perfect and untouchable. All others fell somewhere in between, and their problems, relationships, jobs, and other known laundry was thoroughly wrung out before being thrown across the clothesline.

The men working the ranch did not avoid dissection, but were spared the scrutiny brought from the knowledge of their background. They only faced the assessment of all things physical; Rachael noted a healthy admiration for the backside of one of the young guides. This, predictably, led to her friends pointing out everything that would be lost in her upcoming step of life.

Kelly was ready to add a little bit more to the afternoon. "I found Sarah alone with one of the guides this morning," she blurted, watching Sarah to see her squirm. For the first time all day, the river was the only sound to come between the girls. Kelly had exactly planned the reaction; all eyes were now on Sarah as the women waited for a response. Kelly persisted; "Yeah, I came down looking for some aspirin and ran into them, all cozy together."

Sarah's eyes locked on Kelly. "I would say that's a bit of an exaggeration. He happened to be the only one downstairs — that is, until Kelly joined us."

Kelly liked a good fight and was not afraid to deliver a low blow. "I just thought it looked a little intimate, that's all. What would Greg say?"

~~~~~~~

A year from now, Ben Nichols would complete his final month at some hard-to-pronounce culinary institute just outside of Denver. Huff had discovered this underpaid pool of talent three years ago and arranged a summer program that came with a small salary, no expenses, and an obscure calculation of school credits. Through the director of the school, Huff kept an eye on those who needed summer work. This effort had produced two summers of outstanding meals that otherwise would be hidden behind a long list of reservations at an overpriced restaurant. Ben's talent assured this year would be no different.

The job of preparing the dinner began shortly after noon when he and Terry Wade sat across from each other, working the skin off a mountain of potatoes. Terry was a rangy-haired sixteen-year-old who escaped the hell of putting up hay for the summer by finding this place. Young and cheap, he was right for the job, and Ben needed the help. Terry found a place under Ben's wing, both inside and outside of the kitchen where the meals ran as smoothly as anyone could remember.

The effort of the kitchen was easy to underestimate, given the simple presentation of the meal. Several long tables, arranged end-to-end and draped with white coverings, supported the buffet-style layout of each dish. One by one, the cooks delivered their work to its final resting place, just outside the kitchen.

A 7:00 pm dinner at the lodge normally began forty-five minutes late, giving everyone a chance to find their way out of the day's activities and into a relaxed meal. Most guests entering had wrapped up the day in time for a shower that both reinvigorated and prepared them for the slow slide into dinner.

Tubs of iced beer and other drinks greeted each arrival just inside the door. Anyone who looked would find a little more bite on an unassuming table at the room's edge—it held a full assortment of hard alcohol. The closest thing to "roughing it" came from searching the icy waters for the beer of their choosing or fabricating their own drink. Letting the guests mix their own drinks was intentional; Huff believed this added another element to the setting. The ranch employees shared the dinner with the guests. This was one of Huff's few requirements of the guides, and the intent was to create a comfort between all who shared the ranch. By design, most of the help were social creatures and enjoyed these interactions, despite the propensity to congregate with their own. The more experienced guides recognized the dinners as a time to socialize with those guests most interested in a day of fly-fishing.

Tonight, the guides entered the lodge together, the short walk from their bunkhouse providing just enough time to finish the beers started earlier. This was their nightly routine and usually filled the time slot that otherwise might be used for showers. As they entered the lodge, Billy Talbot, the youngest of the guides, was taking a good-natured assault from the others. Huff had asked that he lead Nancy, Rachael, and several others on a hike the following day. Because they considered any job other than working the river less than ideal, Billy became their target. Stepping into the lodge, their laughter elevated when someone suggested Ted would join the hike in his animal print Speedo.

The atmosphere in the dining room could not help but be enjoyable; only a drink or two separated everyone from the wonderful food whose aroma now teased the air. People gathered inside or on the deck that overlooked the river and lay just beyond the open door.

As the crowd came together, different groups formed around the room to talk about the day. Plates of appetizers were strategically scattered around the room, helping people move in and out of different conversations. Huff was a good host, making sure he found time for anyone who wanted it, moving about the room with an open ear pointed toward anything he construed as a complaint. This was also his opportunity to learn about the visitors. The genuine care for his guest's experience was one of many things that separated Huff from the norm.

Over the years, Huff had watched the ranch sneak into people, touching that puzzling place inside that allowed them to let go. How it did this he never precisely understood, but it was rare when it did not occur here.

The story of an epic battle between man and beast had grown over a beautiful trout caught early in the morning by the groom. There was energy in the story, and those listening were genuinely excited. An expedition to the top of the valley had lasted all day, and the photos taken by one of the men had several in the bride's camp focused on the latest model of Nikon digital camera.

Ted had captured his own small audience in the corner of the room. Huff listened just enough in passing to know the conversation had the expected angle of another accomplishment by Ted Strickland, the Conqueror. Nevertheless, that was Ted's escape, Huff thought, smiling as he eased past.

Over the years, color had begun entering the photographs that adorned the walls of the lodge. These told stories of simple discoveries, such as the beauty of a butterfly resting on a flower that, on its own, would carry a conversation about an impossible purple. Moreover, there were numerous photos of an angler's conquest, holding an exquisitely colored trout just before release.

The large dining room contained its share of these photos. They hung in groups or by themselves on every wall. The black-and-white photographs contained the most history; these were framed in the natural woods that grew all over the mountains. By design or simple result, the frames did more than just surround these dormant windows into the past. Some formulation of oils and stain preserved both the wood and the tracks from the insects that had taken life from it. The irony of how the beauty of the tree was enhanced by the very insect that killed it was not lost on Sarah. Moving out of Ted's conversation, toward her sister Rachael, Sarah was distracted by some of these uncolored pictures. Studying the details captured by an old photo, she stood alone.

Some of the photos were very simple, such as a photo of an old piece of machinery patiently waiting, year after year, to rust into the soil, the grasses reaching up from every free space of earth, seemingly in an attempt to hasten the process. Another picture captured a massive tree that had been set down in the middle of a calm summer stream. The photo elegantly took the viewer to a gentle time in the stream's life but suggested the power of water that had sculpted this paradise.

The one Sarah found herself facing was the picture of a man and a woman standing in front of a small cabin. She was lost in the study of a slice of the early twentieth century. The man must have been in his late twenties, but the sun and life looked to have taken a toll, as he appeared much older. The long sleeve dress shirt he wore looked odd in the picture because most everything else suggested a hard life. Sarah guessed it to be the only shirt of this type that he owned, complete with formal button cuffs and a pocket on the left chest. His pants were clean but otherwise must not have been distinguishable from those worn to work in the fields. She studied the oversized, yet functional, buckles on both his belt and boots.

Two horizontal rails formed a small fence that gave some definition to the property surrounding the cabin. He sat in front of the fence with his back resting against the top rung and the sole of his right boot propped against the lower.

Standing next to him was a beautiful girl who looked too young to be his wife or even to be living in such a remote place. A white bonnet covered her hair; the shape suggested it was fashioned in some sort of bun underneath. Her dress belonged in a far away city with the shirt the man wore. Hooped at the bottom, the dress started tight at her waist, progressively getting larger until it ended inches above the ground. The size of her waist agreed with the youth of her face. The dress carried the center gray of the picture; as Sarah studied it, she wished she could somehow see its true color.

The photograph was mesmerizing to Sarah because of the contrast; these people scraped the earth to survive, but then somehow found a time and then made the effort to dress and pose for such a thing. Their life appeared to be devoted to their simple existence. Sarah stood, puzzled. The fence sheltered a garden that would be unknown today. It was not for hobby or enjoyment but rather demanded success, for its failure could be catastrophic to the family.

She guessed the cabin in the picture sat somewhere near this very spot, which even today was remote. Still, something else did not sit right in the photo. Sarah searched to understand what she found so unnatural.

The man and woman in the picture were not holding hands and appeared distant and cold to one another. Neither offered much of a smile or anything that might hint at something different from what shown. Sarah wondered whether they loved each other or just existed here for the same reason as the garden. Was it just necessity?

Huff noticed Sarah studying the picture from across the room. Two groups had stopped him as he traveled toward her, but in that time, she had not moved. Her eyes remained focused as her mind found questions. He was thrilled, knowing she had discovered something often missed by those only looking with their eyes. "It's the fence, Sarah," said Huff's comfortable voice, not pulling her from the history.

"The fence," she whispered to herself as she realized simultaneously that Huff had both found and answered her question. She now saw that the fence was there for nothing more than its beauty. It would not stop an animal intent on finding anything within its perimeter—the gaps were too large and the fence itself was without a gate. More than that, the top horizontal rung built in a pattern of repeating arcs that had no functional purpose. In this couple's world of necessity, there existed this strange paradox, built only because it was beautiful.

"Why?" Sarah asked, without turning from the photograph.

"He must have built it for her," Huff offered.

"Yes, but why?"

Huff thought he knew, but did not answer that question. "That's Mary and Tom Williams. They homesteaded this place." A brief, contemplative silence followed. "Amazing, really."

Sarah turned toward him. "What's that mean, 'homesteaded?'"

Huff thought of, and then rejected, the formal answer before continuing. "They came here in the late 1800s, found this valley, and decided to build. They would have simply filed some description of the land

and qualified as the owners by building on it and perhaps living off it. For all I know, the Williams did both." He offered more, "It must have been an attractive proposition at face value as, like today, there was lumber to build and water for farming. I suspect having this at their fingertips must have been tempting." Huff thought for a moment before continuing. "Still, the soil is not the best, and it's full of rocks that would make it difficult to farm. And, the winter snowfall is twice what it is ten miles down the valley. I still scratch my head and wonder why they didn't go further down the river."

Huff and Sarah were both now looking into the photo together. "Where did the picture come from, Huff?"

"It was in the old barn that sits just north of the lodge. About three years ago, I decided to dig into the place — threw out a bunch of junk from the folks who owned it in the fifties. Then I came across a leather binder with several letters and this old photo."

Sarah noticed some damage on the edges for the first time. "It's in fantastic shape," she said.

"It was pressed tight against the leather, so the moisture never reached it."

Sarah's curiosity was growing. "Were you able to read the letters, Huff?"

"Yes, well, just two of them. The others did not fare so well."

"Were they from her?" Sarah guessed.

"Yes ... one from her, but the other from him," Huff said pleasantly because he knew Sarah's next question before she asked it.

"What did they say?"

He now toyed with her a little. "What did they say word for word ... or how did I interpret them?"

"Both." Sarah almost shouted, increasingly interested in the letters. "What did they say?" she asked again.

Huff offered a confused smile. She looked at him with the beautiful focus of her intense green eyes. He was smiling because he knew she looked into the picture and found a question so many never thought to ask. Now something deep in her wanted the answer — even more than that, Sarah needed the answer.

"Well, the letters are about nothing more and nothing less than what makes the world go around Sarah — love." Her left eye narrowed a little more than her right, and a smile of contentment came across her lips without opening her mouth. Huff spoke again before she could ask anything else. "I know you want more, but there is not enough time now. If you are awake early, go outside and look south. The only light you will see is my cabin. Come down, and you can read the letters if you want."

Sarah thought through the offer, quickly finding herself looking forward to the letters and the following morning. "Thanks, Huff, I'd like that. What time?"

"Whenever you get up; I'm always awake early." With that settled, he excused himself to his next stop.

Huff lifted his arms and soon had the room's focus; "Thank you all again for choosing the Tres Piedras Ranch. As this is your first dinner, I wanted to explain how things work. "First," Huff pointed toward the kitchen. "Ben and Terry are responsible for everything you're about to eat, so, complaints go their way and, of course, compliments come my way." The crowd laughed as they applauded the cooks' efforts. "Okay, then. Pick up your plates on one end, take what you want, and leave what you don't. If anyone expects more formality than this, you're on the wrong vacation," Huff noted.

The best of diets would not survive the short walk down the buffet. Soon, everyone had a full plate and a place at one of the scattered tables.

Three of the younger guides, including Billy Talbot, found comfort in numbers at a table near the exit. Two others with more experience took a strategic approach, placing themselves by the guests they thought most likely to want a day of fishing. Huff chose to sit near Ted to bolster his role as organizer, and more importantly, as the one who would sign the bill at the end of the week. Sarah settled at a table against the wall, taking a seat next to one of the girls.

The food was as delicious as the aroma had promised and conversations suffered while everyone ate. Dessert had just made the buffet table when Ted stood to say something of no consequence; for him, the message about the bonds of friendship was a distant second to the attention he was receiving from the focused audience. Sarah was half listening because Ted's dash to the limelight, even now, was becoming routine and predictable. Between the Denver airport and this dinner, she had already counted no less than four toasts, all predictably preceded by his run of words. Looking around the room, Sarah expected the guides to begin slipping out at the first possible moment.

Surprisingly, Ted's ability to speak, using hands and body to tie words together was quite impressive. He engaged the entire group, and each felt as if he was speaking directly to them.

Ted's speech drifted further into the background when Sarah noticed the side door open slightly and Rick slip into the room. He slid along the back wall, making sure not to disrupt Ted or his audience. His right hand found Billy Talbot's shoulder, communicating both a silent greeting and a request to move forward so he could continue his stealthy travel behind the scenes.

The bottom of Rick's khaki shorts were wet from the river, saturated up one leg slightly higher than the other was. Into the kitchen, he turned, his thin shirt exposing every detail of a contoured back. Feeling her stare obvious, Sarah quickly scanned the crowd to ensure that Ted's skill had left her alone, in appreciation of the sight that demanded the return of her gaze. The fabric of his shirt fell into a valley that began at his shoulders, formed by the symmetrical muscles on each side of his back. Holy crap, she thought, almost feeling guilty for her enjoyment.

In the kitchen, Rick was less encumbered and moved from cabinet to cabinet, pulling pans and other things out as he searched for something. He knelt, disappearing for a moment as Sarah heard the opening of a cabinet. He stood again, looking into the dining room before quietly approaching the buffet. She watched him fill his plate, and it became obvious that volume was the primary concern. Then he disappeared back into the kitchen and found a quiet place to eat.

Rick and Ted finished about the same time, and a small round of applause ensued before the individual topics around each table took over again. While Sarah clapped, she again searched, quickly finding Rick back at the buffet with a plate of dessert. He covered it with a thin piece of plastic before picking up something else from the table, now fumbling with exactly how to carry everything. Sarah lifted slightly in her seat, bending to get a better view and resolve her curiosity. Rick edged his way along the back wall and back toward the door. When he was behind the guides table, a space opened, and Sarah caught a glimpse of his right hand. The sight made her immediately curious and strangely disappointed. She did not want to confront this disappointment because it made no sense — two large wine glasses, held by the stems in his hand, should not make her heart sink.

The girls would be disappointed, Sarah realized, finding she was sharing the same feeling. Silly, she thought, scolding herself for letting an enjoyable morning take her to this point. "It makes sense," she whispered, the two glasses convincing her that somewhere on the ranch another woman had been occupying his time. A minute later, she had a completely different idea; was the other glass actually intended for someone in her own group? Wow, she thought, could one of the girls really have worked that fast?

Ted's speech allowed Rick to come and go without notice. He used his back to push open the screen door before hesitating to scan the room. Sarah believed she was alone watching; everyone else seemingly consumed in conversation. She followed his eyes from table to table, the search piquing her curiosity. He was deliberate, taking time to study each table before moving on. Then he found Kelly's table, scanning it too before moving on to the next.

Sarah was watching this so intently and with such interest, she had not considered the next thing that happened. Rick's eyes found Sarah's table, then they found her, and then they stopped searching. She almost startled, suddenly being in the moment where it was just the two of them looking at each other. There was a long pause by both, as if trying to understand one another, before he delivered a subtle but clear message, lifting his chin up slightly and turning his head in the direction he was going. Come on; let's go.

The signal was obvious, but Sarah sat motionless, waiting for the assurance that would allow her to believe he wanted her. His chin moved again. This time Sarah turned to make sure that she did not stand just in time to run into his intended recipient. Her back was to the wall, so there could be no one else.

The adrenaline began pushing through Sarah's body the very moment his eyes stopped on her. It had now saturated her bloodstream, and she knew it, the rush making a stealthy departure from her seat almost impossible. Then she let herself think, fighting off the reasons she should not go that were now racing through her mind. She arrived at one prominent question: How could he be so confident that she would go with him? This simply resolved itself, mostly because he was right.

Slowly standing, Sarah turned to place her napkin where she had been sitting. In this motion, she came to face the wall behind her; her expression, hidden from the room, opened up like a five-year-old on Christmas morning. Contained again, she started slowly toward the door that Rick had released moments earlier, allowing him to disappear. The woman seated next to Sarah scooted her chair under the table, allowing room to pass. Sarah whispered something obscure about the bathroom as she slid by.

Rick was standing at the west side of the lodge waiting for her. "You like wine?"

Who in the hell cares? she wanted to yell, but throttled the response. "I do. Red."

Rick motioned to a bottle of cabernet that he had placed on the ground next to the wall. He stepped down from the stone walk to the dirt road, one hand holding two wine glasses, the other a plate of dessert. "Good. Mind grabbing the bottle?"

She picked it up. "Where are we going?"

"Are you a fan of a good sunset?"

Sarah was already comfortable and feeling her oats. "Well, I do like the sun," she said, presenting her response so he knew she was playing.

It was Rick's turn. "Yeah. This is kinda like that, but in the end, there's no sun."

Sarah liked that he jumped in, so she continued. "Well, now, that would be night, right?" Sarah put one finger to her chin and looked up as if she were trying to remember something.

His smile told her that he shared her enjoyment. "You're getting close. Come on. I'll show you." They turned north on the main road as it gently climbed away from the lodge.

It took ten yards before Sarah was certain she was in heaven. The smells of sweet grass and pine dominated the air, and the fading sun had already begun playing with shadows. Stealing a glance, Sarah could see he was tall and strong. She desperately wanted to just throw her head back and spin around in a circle. She closed her eyes briefly, looking toward her feet as she realized this was the first truly happy moment she had in months. Moreover, she realized, there was already trust because, somehow, all things seemed properly placed. It was all combining to be the best surprise yet, and she was feeling completely free in this spectacular place.

"So how's Colorado treating you so far?"

It was easy for Sarah to be honest. "It's one of the greatest places I've ever been, and the sound of the river, it's so relaxing. I always know when I sleep well because my dreams are crazy. I need this river in my home. Can you arrange that?"

"I'll see what I can do," he said, stopping briefly to make sure he was not walking too fast. "So, tell me about your dream."

"Okay. Really?"

"Yeah. Hit me with it. What's your mind working on?"

"I dreamt that I was skiing in Colorado and there was an elephant skiing next to me, complete with a scarf."

Rick thought for a moment. "Two skis or four?"

"Ha, funny! Four, I think."

"You know elephants can't ski, right?"

Glancing up, she said, "Really?"

"Squirrels."

Sarah thought she had heard him but wanted to make sure. "Huh?"

"Squirrels. Squirrels can ski. But they are better on water than they are on snow."

Laughing, Sarah replied, "Are you goofy?"

"You're the one that said she saw an elephant skiing."

"I ..." The smile on Rick's face stopped her cold. Returning the smile, she again looked down, realizing how much fun she was having.

They turned off the lane and onto a steep trail that led up the west side of the valley. Animals on their nocturnal trip to the river had trampled the narrow path they followed. Limbs from oak brush slowed the pace. Rick pushed them aside, holding them with his shoulder until Sarah passed. A short distance up the trail, they came to the top of a narrow ridge. Their walk eased as the trail flattened and the brush around them opened.

Their destination was evident before Rick pointed it out, marked by a large tree with an unobstructed view of the western ridge. The limbs, once occupying a place near the earth, had lifted with age and now offered shade from the day's remaining light. The tree was positioned so that the setting sun could be watched falling perfectly between two ridges of the western wall, the gap squeezing a few more minutes of the day into the valley. Beams of light found the base of the tree where they now sat. The tree's shadow reached long behind the two of them, to the east. The details of every mountain, visible at midday, now fell to a featureless color of purple in the diminishing light.

Sarah needed this, an easy time, warm and uncomplicated beyond the enjoyment she was finding in this exact instant. It was almost lost when she began anticipating the complications Greg would bring the next day, but she discarded the thought, careful not to ruin the coming sunset.

Rick's search of the kitchen had produced a functional but outdated tool to remove the cork. It did not compare to the overpriced technical gadgetry that had become so popular in most kitchens, but it accomplished the same task. Remembering it in the side pocket of his shorts, he opened the bottle and poured two glasses. He quietly handed Sarah a glass without the pretentious commentary offered by someone who thought themselves a connoisseur of the world's fine wines. The contrast brought Ted briefly into Sarah's thoughts.

Rick extended his feet directly in front of him and rested back on his elbows, his eyes closing to let every fleeting ray warm his core. Sarah watched this, feeling he would be in this exact same place, at this same time, whether she had come along or not. She sat next to him with her legs crossed, her back resting against the trunk of the old tree that had watched over this same sunset for many years. Rick was quiet, seemingly lost in thought or just enjoying everything. Respecting his peace, she said nothing. In the silence, with the feel of the setting sun on them, each reflected on life, their busy thoughts narrowed to only those important enough to find their way to this place.

The reason the wine tasted so good did not jump out at Sarah, but that the first sip was enjoyable made her look into the glass. It was a natural reaction, but it would not produce the answer she sought. To find that, she had to realize that her senses had been left alone and unencumbered by the loss of her job, Greg, and most everything that had been occupying her thoughts. Sarah's excitement about leaving the lodge had much to do with her company. Now, lost in this moment, there was so much more to enjoy. For his part, Rick appeared solitary, following the drifting path of his mind . This place had touched both of them as the weight of the world briefly felt distant.

"Do you think it was a god who created all of this?" Rick phrased his question intentionally, offering the possibility of all gods or none. He did not move from the position he had taken, except that his eyes were now open.

Sarah studied the simplicity of his demeanor, it somehow adding power to his question. She wrapped her arms around it all, enjoying the cleverness of his simple presentation. Sarah did not answer right away, taking his question in and toying with it briefly. "It could not be anything else," she replied.

Rick's eyes closed. "How about a huge explosion a billion years ago and some evolved arrangement in time?"

She liked this question but knew the trap of a conversation that did not have an answer without faith. However, his question did have an answer, and she delivered. "Isn't that someone's god?"

Sarah's answer fell into the silence as Rick thought. Her response was masterful and easily could have been overdone. It was not. There was no better way to answer, and he knew it. He rolled onto his side so he could look into her eyes. "Yes, I think it must be someone's god too," was all he said. However, a clear understanding arrived from the one weapon she knew was hard to dismiss: the smile of Rick Wheeler.

He looked back to the sun nearing the mountain. "Beautiful, isn't it?"

"It's spectacular. Thanks for thinking of ... for asking me."

He sat up and reached for the dessert. "Of course, Sarah. Of course."

Ten minutes evaporated with little conversation, both enjoying the incomparable beauty surrounding them in the fading day. Seconds after Sarah closed her eyes, a rare yet familiar sensation began where her neck met her chest. The comfortable warmth traveled slowly through her body, seeking every extremity. A deep exhale and she realized she was about to be lost within herself. Her eyes flew open just as the first colors darted across her being. Searching all around, Sarah was back, aware that Rick had no idea of what had just happened. Why would my colors come now?

Chapter 12

The morning was quiet and dark, the only hope for light coming from the moon, caught in an island of clouds sitting over the western ridge of the valley. The sun was far behind the moon, and its rays would not reach the top of the eastern rim for at least another hour.

Sarah slipped out of bed, located a thick pair of sweatpants, and began feeling her way downstairs — an exercise that would be well practiced by the end of the week. She moved cautiously — at this hour, each noise measured against the sound of the river. Pulling the door slowly into its jam, Sarah was out onto the lodge's walkway and into the dark morning. Almost by instinct, she took the cool, fresh air deep into her lungs. The smell of an evening rain permeated the air, so she took another deep breath to better sense everything.

Walking to the edge of the building, she looked south, just as Huff had told her. The light from his cabin appeared tiny and bright against everything else black in the valley. It was the destination she had thought about since seeing the pictures and learning about the letters. What more would the letters say that the pictures had not?

She wanted to believe it was the letters that had kept her eyes open long after the crowd's noise had faded into the sounds of the river. She wanted, and even tried, to ignore Rick's contribution to her insomnia, but she could not.

Though the light appeared far off in the distance, Sarah worried that her passion to read the letters would bring Huff out of bed. She briefly contemplated his surprise at finding a crazy girl at his doorstep so early in the morning. Still, it was his invitation, and he told her to come early, so she convinced herself to go — except now thoughts of wild beasts, and, frankly, snakes, weighed in on the journey down an unlit, dirt road.

Her steps were deliberate, listening more intently to compensate for everything her eyes could not see. Her pupils were in full, yet futile dilation. An extended right hand led her forward each time she suspected a limb or something else in her path. The noise of a small animal moving through the grass caused her heart to race for a moment, before she continued.

Sarah's eyes continued working hard to make out shapes in the darkness. The ridge tops of each side of the valley came into focus as dark outlines against the very dim sky. The light of the small cabin grew as she approached. Near the structure, she saw the light was coming from Huff's porch, and the light lit the area enough to identify the opening in the fence. Reaching the lawn, Sarah swung wide of the picnic table, remembering it from their arrival at the ranch.. Climbing the wooden steps, she was relieved to see another light and movement inside the house. Huff was indeed awake.

She knocked twice, very softly, bringing footsteps, the sound of an old doorknob, and the friendly face of Huff in front of her.

"Sarah, good morning," he greeted her.

"Good morning, Huff. I hope I'm not too early?"

"Never. The birds are still asleep long past when I'm up," he chuckled.

Huff was expecting her and was certain she would arrive early. He had seen something different in her, something that intrigued him, and whatever it was, he knew she would not be late. He looked forward to her visit, wanting to know what else she might have seen in the pictures. Huff enjoyed good conversation and suspected there was something special behind the beauty of her curiosity.

"Come in, come in. It's chilly this morning," Huff insisted. "The mornings are cool even on the warmest summer days, but with the rain, the temperature has really dropped."

The shortness of the walk was the only thing that kept the warmth contained within the cocoon of Sarah's oversized attire. Nevertheless, as she reached the door, the morning air had penetrated to her skin, the chill causing her to cross her arms in an effort to keep warm. Happily accepting Huff's offer, she stepped inside. "I could smell the rain after I was in bed. It was so pleasant," Sarah said, enjoying how easy their conversation already felt.

"Do you like tea?"

"I do. Would you mind?"

He turned and waved for her to follow him, headed through the front room. "Please."

Huff's cabin was inviting and comfortable. The small living room was full of furniture but not overdone. It was comfortable — just like Huff was comfortable — but there was something missing, something that Sarah could not place. The ceiling was low, the black pipe of a small stove easily reaching it before disappearing to the roof. The heat from this stove had willed Sarah's arms to unfold and relax into the warm space it provided.

She watched Huff walk as she followed. His right leg had some sort of injury, but he was proficient in his movement, and she guessed it did not slow him down. This brought memories of her grandfather. His home was comfortable, like this one, forever marking her memory with the pleasant smell from the pipe he smoked. It was funny how that simple smell was so tied to everything she could remember about him.

Moving through the cabin, she noticed sporadic Indian décor — several rugs mounted on the walls and others placed over the wooden floor. Like the floors, the walls were familiar now, made of the same woods as those in the lodge. A large bookcase covered every inch of the east wall, except for the opening of the door she had just come through. Books and several pictures filled every space in the case. She followed Huff but continued to search the bookcase, now incredibly curious about the subjects that occupied the owner.

Huff led Sarah to a small closet door, again made of the same natural woods from which everything else was constructed. His hand searched through the air, grasping a small string hanging from the ceiling. Pulling it revealed an inconspicuous long room, each wall covered with shelving. To Sarah's astonishment, hundreds of glass jars packed every nook; the variety of different sizes and shapes in itself consuming. The original purpose of the majority of the jars seemed to be canning homemade jams and other food. Complete with tin tops, each jar sealed tight with a small white label taped to the front; the contents within were described in thick black ink. Sarah began reading the labels to herself: *Herbal Apple w/ Spice, Black Tea/China East.* She confirmed her discovery. "Huff, you're a tea collector." She was surprised because this discovery did not fit the image of the mountain man she had since arriving at the ranch.

"I like to say I am a tea drinker who just happens to have an awful large selection," he replied, his grin big and friendly. He continued. "It started a long time ago, after meeting some people who made it a habit to travel the world. They introduced me to the art of a good cup of tea, and it turned into one of my favorite things. Even today, I receive unannounced packages in the mail from all over the world. Now their kids have even taken to sending teas they find and think I will enjoy." He hesitated in thought. "Can you imagine that?"

Sarah looked at Huff, who had drifted away in reflection of receiving tea from the children of long ago friends. He's so happy, she thought. "Why the jars?"

"It helps them stay fresh by keeping the air out, but I keep their boxes too, for information that might be important." Huff considered what he just said, concluding to himself that the boxes were never important.

Sarah read one aloud. "Herbal apple with spice. What's the spice?"

"Cinnamon," came from Huff, soft and slow, as if he were revealing an international secret. "Made that one and several others myself, mostly the herbals, from right around the ranch."

"Really, Huff?"

"Yeah. I guess I enjoy seeing what I can come up with. Herbals aren't just made from the leaves; they're made from the entire plant — the flowers, roots, bark, and even their seeds. It can be a bit of a concoction, but I like them because most of the herbals don't have caffeine, so they are very smooth."

Huff never presumed that anyone other than himself had an interest in tea, so he rarely spoke of the subject. This morning brought him a pleasant surprise, as his guest seemed genuinely interested. Sarah continued to read the labels while he picked up one of the jars and opened the lid. "The herbals are good just before bed," he said. "Here, smell this one."

She brought her nose toward the jar but needed nothing more as the scent seemed to pour out. "It's wonderful. It smells like a flower?"

Huff brought it back to his own nose and agreed. "Yes, flowers, from China. The teas from China are both unique and fantastic. They're my favorite."

Sarah read another label. "JAS green tea/ first harvest. What's JAS?"

Huff had managed to get to one knee and was looking under the first level of shelves. He pulled out and looked over his shoulder to answer. "Ah, good question. The JAS mark is the certificate given by Japan's Ministry of Agriculture. Do you see the 'First Harvest'?"

Sarah looked again. "Yes."

"The First Harvest teas have always been prized and recognized for having better flavors and more nutrients. It's a good fact, but I'm not sure I can tell the difference myself." Sarah laughed.

He began opening jar after jar, unleashing smells from around the world into Sarah's senses. After her nose had its turn in each jar, Huff would wave the fragrance to his so he could remember each one. The two were enjoying both the tearoom and each other. Huff glanced at his watch. "Oh, how rude of me. I trapped you in my little hobby and became lost in the tour. Let's pick one and get to the letters."

"No, no — this is great. I have all the time in the world."

"Well, I'll tell you what. Let's get to the letters and promise to sit for another tea this week?"

"Done."

Huff held up a jar. "Chinese flower tea?"

"Perfect."

In the main room, shadows danced on the walls from the yellow flicker coming from the port window of the old stove. It was made of black iron, the top flat and supporting a small metal kettle. Steam drifted easily from the spout before evaporating into the air. Sarah loved the cozy setting, remembering her grandfather's home. She had always enjoyed little treasures such as this. Taking a deep breath, she exhaled in appreciation of this wonderful morning and this beautiful place.

Huff took the tea into the kitchen, grabbing two cups. In his absence, Sarah drifted to the bookcase for a quick glimpse at the interests of what was turning out to be a unique man. She walked along the bookcase and read titles off the spines that caught her attention. It appeared he enjoyed a wide variety of subjects and authors. There were a great number about World War II. Truman Capote, Robert Frost, Alfred Hitchcock, and other authors also claimed their space on his shelf. There were biographies of Republican and Democratic presidents as well as Ford and other American barons of business. Books about the Rocky Mountains, native flora, and, of course, tea all held their space, too. Sarah counted at least three books about nothing more than tea.

In the middle of the bookcase, a square shelf was reserved for a picture taken several years earlier of Huff, what looked to be his wife, and another younger man Sarah guessed was his son. His wife had beautiful brown skin and penetrating, large brown eyes. A red cloth, adorned with bright yellow print, pulled back and tightly held her black hair. The red lipstick she wore matched that of the fabric and created a beautiful contrast with her skin. Laughter exaggerated wrinkles on both sides of her and Huff's eyes. The younger man appeared to be on the outside of whatever was giving them enjoyment. Nevertheless, it was clear that he, too, was happy and sharing the moment.

Huff's wife wore a magnificent dress that Sarah guessed was reserved for special occasions. Sarah looked at the colors of the dress and noticed how the photo vividly captured their full detail. Each color was rich and bright and she thought it an art to bring these alive in the fabric. Unknowingly absorbed, she was unaware Huff had come into the room. "My wife, Maria, and son, Mateo."

"It's a great picture. Your wife is very pretty. I was looking at the red and turquoise colors — both are so striking."

"They're even more brilliant than what you can see in the picture. There is some real pride in that dress, let me tell you. The Mexicans love their colors. Maria is always complaining that there aren't enough fiestas … parties … so she can't wear all of her dresses. I've taken to hosting a party every fall at the lodge just to have her show another one off," he chuckled.

"Was the picture taken here on the ranch?"

"No, that's on our farm."

Sarah was confused. "Your farm?"

"Well, it used to be a farm. Now I guess you would call it a house with land ... or a farm with weeds. Anyway, it's west of here, about twenty miles."

He moved to take up position in front of the stove. A small couch sat across from an old leather chair, perfectly worn to accept the shape of Huff's body. To the right of his chair, an open book lay face down on a small table. Sarah saw the book and felt bad for interrupting what looked to be Huff's morning read. She noticed a set of reading glasses resting on top of the book as Huff bent slowly to take a seat in his chair.

The news that Huff had another home did not surprise Sarah because the small cabin had not made much sense to her. Although it did not strike her immediately, she was aware that there was not enough life in this place. There were too few pictures and other things scattered about for this cabin to contain the sum of someone's life, certainly not a man like Huff. And, of course, where was his wife?

"How long have you and Maria been married?" she asked.

"Hmm, well now, around thirty-two years. Yes ... thirty-two years, thirty-three in September, the twenty-fourth." Sarah smiled; simply enjoying that two people could be in love for such a long time. She looked again at the picture.

Since Sarah had been a little girl, she sorted things slightly differently from most people. Things that others would casually disregard were somehow important and placed in her mind for remembering. At that moment, her list of important things had just grown. Huff and Maria were now certain to receive a card around September 23, because Sarah was never late.

"It's funny. When we met, I didn't speak Spanish, and Maria did not speak English," Huff thought for a moment. "Hmmm ... maybe that's why we have been married so long?" Both enjoyed the humor.

Sarah was now intrigued about Huff and Maria's story, reflecting on Greg and their recent relationship. She asked herself, "How could a relationship ever grow when they could not even understand each other?" She walked over and sat on the couch across from Huff, ready with a question that was causing a curiosity even beyond the letters.

Huff had brought two cups and a small glass container from the kitchen. In the bottom, he placed two perfectly round and dried flowers. Over these, he poured the steaming water.

"You could not speak each other's language? Not a word?"

Huff's white eyebrows lifted. "Well, I knew 'Si,' and she had a few select words up her sleeve, but mostly that's right. There was a lot of comedy in the early going."

"Comedy?"

"Oh, yeah, Sarah. Lots of funny things." He drifted off as a smile from the past came across his face. "Her father was bilingual and helped us communicate. Just think of that. I'm courting his daughter, and he's the translator. That alone is comical, don't you think?"

Sarah loved Huff using the word *courting* and all the good things it seemed to imply. "I think her father helping you two is sort of romantic."

Huff continued. "She lived with her parents, and soon I was invited over for a dinner Maria had prepared. Guess she was going to show off her cooking, or maybe her mom wanted her to. Anyway, somewhere along the line she burned the heck out of the thing—burned it black to the bottom of the pan. She knew it and started her apologies long before we all sat down, but. I didn't know what she was saying, and her dad made up some other story to account for the look of embarrassment she had on her face.

"I knew something was off; I just didn't put two and two together because I was nervous too. Her father was playing with us, convincing Maria and her mom that it wasn't that bad and should be served. That was the joke as I didn't know what was going on. Maria knew it was awful, her mom and dad knew it was awful, and I knew it after the first bite, but her dad managed the conversation between us, keeping quiet about the common knowledge of the ruined meal. I guess he wanted to see how I would react." Huff thought back, laughing aloud and sitting up in his seat as his face reddened. "He looked so damn happy," he said between his laughs, remembering Maria's father.

"A real joker, that guy. He was having a great dinner without even eating. I, of course, ate my entire plate and asked for seconds of the most godforsaken taste on earth — missing that no one else had touched their plates or that her father had tears in his eyes when I asked for seconds. Maria later told me she thought I was crazy, watching me eat so much. Her dad told that story for years. There were a lot of things like that in the beginning."

Sarah liked how Huff had worked to encourage and appreciate Maria's efforts. She shifted in her seat, biting her bottom lip. "How did you know? I mean, how did you know you should give the time to work it all out with Maria?"

Huff thought for a moment. "That's a big question, and maybe I'm not the best person to try and answer. I have only ever loved one person — Maria. I have only ever had to ask myself that question one time, and it was a long time ago."

"You have been married for thirty-two years. I'll gladly take your perspective."

Huff was quiet while he contemplated the qualification just noted. His right hand rubbed his chin and wondered about Sarah's curiosity. He then bent forward to inspect the tea. In turn, Sarah looked into the glass and saw that the balls had opened up like springtime flowers. Inside were the fragile, detailed structures that seemingly came to life again. Huff lined up two cups and filled each. He turned Sarah's handle toward her before picking his cup up and sitting back into the well-worn chair.

"Here's what I know, or at least what I think: it begins by both people knowing there is no other place they want to be or other person they want to be with. It must start there. That's what gives it a chance. If that's not the most honest and exact feeling of both people, then it will never start, right?"

Sarah sipped her tea while she listened to his words. Moving the cup an inch away from her lips, she hurried the next word out. "Start?"

Huff contemplated the word he had used. "Yes. Start discovering each other. Somewhere inside both people, the need and want to discover must take over. If that happens, it's easy, because it's natural."

Both were again silent as they held their cups. "Before I spoke Spanish, I would listen to Maria's words, spending hours on a single sentence. A word or a sentence would stick in my head, and I would ask her to say it repeatedly, until I could remember it on my own. It was not just the words, but how she said them—the inflections in her voice, her tones, and even the look on her face all drew me in. A simple word, easily understood, had so much more to offer. It told me something about her, so I would play it over in my head many times. It let me discover how she saw the world. It's all about discovery."

Sarah thought about everything Huff had said before she asked her next question. "There are many people who love each other and don't know it until long after they meet?"

"Yes. Certainly. In fact, Mateo's wife was the sister of his good friend, and it took them a long time to know they could even stand each other. But somewhere along the way, discovery took over. I was only talking about Maria and me. I was lucky because I knew the first time I saw her. Probably with most people, it doesn't start right away like that,but in all cases, there must be a time where the need of discovery is prevailing. Don't you think?"

She thought about his question as she watched the steam from the kettle disappear over the stove, coming off the thought for a moment to look into her cup. It held a taste she had never encountered, and she decided it was a tea to sip and savor slowly over conversation. So far, it had been the perfect morning.

"Do you think love can happen without discovery?"

"I don't know how it could. I know it might not happen right away, and that each discovery is different, but I think before love there must come a need for discovery."

It was a good topic for both, and they appreciated the other's consideration. "You used the word *need*. Do you really think it's a need?"

"I think it's an appropriate word here, Sarah. Have you ever heard that 'necessity is the mother of all invention?' I like that saying and think it's not too different. It says that only when there is a real need does the true discovery happen." Both Huff and Sarah took drinks at the same time, equally enjoying their thought-provoking company.

"I know some people who developed a list of everything they were looking for in a partner. For instance, they must be tall or must like sports or the outdoors, read this, like that — whatever it is they think they wanted. So, they looked and sorted according to whatever criteria they had arrived at. They found the perfect person who had everything on the list. Still, there is something wrong or missing and love never grows. Then there are those who are so different that it was hard to imagine they were even friends, let alone so perfectly in love. You know couples like this, right? Why?"

Sarah considered everyone she knew. She thought about her sister and Andrew. Were they truly in love or was it just that the criteria had been met? Most of all she thought about Greg and everything that remained uncertain in her head; had she made the right decision moving out?

"You have me talking; that's a dangerous thing because it's a well-recognized fact that I'm hard to shut up sometimes. Maria will tell you this."

"Huff, I am having the best morning ever! You talk all you want because I am enjoying every bit of it. You're making me think."

He responded with an infectious smile. "Well anyway, my point is that you can meet someone that has everything on the list, but there must be a need for discovery. That's what takes you through the course naturally. In fact, you can't help but go through it because, of course, you need it. Then you discover the magic of discovery."

"The magic? What's that?"

Huff smiled because he had brought Sarah to the most important thing he knew on the subject of love. "The magic is that you discover yourself. You discover yourself, Sarah."

This sent Sarah deep in thought again before she simply added, "Thank you."

He was not sure he had helped — at least he was not sure how he had helped. His mind shifted, remembering why Sarah was here. "Oh, the letters," Huff said suddenly. He leaned forward, standing up in a single motion that brought him out of his chair.

A small pile of split wood sat to the right of Huff. Pulling a metal bar above the stove's window, the door swung open. A log that had been burning slowly for hours flared with the available oxygen. Sarah instinctively reacted to the intensity of the heat, moving back slightly. Huff added another log, pushed the door shut with a glove he did not bother fitting onto his hand. He made his way to the bookshelf, searching the upper shelf. "Ah, yes. Here it is," he said, reaching up and bringing down a thick book.

Sarah could not read the title of the book, but she could see the cover contained a black-and-white picture of an old train engine. Huff's attention turned toward the small table to his right, picking up the pair of reading glasses and bringing them to his nose. "Okay, now, that's better," he said while adjusting the book's distance from his glasses. Thumbing through it, the book fell open where two envelopes had created a space. Taking these out and reading the first, he was quiet as his memory caught up to the words. Picking up the second, he slid the letter out, unfolded it, and handed it to Sarah. "Here, start with this one." The paper was thin and old, reminding her to handle it with the greatest care.

October 3, 1883
Territory of Denver

Dearest Thomas,

As this letter is written, I sit in the front parlor in Aunt Verna's home. It is a wonderful and comfortable place, overlooking a small yard and iron fence. The street just outside is bustling with activity and it is an exciting contrast to the ranch.

Clayton enjoyed the train ride but soon took to sleeping until our first stop where the engine took on water. The work accomplished by the railroad in such short order is inspiring and gives a person great hope for the future of this vast territory.

We were not able to depart the train until reaching Antonito. I was so tired of that seat that I remained on foot until we boarded again. All of the passengers suffered commonly and wished for a longer stop.

The wind carried the coal smoke right over the train for much of the journey before Antonito. We heard from the conductor that this is not usually the case, but the black dust inside the cabin made me wonder otherwise. I do believe your son was in great need of fresh air because of his tiny lungs. He developed a small cough, but it has cleared up after we reached the city of Denver.

Aunt Verna was at the station when we arrived. She had chosen to wait for us even though the train was past the schedule by more than two hours. We had a fine conversation late into the night and once again that first morning, until Clayton awoke.

Aunt Verna is doing well and occupying her time with activities to keep her mind busy. She has told me that Uncle Henry provided well so she will be comfortable without the need of further work. She and several other women have taken to caring for an elderly couple from the church. I believe Aunt Verna is truly enjoying helping, and it clearly is busying her thoughts.

I'm afraid that everything I had hoped to help my Aunt with may be lost, and all that I provide is another place to occupy her time. You see, my husband, I write this while in the greatest despair of longing for you.

I have never missed anything more than in those moments when the train left Durango and your figure became obscured in my tears. It was an awful feeling that I hope to never again experience. Even this letter causes me to ache, but now it is dull and not wrenching in my throat as it was in that moment.

I will confess that the excitement of this city did cause me to forget what it is about home that so draws me. For it is not the mountains, the trees, nor the river that have held my thoughts since boarding the train. The ache in my belly is that I miss you. I truly miss my husband.

You have always told me to be practical in my path. But to practice this, I must keep your words near and take each day for its own. I know time will speed with gained routing, but I am already waiting for the moment I enter your arms again.

Although it is winter, I often drift back to the ranch and to you in the fields. It warms me to imagine you in the middle of everything you have built and to see what it means to you. I would be amiss and untruthful if I left this letter without a mention of the Cascade. A swim in the pool with you puts me to bed most nights and is only followed by the Lord's Prayer.

To lie beside you with your arms wrapped around me is a security that can never be properly described. You see, it is not this security that is so missed, but the word it makes me know, and the one I will leave to you in this letter,

I love you.

Your Wife Mary

Huff had watched Sarah as she read, sipping his tea and enjoying the slight contortions of her face caused by questions and feelings produced by the letter. After she finished, Huff added to the letter. "She and her baby left for the winter. It looks as if they had gone to stay with her Aunt in Denver. I tried to look up some history on a visit to the capital a year ago, but there wasn't much there. I did find that she was staying with her mother's sister. Best I can tell is that her mother lived in St Louis about that time. Henry Brooks, her aunt's husband, had died in the middle of that summer."

"It sounds like she went to Denver to comfort her aunt," Sarah observed.

"Yes, well, for two reasons. That was one of them. The other was because of the child, Clayton, and the hard winters here." Huff thought for a moment. "Guess I'm ahead of you here. I get most of that from the other letter, his letter."

Sarah was immediately curious. "He wrote too?"

"I think they had both written each other many times, at least that's how I feel. But I only found two letters that survived — just one from each of them." He considered what he had just said. "It's better than two letters from either one of them; at least it's more interesting.

"What's the Cascade that she talks about?"

"Ah, yes. That's a creek at the top of the ranch. It meets the river above the old cabin. I've always known it as Cascade Creek. They must have given it the name."

"Can you tell me about the railroad — is it still there?"

Huff was excited at her interest in the history of the area. "Oh, good, yes. It was built for the mines around Silverton."

"Silverton?"

"Around 1880, the Denver and Rio Grande Railway had reached Alamosa, which is about a hundred miles from here, on the other side of the Rocky Mountains; you would have flown over it coming from Denver. They decided it was in their best interest to service the mining activities in the San Juan Mountains above Durango, you know, chasing the silver and gold. The railroad is why Durango is Durango. Before that, it was a small place called Animas City, along the Animas River. The railroad liked building their own towns back then when they reached new areas.

"In July of 1881, the first track reached Durango. Thomas Williams was a surveyor for the railroad; he took out on his own to discover this place. His plan was to float wood down to Arboles to meet the train before hauling it up for the mining and railroad construction.

What the railroad accomplished was amazing — building almost two hundred miles of track from the central valley to Durango in a little more than a year. They went over the continental divide and in and out of Colorado and the New Mexico territories seven times."

Sarah cut in. "In her letter she said something about the railroad's work."

"Yes, that was it — must have been impressive then." Huff gave it some thought. "Hell, it's impressive now."

"Is the train still there?"

"Just the section from Durango to Silverton. Tourists, tourists, tourists — the lifeblood of Durango's summer now. It's a good trip if you can find the time.

"By the summer of 1882, they had completed the tracks from Durango to Silverton. They went straight up the Animas canyon. You can't imagine what that canyon looks like, Sarah. If they told me they were going to do it in one year today, I would still tell you that it's crazy." Huff caught himself slipping into his excitement of the area's history. He pulled away.

"Anyway, there's my history lesson. Mary Williams boarded the train in Durango. He saw her off, and it sounds as if it was not easy on either one of them. Ooh, there I go again, more hints about his letter."

"Her letter was beautiful."

Huff was curious. "What did you find in it?" This is what he wanted to hear from Sarah; it is why he had suspected a conversation with her would be enjoyable. She had looked into the pictures and found questions beyond the frozen figures. He wanted her thoughts because she saw something too.

"I think it was interesting to step back in time. But most of all, I believe what she said, that she loved him, and her heart must have really hurt."

"Yes, exactly," Huff agreed before moving up in his seat, charged by the same clarity she had found. "But how do you know she loved him? She says it, but it's more than that, right?"

"Yes, yes, you're right," Sarah agreed before continuing. "What's interesting is that she is alone in her writing, only talking to him, and she feels a physical pain. She sees it as love, and it hurts her."

"But is it really love?"

Sarah's brow wrinkled. "What do you mean? She says it, right?"

"That's true, but what if she doesn't know? What if she is just reacting to her change in circumstance? What if that is all she is feeling?"

"Huff, she loves him. She loves him." Sarah said, again fidgeting in her seat.

Huff energized, seeing Sarah had thought through the letter and now felt something beyond just the words. She knew Mary loved Thomas, knew it so well she was ready to argue the fact with Huff. She knew it from the letter — knew it not because of the word itself, but because of the pain it caused, the pain Sarah could see and feel. "Yes, yes, yes, Sarah. You know it because you feel it. That's why I see it too." Huff added more thought. "But what if it was just a word? What if she did not speak of the hurt? What if she just signed off with the word *love*?"

Sarah sat quietly thinking of Huff's questions. She thought and thought but did not answer before his next question.

"Give me the definition of love, Sarah."

"Well, isn't it when you really care for someone, or they mean so much to you, you need them, love, well no ... shit. Huff?" She realized every time she tried, or thought she knew how to express love, it was completely wrong. It was not enough, always short of the meaning that could only be contained within the expression. She sat back on the couch and crossed her arms in a playful pout, glaring at Huff before simply adding, "Uncle."

Huff started to laugh and Sarah smiled at the reaction she had hoped to bring. "Yes, she loved him, and you will see that he loved her, but you won't know it by a single word. You will know it in the same way you saw it in the picture. Something you see that is for no other purpose than to please her. Something that was so well done that it had to embody the want and need of giving. That is what the fence is to me."

"After you mentioned it, I went back to look again. You were right: the fence is what was out of place in the picture. Almost everything else had a practical purpose."

Now it was Huff's turn to be curious. "Almost everything?"

"The picture itself is like the fence, hung in their home only for them to look at and remember, perhaps?"

"I see. Perhaps just for them," Huff agreed. He shook out of the thought and brought the other letter forward. Sarah opened it carefully and her curiosity was again overflowing.

Thomas Williams
This 10th day, October of year 1883

My Dearest Wife,

I have convinced Mr. Charlie Isgar to ride along with me into the town of Durnago. It took almost a full day just to reach his farm from the valley. His wife was courteous in feeding me and putting me up for the night. The first snows have been very wet and lent to the perfect muddle of top soil. It was not an easy journey for the horses. They seemed genuinely relieved when stabled after finally reaching Durango.

I retrieved your letter dated 3 of October and have only just read it as I now write. Mr. Charlie has found a good beer and left me to the small table in our hotel. I suspect it was his wife's urging that brought me his company. He accepted my eagerness to gather your letter without a single question and the job of buying supplies appears to be a forgotten task.

I stood in the middle of the tracks to watch you and my son disappear, because my eyes did not want to leave the two of you. I will never know a pain as deep as that brought to me by watching the last car fade away down the Valley of the Animas.

The preparation for the winter has kept me physically busy, but my mind has not left you. You and the baby have been in my thoughts every day and long into the nights. It is the only reason I sit here now and not in three weeks, as I had originally planned. It was my guess that I would find an early letter, and now my greatest delight. It is these thoughts that have brought another prayer to the Lord. Each night I ask for a mild winter in the hopes of reducing the impossible time that you are away.

On our ride, I spoke to Mr. Isgar about trading some labor. I wondered if he might watch the ranch and animals long enough for a visit to Denver. It is a tall request as his son is not old enough to be much help, but he did say he would give it fair consideration. He is a good man, and I can't ask for more than that.

To write this letter is taking every trace of my emotion. I have read your writing three times over, and each time I have been caught at the same places, for we have been thinking of the Cascade together but from two places so far apart. I have stopped each reading when you speak of being in my arms, because it's this thought that extends each night's prayer. I need to hold you so that my heart will beat in the proper rhythm it has come to know. I love you.

Not much has changed in the valley. The early snow brought two very cold nights. The temperature drop hurried the aspens from yellow to red. The animals are still able to reach enough feed in the fields so I have held the alfalfa off. Each day this is possible will mean a lot in the coming winter.

Most mornings, I have seen elk and suspect they are all moving down with the snow. I'll soon take one for the winter, when the temperature will keep the meat.

All else pales in the light of your letter and the thoughts of you and my son. I will return in three more weeks to collect your favors and forward mine. It is not simple that I tell you how I will wait to hear your words or, most of all, to hold you again. I too will leave you with the words only my heart can describe.

I love you.

Your husband

Huff had watched Sarah read again while trying to guess at where she might be in the letter. What made her stop and consider? What made her feel? This time, after his letter, he waited for her.

She sat contemplatively, reaching for the cup of tea that had also waited patiently for her to read. The water had cooled but felt good and sweet when it wet her throat. She needed this time so her words would not stumble as they came out. "What happened to them, Huff?"

"They're at the top of Tres Piedras, the top of the ranch. It's where they are buried, side by side, not too far from their home."

Sarah was instantly interested in the possibility she just heard. "Is their home still there?"

"Not much of it. Two walls of the house, some metal left from equipment, a horseshoe here or there, that kind of thing. Would you like to see it?"

"I would love that. Can we?"

"Sure." The logistics of seeing the old cabin now came to Huff's mind. "Have you ever ridden a horse?"

"Wow, that's a thought. A long time ago, with my father. Not much of that either. I'm sure it was a real old horse, you know, the safe kind for kids."

"Don't worry. I have a great horse for you. She'll take care of the work. All you need to do is stay on her."

"I bet I can do that."

"Let's go around 4:00 this afternoon." He drifted in thought. "Oh, wait. Tonight, Maria is cooking dinner." Huff searched for another time, "How about tomorrow at 4:00?"

"I have almost no schedule this week, so I'm sure that would work great."

"Come down to my cabin, I'll have the horses ready. Make sure to wear some long pants or you'll remember the trip for two weeks." Sarah laughed aloud at this, already excited about a horse trip through the ranch, knowing that the memory would last in years, not weeks, as Huff had joked. More than that, she thought she had found a friend and the invitation relaxed the urgent need for more questions. Without this pressure, they began to talk of other things; Sarah's childhood, her sister, and others topics drifted into the morning's conversation. A shopping trip over the holidays, almost two years ago, that took the lives of her parents. "It will always be painful," she confided. There was relief that no one else was injured, but also some guilt by Rachael and Sarah that they had survived unscathed. Huff found a tissue for the tears that rolled down Sarah's face and opened her heart.

Although Sarah did not offer it directly, Huff found that she felt awkward within the group of her sister's friends. Her pursuits were different from most people's and had always been measured by things less tangible than the best car or the largest home. Her world was valued differently, and Huff suspected this made her feel a little outside of the others at the ranch.

During last night's dinner, Huff wondered whether there was more to this curious young woman. This morning, he found that Sarah was unique in her thinking, views, and caring; it came through in everything they talked about and in how she listened. The morning had taken Huff back to the mountains, the hunts, and the wonderful people who had entered his early life. Places and people came out because she coaxed them from him with her curiosity. It ate away at time, as all good things do, until the sun had pushed its way down the valley, through the small window, and into a warm comfortable space they had shared.

Sarah stood and Huff followed as she made her way to the door. There they confirmed the horse ride the following afternoon before she thanked him for the tea and the wonderful time. He reciprocated as she eased her way down the steps and through the dew-soaked grass. Sarah was halfway up the lane when the river came into sight. Steam rose from the water until it obscured the bottom of the trees on the far bank. Without light, the river might have appeared mysterious or even scary. However, with the sun now charging down, it let her stand and look through the mist and think about the last several hours. She asked herself why she had not brought up Greg in the midst of a conversation so pertinent.

Huff watched Sarah through a small window as she walked back toward the lodge and was not surprised when she stopped to gaze at the first view of the river. He, too, had a question that had not come into the morning's conversation. This had caused him to worry since it first came to him as he watched her follow Rick out the lodge's door the previous night. Should I be relieved or even more concerned? Huff asked himself.

Several hours later, Huff called Maria, as he did every morning when he stayed on the ranch. He told her about the morning with Sarah and about the pictures the previous night. She, like Huff, thought there was a tremendous value in people who were unique. On the phone, he struggled to find just the right words to describe his guest, and then it came to him. "Maria, I wonder if she has the colors."

<u>Chapter 13</u>

Ben Nichols and Terry Wade had made the mistake of thinking they had an easy night's work in front of them. It was understandable; Huff let them know that his wife Maria would handle the evening's dinner.

The older guides could have warned the cooks, having previously watched Maria take control of Mexican Night at the lodge. She took dinner very seriously, and shortly after opening the car door, there was no doubt about who was in control of the kitchen. The two cooks immediately began unloading plates, groceries, and several miscellaneous things that made them scratch their heads. Pulling out and holding up a tangle of white Christmas lights, Terry shot Ben an inquisitive look. Ben tilted his head to the side, lifting his shoulders. "I don't know. Maybe she's going to wear them tonight?"

Terry hunched over and awkwardly shuffled his feet. "Yeah, we'll need to follow her around with an extension cord." Both laughed, but Maria, who witnessed the demonstration, did not. She quickly had them stringing the lights along the railing of the outside deck.

An hour into the dinner's preparation, Ben decided to get serious. He had already seen enough to understand the opportunity that Huff's wife presented, so he settled in for an education about the subtleties of Mexican cooking. Maria appreciated his approach, and soon their common interest brought about a smooth operation.

When Maria cooked, there was always a battle between quality, volume, and variety. A Mexican casserole, white bean and chicken enchiladas, pavo quesadilla with fruit chutney, red chili sauce, and rice were part of the menu. In addition, homemade taco shells and a full accompaniment of toppings were prepared so each guest could build their own plate. Of course, the proper drinks were required this night, so the emphasis was on Corona and Pacifico beer, and another area was set up specifically for margaritas. Five hours after they received their first instructions, Ben and Terry were almost too tired to enjoy the fruits of their labor.

Reducing the burners to a simmer, Maria left the meal in her new companions' trusted hands, heading to Huff's cabin to get dressed. Ben took the break in the schedule to reward Terry; they disappeared to a quiet place in the back of the kitchen where he handed the underage Terry a cold bottle of respect. It was not much of a reward, unless you were seventeen years old and hoping for acceptance. Then it was the world. Ben knew what it meant for the two of them to drink the beer together, as friends.

Around six in the evening, a single car arrived at the lodge, driven by the same pony tailed man who had driven the lead car two days earlier. A single passenger sat in the rear seat. Ted had been expecting the car and made sure he was at the lodge for its arrival.

Greg Watkins's trip had taken almost seven hours. He was irritated for almost six, because he had slept for one. The driver somehow became the focus of this annoyance, and it came out in his tip — or lack of tip. He stood for a minute, waiting for Greg to do the right thing. Then he brought the hatchback down, climbed into the driver's seat, and muttered the next words out just loud enough for Greg and Ted to hear clearly. "Asshole."

Both men hesitated only briefly before brushing it off as the problems of another long-haired hippie that their hard-earned tax dollars were supporting.

Greg was glad to see Ted, as they had become chums some time ago. Although a difference in age existed, they had established common ground early because Greg's father and Ted were business partners. A shared enjoyment of large cigars, politics, and an approach to the business world had made them fast friends.

Ted brought Sarah into Greg's life, but ultimately it was Greg's friendship with Ted that prompted his invitation to the Tres Piedras Ranch. The trouble between Sarah and Greg resulted in a week of discussion between Andrew and Rachael about extending Greg an invitation. Andrew was in a terrible position, knowing that his dad would insist on Greg coming and would not hesitate to point at the large checks he had written to get his way.

Greg brushed off his dress slacks the moment he climbed out of the car. He shook hands with Ted, and quickly jumped into business. Greg was sure he was important, as was Ted, and the reciprocated affirmations rarely stopped when they were together. "Working on a really big deal; it was tough to get away from the city. The office slacks when I'm not around to kick some ass. You know how it is, Ted."

Ted nodded his head in approval, placing his hand on Greg's shoulder. "Come on; let me show you this place."

Ted had made sure that Greg's room was near Sarah's, believing that proximity would cure the ailment that afflicted their relationship. His invitation to the ranch also followed this same line of logic. Fifteen minutes after arriving, Greg had changed into a pair of khaki dress shorts, removed his socks, slipped on his Armani loafers, and met Ted on the back deck.

People were beginning to arrive for dinner as Greg stepped out of the lodge. Nancy met him with a distant hug and a fake smile. She felt trapped, listening as the two men quickly jumped into conversation, seemingly about everything that was wrong with the world. Ted pulled two Coronas out of the tub and handed one to Greg, both turning to peer into the clear water below.

What would have been wrong with a beach? Greg thought to himself, looking into the uninviting river. He held his opinion. "Nice place here. Well done, Ted."

"Thanks. It's a special place." he responded, his right hand patting the shoulder of his companion. "I'll give you a good tour tomorrow. It's a great place to let the mind clear. Guys like us need that now and then to keep everything running."

"Here's to that." Greg lifted his beer, meeting Ted's before a long swallow. Nancy rolled her eyes at the growing absurdity, turning toward the lodge to see whether anyone needed help —anyone.

~~~~~

Entering the deck, Andrew immediately noticed Greg standing with his dad. At six two, handsome with his blond hair and blue eyes, Greg was hard for anyone to miss. Putting on his best face, Andrew came over and shook his hand, welcoming him to the ranch. Rachael followed, offering a cold hug and feeling much less pressure to make him feel comfortable. Only a select few knew the real story behind Greg and Sarah's breakup. Although speculation continued, the distance between Rachael's friends and Sarah let this rest, most knowing only that the engagement had ended abruptly. Rachael, of course, knew he had cheated and had hinted just enough for most of the girls to have a solid opinion.

Kelly Rogers and two other girls spent the afternoon tubing the river, repeatedly hiking up to float down in the cool water. Uncertain of the river, on the first trek up they asked the younger guide, Billy Talbot, to accompany them. Entering the water for the first time, Kelly noticed that Billy had quickly developed an obsession with the bikini tops worn by the girls. This led her to a little plan, and she quickly recruited the other two girls. Shortly after splashing onto the tube, she removed her top. Somewhere between Billy's initial shock and his subsequent hyperventilation, the other girls removed theirs too. They excused him after they completed the first trip, laughing for hours as they recalled the look on his face.

Kelly's eyes widened as she noticed Greg standing with Ted. Like a skilled boxer, she took a position at the opposite corner of the deck. Her greeting would wait. Half an hour later, when the alcohol primers had begun their work, Kelly led the group through their little bikini trick, emphasizing the shock of Billy's face. Two of the groomsmen bent over at the waist in hysterical laughter.

Billy himself had a story to tell. This time however, he had the full attention of the other guides. None of them would pass on a hiking or tubing trip the rest of the week. This was one of the better groups to visit the ranch; they were convinced.

~~~~~

Huff sat quietly on the small couch in his cabin, patiently watching for Maria to add the final touches to her makeup. In the small mirror, she could see he was in thought. "Your mind is working?"

"You are especially beautiful tonight," he replied.

Hand in hand, Maria and Huff walked down the lane toward the lodge. The day of cooking had passed Maria's test and she was in a very good mood. They were now talking about Ben. Maria was very complimentary of his work and pleased with his manners. Even Maria knew it was hard to work around Maria.

Huff knew his wife had had a good day at the lodge simply because she was speaking Spanish. On days like this, the words came from her faster and with more energy than normal. Moreover, when her words came at the same speed as her thoughts, Spanish was the only possibility. Huff loved these times.

The years of walking hand in hand with his wife never changed for Huff. Since he had met her, it always made a cold day warm and caused his arm to tingle. Nevertheless, when she wore one of her dresses, and felt the energy to speak in her first language, something extra was there. He recognized why this was but could never put a word on it or describe it appropriately. He just knew it contained the *énergia de la vida*, the energy of life.

When the dinner was planned, so too was the dress, and thus this very time had been anticipated. Together they now walked, Huff smiling at Maria's smile, the surrounding colors of nature providing the perfect backdrop to the ornate and vibrant display of red, orange, yellow, and turquoise. She was happy with the day, and now, wearing a dress that had begged her attention for months, the evening felt magical. Every couple of steps she would look at Huff and see that he was pleased and that would bring more joy to her. The *énergia de la vida* flowed like the Tres Piedras.

Greg had come to this place for one purpose, and thus had no reason to put much effort toward Huff or Maria, whom he perceived as the owners of a business obligated to entertain him. The hosts sensed this immediately, affording him the appropriate time: none.

~~~~~

Sarah was not aware that Greg had arrived. Although she knew he was coming, the specifics of his schedule never reached her calendar. After her early morning with Huff, she ran into Nancy at breakfast. The two made plans for a walk, which lasted until the early afternoon. After that, she sat on the back deck with several others before digging a book out of her bag and sneaking to the place where she and Rick had watched the sun set the previous night.

When she saw Rick next, she would mention this to him to make sure she was not trespassing onto a secret place of his. Sarah found the spot he had shown her to be as beautiful under the midday sun as it was at sunset.

When she entered the deck, Sarah immediately knew who Maria was because she stood proudly by Huff and because of the dress. It was a different dress than the one in the photo but extraordinary in color, like the other. This brightened Sarah's eyes and put a noticeable bounce in her step. With her focus narrowed, she missed Greg, who had finally seen her. He walked away from a conversation, heading straight toward Sarah.

"Greg ... Greg." Sarah said, surprised at his sudden presence.

"Did I surprise you?

"Yes, you did. Sorry ... I knew you were coming but lost track, I guess."

Greg had hoped Sarah was aware he was coming today and that his arrival was her priority. However, he was unfazed, certain she was just playing a little game.

"How are you, Sarah?"

"Actually, I am doing very well. I mean, in the middle of this beautiful place, it would be hard not to have a great time. It's all so amazing — maybe the best trip I've ever taken."

Greg was quiet briefly, "Better than Jamaica?"

Jamaica had been one of their better times. Early in the relationship, they had rented a very large estate on the ocean and both sets of parents joined them for a ten-day vacation. Sarah took his question as rhetorical and offered only a nice smile in acknowledgement.

Seeing Greg was more difficult than she had anticipated. Since moving out and after his last appearance in front of her apartment, there had been moments where uncertainty crept into her mind. Had she made the right decision? This debate accompanied her to Tres Piedras; she hoped the solitude of the mountains might help resolve things.

In the first brief moments, Greg reminded her of why she loved him. He could be cold and sharp when he was disinterested in someone or something but also warm and engaging when he was interested. When Greg wanted something, it was hard to say no, or difficult to believe that no was the right answer. Still, there were many things to sort through, and now was not the time. "Greg, I wanted to say hello to Huff's wife before we all sit down, so I'm going to slip over. I'll talk to you later, okay?"

Being careful not to be too obvious, many on the deck watched Sarah's exchange with Greg. The guides watched this too, not because they knew anything of their relationship, but because they were all trying to guess whether Sarah was one of the three topless girls.

She waited patiently for a gap in the conversation between Maria and one of the older guides. Sarah extended a hand and introduced herself. "Maria, I'm Sarah Field."

Long ago, Maria learned her husband had a good instinct about people. His opinion of someone was evident in the energy of his descriptions. When the person was unremarkable or struck him the wrong way, he might only offer a passing comment to Maria. On the rare occasion when someone offered a little something different to life's table, he would deliver a rich descriptive and contemplative conversation to his wife.

"Sarah," Maria exclaimed, as if they had been friends from long ago. She, like her husband, had a way of quickly removing the formal edge of the unknown. "Huff told me you had a nice morning. Did he bore you with 'tea this' and 'tea that'?"

"No, no, quite the opposite. It was wonderful. The morning was a fantastic start to my day."

"Oh, good. You never know when he gets started on his tea," she said, before coming in close; speaking just loud enough for Sarah to hear. "He could not stop talking about his morning with you." Then she gently put her hand on Sarah's forearm and slid it down to her hand before squeezing. "My Huffy says you're special."

Huff naturally garnered respect. Sarah felt it shortly after arriving at the lodge and again over the letters. She was delighted. "That's very kind of him."

Like Huff, Maria was an easy conversationalist. It would be easy for the two of them to isolate themselves for hours over a conversation about her dress. However, asking for everyone's attention, Huff introduced Maria as both his lovely wife and the evening's cook. Dinner officially began following a round of applause.

White tablecloths and simple candles transformed the picnic tables covering the deck. The white Christmas lights strung along the railing added to this odd formality. Against the night, they provided just enough light to make the dinner area seem isolated against everything else in the valley.

Like the previous night, everyone filed down the buffet before returning to find a seat. Maria and Huff's table filled quickly, leaving no room for Sarah. However, Maria made arrangements so that the two women sat at the end of adjacent tables. Their backs faced the center of the deck. Huff sat across from Maria so he could be near his lovely wife and keep an eye out for the guests.

Greg had waited for Sarah to find a seat, wedging his way in next to her. Soon however, the conversation between the two women was trying his patience. He wanted Sarah's time and felt all this talk about dresses was a complete waste. Ted took a seat across from Greg, the criminal behavior by the opposite political party chewing up time.

Everyone quickly ate and returned for more — the rumors about Mexican Night were not exaggerated. All diets were off as everyone enjoyed the freedom to fill their plates and glasses as often as they wished.

This brought the tables to life — again, conversations and laughter roared from everywhere, requiring the music's volume to be increased.

~~~~~

Away from the lodge, Rick noticed the white lights when he rounded the north bend of the river trail. He had spent the entire day on the water and lost track of time as well as how far he had traveled. It was not until he saw the lights that he remembered that Maria was cooking. He removed his wading sandals and hat at the bottom of the deck, hanging his fishing rod on the side of the lodge. He quickly combed his hair with the fingers on his right hand, a last-minute attempt at decency.

~~~~~

He entered the deck in his bare feet, his clothing still damp from an earlier fall in the river. Huff noticed him first and began to motion for Maria just before Rick's finger slid in front of his lips. He snuck up behind her as she sat talking with Sarah. He bent over and forward so he could whisper into her ear.

"Once again, I see Huff has brought the most beautiful girl to the party."

Maria startled, turning quickly to the sound of voice. At his sight, her face brightened, and she came out of her seat. She reached up, cupped both sides of his face, and pulled him closer. "Ricky, Ricky, how are you? I heard you were here. Do you ever think of calling ahead?" Before he could answer, she pushed him back, peering into his eyes before pulling him close again. "How have you been? Are you eating well?"

He tried to answer both questions. "Life is always busy," he said, patting his stomach to show her how well he was eating. Maria clearly thought he was too thin, delivering a scolding look.

Rick held on to Maria's hand and led her to the center of the deck, open and practically begging someone to dance. He had not seen her for some time and knew she would want more than just casual conversation, so he brought her here, where she could ask and he could answer the private questions first. He lifted their hands and Maria instinctively twirled under as she brought her dress to life. Continuing to dance, they naturally came together. "Ricky, I know things are busy. Always busy. I'm trying to ask how you are."

He pulled Maria close after he had spun her again. He bent so his mouth was close enough to her ear to make the next words clear. "Fine, Maria. I'm doing fine."

Again apart, Maria's eyes caught his and coaxed out a further response: "Really, I'm doing well." Then he changed the topic. "How's Mateo? We haven't spoken for several weeks."

"They're all doing fine."

Their two figures twirled and moved under the black sky. Maria's dress appeared magical against the white lights of the deck, reflecting just enough color to tease everyone with its beauty. They spoke as they danced, catching up on all things new and exciting in their lives. Those seated furthest away were compelled to stand for a better view. Most everyone watched the captivating movement of the dress. Everyone except Kelly — she watched for a more selfish reason.

Huff tapped Rick on the shoulder. "Mind if I have a dance with the most beautiful girl in the world?"

Despite his bad leg, Huff moved with the grace born over years of dancing with his partner. Nancy and Ted soon joined them. This led to Andrew, Rachael, and others who felt compelled by the setting.

Rick returned to the table, moving to Sarah. She too had stood and now watched Maria and Huff intently. She teased the obvious, "You forgot your shoes."

He glanced at his bare feet, bending to her ear with a secret. "I had them on when I started dancing. Do you think I'm so good they just flew off my feet? Or maybe someone stole them because of how elegantly they moved me?"

Sarah smiled and jumped in, "Those bastards. They've caused you to break a very strict dress code. The staff may want you to leave."

"Let me know if you see them coming?"

"I'll keep an eye out," she finished before moving on. "How was your day?

They drifted into an easy conversation; Rick forgetting about his hunger, and Sarah about Greg. Inside the lodge, Terry had rallied from a day of Maria's orders, deciding to take control of the music. Aware of the dancing, he decided the mood called for John Mayer, starting the song "Say."

"Have you ever danced with a barefoot man?"

"That's the oldest line ever."

When Maria and Rick danced, it caught the attention of everyone because it changed the evening's momentum and because of the dress. Rick and Sarah's entrance caught everyone's attention for a different reason. Rick gently led Sarah out by the hand, the surprise immediately taking Rachael's gaze to her sister's face. For a very brief moment, the sisters found each other, Rachael seeing enough in Sarah to understand how she felt. A blissful joy, even more rare than Sarah's colors, was unmistakable. Rachael turned away, simply mouthing to herself, Oh my God.

Kelly watched too, but understanding the significance, shifted to catch Greg's reaction.

Sarah leaned in. "I spent the afternoon reading under the tree you showed me last night." She considered it might be a special place, "I hope that was okay?"

"Was it you I took there last night?" he teased.

Her elbow skillfully caught his ribs. "You're funny, real funny."

"Yes, of course it's fine. That spot fits you well."

"It fits me well," she recounted his words, smiling as she turned under his arm.

Sarah was not uncaring or unaware of Greg, but she was not going to let the pressure of his presence affect her either. Still, she was careful of everyone's perception and danced with caution. Rick too moved and held Sarah with the presence of a good friend. However, the caution that they both exhibited broke down somewhere in the next song, when the topics of the day gave way to the music. The rhythm was just right, and Sarah's cheek came to rest gently on his chest. Reminded of the previous night's sunset, she carelessly closed her eyes, pressing her ear to his chest and hoping somehow to hear his heart.

It did not take long, a few verses of the song, before the colors started flowing again. This time, she allowed the calm warmth to radiate to all parts of her body, aware what would be next. The colors built as she watched; the energy they contained growing before finally exploding into her senses. She demanded her eyes to open, coming away from Rick in an effort to understand what was happening.

"Are you okay?"

"Yes, I'm sorry. I just ... I just remembered something." She wondered why the colors had even come, but then to have been so powerful too; she tried to gain her composure.

Although the moment was short, everyone had witnessed her lay her head against Rick and let go. When her eyes closed, Greg almost came out of his skin — a predictable reaction for a man who expected to have control of everything. "Who's that guy?" he demanded from Ted.

As if he had seen nothing out of the ordinary, Ted responded, "Which guy?"

"The tall one with Sarah," Greg shot back, irritated that Ted did not immediately answered his question.

"Just one of the workers. I don't know. A fishing guide." This reassured Greg, who measured himself against others by income level or any other way that was in his favor. "Just another broke asshole," he decided.

Maria and Huff had seen everything. They had danced the same song and watched when Sarah's eyes closed, knowing where she had gone but shocked to see Rick slip away there, too. Huff whispered to Maria. "¿Ves?" (Do you see?)

"Si, Huffy, si. La énergia de la vida." (Yes, the energy of life.)

"Si, la énergia. Está allí." (Yes, the energy. It's there.)

Huff's next words were heavy. *"¿Maria, deberíamos estár preocupados?"* (Should we be worried?)

She thought for a moment. *"No nos tenemos que preocupar por esto."* (It is not ours to worry about.)

They were both quiet in thought. Maria quietly whispered. *"Ella tiene un espíritu hermoso."* (She's a beautiful spirit.)

Huff responded. *"La energía puede traer el mayor dolor."* (The energy can cause the greatest pain.)

"Si."

Rick's left hand was on Sarah's back as he followed her toward the tables. As she turned to settle into her seat, his hand caught the top of her arm. Slowly, it slipped down her arm until their hands briefly met. They both squeezed quickly, just before her last two fingers slipped away. Sarah felt something that brought her eyes immediately down to his hand. Although the night was dark, one of the small lights reflected the unmistakable shape of a ring worn on his third finger. The breath came out of her immediately. She dropped into her seat as both legs lost their strength.

Rick took the seat Maria had occupied. He was already in a conversation when she looked again. Now holding a glass of water, the condensation caught the candlelight, flickering just above a small pool of wax. Sarah put on a good face but now sought to confirm what she hoped was her mind's mistake. However, the droplets of water reflected the flickering light in every direction, making the ring appearing as if it were on display, sinking her even further.

Greg was saying something to her, but it had tangled in the background noise while she asked and answered her own questions. How could I have missed it? Did he have it on yesterday? She searched her memory but realized she had never taken the time to look. There was no reason to look; he had done nothing, and had suggested nothing, she thought. "You dummy," she whispered.

Greg was not used to losing and did not like any suggestion, or perception, that this might be the case here. He strained for understanding when he saw Sarah's face change. Whatever had just happened, it caused her to deflate. That thrilled him; the carpet yanked from beneath her feet. Still, Greg felt that was not enough and searched for an opportunity to correct his world. He stood because height had always been his benefit, and he enjoyed the advantage of talking down to people, both literally and figuratively. Now standing, he introduced himself. "I'm Greg Watkins," he said, presenting his hand uncomfortably close to Rick's face.

At the same moment, Maria appeared, insisting that Rick follow her to the kitchen so she could put a dinner plate together. He shook Greg's hand as Greg stood to follow Maria. The height advantage Greg had always enjoyed disappeared as Rick straightened up. Although he had seen the guy was tall, Greg had not anticipated delivering his question while looking eye to eye. However, with the words already chosen carefully, he continued. "Maybe I can employ you later in the week for some fishing?"

Everyone heard the words, shocked that he would ask this way. Unconcerned, Greg had delivered them exactly as intended, without respect and with the intent of stripping dignity. Rick waited to respond, trying to understand Greg's intention. His body shifted and his eyes narrowed, still uncertain why, or even if, he was being challenged.

Greg left little doubt, moving in even closer. "A few extra dollars would be important to you, I bet?"

Sarah had heard this and, knowing Greg, she instinctively reached toward him, somehow trying to diffuse whatever it was that he was attempting.

Rick handled the encounter carefully, "Perhaps, but I am very selective about my clients," he responded, looking directly at Sarah so his message was clear. It was subtle and precise, and it left Greg stuck without a thing to say.

Blood pulsed through Sarah's system, exaggerated by the emotion that was set in play by Rick's ring in the preceding moments. A rare anger overwhelmed her, and, without thinking, she followed Rick's words. "We still have our plans for Wednesday?"

Rick was surprised. He thought the situation already diffused and was now walking away with Maria. He turned, finding Sarah had stepped off a cliff and instantly knowing he was the only one who could catch her. "Yes, Wednesday, I'll pick you up at eight … as we planned."

Greg's attempt to straighten out his world had backfired; moments earlier, he had miscalculated that the financial contrast between him and this guide was enough to align things according to his interests. Now, he found that the guy and Sarah would be sharing an entire day together. "Wednesday at 8:00 AM," he considered.

Sarah, surprised by what had just happened, wondered if her Wednesday now had a schedule. She would apologize and let Rick off the hook.

~~~~~

Maria brought Rick to the kitchen, insisting on coordinating his dinner plate. The cooks had begun putting the food away, but she reversed this process and began pulling plastic wrap off dishes. Rick offered an apology, silently shrugging his shoulder when he caught their eyes. They accepted it and let him know it was no big deal.

"You're taking that pretty girl fishing?" Maria pried as she put his dinner together.

"I'm not real sure about all that."

He had spent the entire day alone and without a lunch. He had not eaten since the morning, but even with that hunger, the plate of food Maria put together challenged him. Huff came in and the three sat around a table and talked while he ate. Huff sent one of the cooks to the cellar with specific instructions. A short time later, he emerged with a bottle of wine worthy of "catching up."

~~~

Greg's anger had led him down the back steps after he received a cigarette from one of the workers. Alcohol and anger often led to a smoke. The cigarette's embers cut through the night, allowing Kelly to locate him within the vast darkness. "I was dumb enough to think that you might have come here for me," she said.

He offered nothing, the brightening end of his cigarette making it clear he had taken another long drag.

"You're here for her, aren't you?"

Tapping the cigarette on his hip, the embers dropped, "What did you expect?"

"You told me you didn't think it was going to work?"

"Don't act like a fool; you wanted exactly what you got."

"Fuck you! I quit my job ... and ... and ...no one even knows what I've done ... because I thought ..."

"You thought! You thought what?" he said, before his eerie laughter cracked the darkness.

"What is it then? Why her?" Kelly stopped, realizing both the absurdity and futility of her questions. "Maybe what you see in her is what she's found in that guide."

~~~

When he finished eating, Rick insisted that Huff and Maria return to the music. Disappointment would follow if she did not properly exercise her dress. Rick excused himself, promising some time together in the coming days. Following them outside, he slipped along the wall and disappeared down the steps. Reaching the bottom, he fumbled through the darkness until he had found his wet sandals. He decided he would return in the morning for his fishing gear.

Shortly after he began walking, Rick heard a woman's voice. "Hi, there."

"Whoo, you scared me."

"Sorry. It's Kelly. We met the other morning."

Rick took a moment while he rid himself of the adrenaline that had just raced through his system. "Right. Yeah. I'm Rick. You surprised me. I thought everyone was at the party."

"Everyone except you and me. Mind if I tag along for the walk?" Kelly asked innocently.

He noticed something in her voice, "Are you okay?"

"I'm fine — just needed to get away from the party."

"It's a dark walk back. Won't you be scared?" Kelly would be scared under normal circumstances, but the same tequila that had sent her after Greg had also calmed her nerves. Recovering quickly, she did not intend to walk back until sometime around midmorning.

"I'm not scared. Should I be?"

"No. There's nothing out here."

The trip to his cabin took ten minutes. Kelly was a natural talker, speaking several decibels above that which was comfortable for the ear. He was happy to let her go on about nothing, certain she was driving any animal life from the immediate area.

A small light came into sight just as the road dropped away from the mountain. Built into another fold of the ranch's landscape, a dense collection of trees and brush concealed the small structure. Kelly inspected the setting, pleased that there would be no apparent reason for anyone to disturb them.

Rick pulled up and stopped just before taking the path down to the cabin. "This is my place."

"Yes, there it is. It looks ..." Kelly searched for just the right word. "... lonely."

Rick affirmed that not a single light was on inside. Internally, he agreed with her assessment but took a different direction. "No, just dark. Makes for a good night's sleep."

Her experience told her that the gorgeous ones were always a little slow. Dumb but certainly worth the trouble. She tried a less subtle approach. "Can I take five minutes to warm up before you kick me out?"

Rick's early height had made him an awkward teenager. Among other reasons, this slowed his read of aggressive women. Around nineteen years of age his growing slowed and his weight filled in, realizing the full potential of his good genetics. Heads began to turn as he walked by, and he soon learned how to deal with an infinite number of personalities and agendas.

Kelly's intentions were no longer a mystery; he understood them somewhere before they reached this spot. They neither put him off nor excited him with the possibilities. They were just what they were. He responded to her request, knowing he could handle whatever situation presented, and do with it what he may. Besides, he thought there might be something to the suggestion of warming up; his own wet shorts had chilled him beyond comfort. "Sure, come on."

The cabin was small and simple, its tiny kitchen missing any appliance upgrades since somewhere in the 1960s. Off the kitchen was a small room with a hard tile floor. There was no TV, phone, or even a stereo. The main area doubled as the family and dining room. Reading the room, Kelly observed five chairs with their legs facing up on top the table — only one taken down. This was too easy.

"Please sit down and give me a chance to change."

He disappeared into a small bedroom. Kelly then spotted the only redeeming feature in the entire place—a comfortable couch. A neatly folded blanket rested on the arm; this will work, she knew.

From the bedroom, Rick moved directly across the hall and into the bathroom to hang up his wet clothes. Shoeless, he returned to the living room in a pair of jeans and a white t-shirt. As he approached, he found Kelly with a blanket pulled up to her neck, both legs folded and tucked neatly underneath. A long stride was necessary as he avoided the pile of clothes left just in front of the couch. Kelly's message was unmistakable, revealed by a black thong and bra topping the pile. He took a seat next to her, careful with the wrapping on the gift she presented.

"Warming up, I see?"

"Yes, you might even say ... getting hot."

Rick was a good-looking man. He had been aware of that for many years but thought little of the fact. It was not something that he ever cared about or let go to his head. Most of the time he thought of it as luck, but then sometimes it was a curse too. Whatever it brought him, it was not within him to be rude or taken for granted. He was careful handling his guest. "Kelly, look, I'm not sure whether you are making an offer, but if you are, I'm not sure it's the best idea."

She had seen the ring; it was one of her first assessments whenever a man intrigued her. It made very little difference to her — an obstacle within the game. "Rick, I am making you an offer ... and I can assure you, it's a very good idea!" Experience brought the next move: She shifted slightly and turned toward him as the blanket fell to her waist, revealing a flawless set of keys that had never failed to unlock the strongest man. Her right index finger touched him on the shoulder and began slowly moving down his arm, masterfully pacing the words she spoke. "I'm making an offer for you to do whatever you want to me, as hard as you want, and for as long as you want." She let this settle in before continuing in a low, provocative voice. "I might make some noise, but I won't say a word to anyone. Got it?"

Chapter 14

Rick stood on the bank above the river, studying the water, yet aware that his mind was elsewhere. Reflecting on the evening, a confused tangle of emotions emerged. Without focus, the hypnotic movements of the water took him back.

His mother, Cynthia, had been a strong woman. Her marriage to Dale Wheeler, Rick's father, was a mistake by any measure, except that it produced Rick. She had given up her plans to attend college, choosing to marry Dale and follow his military career overseas. Still, she always wondered about passing on her plans to attend college and, in time, it became Cynthia's one and only regret in life. Fortunately, the resolution was simple and clear: with the strength and resolve of his mother, Rick and Cynthia developed the Stanford Plan.

The Stanford Plan came about simply because it involved Stanford University, in the Bay Area of California. Rick, his mother, and no relative knew much about either the Bay Area or the university, beyond its reputation. At a base in Japan, Cynthia happened to pick up an English magazine, reading an article about the many bright minds Stanford had produced. She rushed home and sat down with Rick, who was too young to know or care at the time, and put the plan in place.

It required a bank account, time, and persistence. Even before Rick was old enough to know the plan was for him, his mother began tending to it religiously. With each payday came a small contribution to the account, large enough to make a difference, yet small enough to go unnoticed by

154

Rick's father. Cynthia found odd jobs at most places they lived and was able to add even more when she could. Eventually Rick caught on to the importance it held for to his mother. That is when the Stanford Plan became his plan too.

Blessed with his mother's intellect, success in the classroom came easily at every new school. His parents were aware their son was sharp from an early age. However, while Cynthia preached the importance of working harder when things seemed effortless, Dale was somehow intimidated and promoted the easier path. Fortunately, Rick had the vision to make an accurate assessment of his parents' different ideas, evaluating the results each night when his father stumbled home from the bars.

Dale Wheeler left for the final time during Rick's sophomore year of high school. By then, he was tall like his father but so skinny he appeared disproportionate. Rick and his mother benefited when the family's tension followed Dale out the door. Life was necessarily modest in Killeen, Texas, but also more valued and enjoyable than either had known in years. Rick stayed focused on school, and his mother began rediscovering some of the simple pleasures of life. One of these was poetry, a subject of uncomplicated enjoyment when she was a teenager.

As eating out was an unaffordable option, each meal took place at home, served on a small table in the kitchen. After dinner, Cynthia would read aloud one of the offerings from her favorite book: *Poems, Rhymes, and Other Curious Things.* She and Rick would discuss the author and their interpretation of the writing. They both enjoyed this time, further developing the bond of a mother and only son. Cynthia also liked it for another reason;

she felt the education of her son required an exercise of the other half of his brain.

The peace that Rick and his mother enjoyed after his father left did not last long. She ignored a funny twitch in her neck and some difficulty swallowing. Nevertheless, eventually she made her way to the doctor. Diagnosed with muscle spasms, the doctor prescribed something to help her relax. The spasms made sense to everyone given the recent changes in her life, but the medication only seemed to make her tired. The symptoms persisted, and a month later, she was back to the doctor's office, this time with a strange loss of control in her leg. This led to some head scratching, a series of tests, and eventually a diagnosis that changed Cynthia and Rick's world again, this time for the worse.

Most of us live life without the knowledge of how or when we will die, but Cynthia was not that lucky. The motor neurons that sent and received messages to the brain were under attack, and they had no chance. Her respiration would be particularly susceptible, and, ultimately, that would end her life.

Rick was in the doctor's office with his mother for the final piece of the awful puzzle—the one that estimated she had only sixteen months to live. To the doctor's amazement, neither of them broke down, cried, or asked why; it was not Cynthia's way, so it was not Rick's either. Together, when they were alone, they had time for all of that, and, Rick, a boy of sixteen, proved to be the strongest man his mother had ever known.

Cynthia understood her final lesson, delivered without ever speaking a word: grace and dignity could exist in the worst of circumstances. This would prove to be one of the most powerful things she ever gave her son.

There is a business to leaving this earth: things must be organized, planned, understood, and eventually resolved. In her last months, these responsibilities occupied much of Cynthia's time. There were too few assets to cause any real trouble, save for the Stanford Plan account. Because Rick was only seventeen, his uncle took control until he was ready for the money. The other planning was concentrated on his final year of school — this, too, under his uncle's watch in Oklahoma.

In Cynthia Baxter's final days, she eased off the pressure associated with attending Stanford. She did this to give her son some room, in case it was all just too much for him. Rick understood his mother's intentions, but now more than ever, knew he would remain focused on school, work, and a schedule to make everything happen, just as they had planned.

The estimates of life expectancy are inexact, sometimes wild speculations and often surpassed by sheer will and determination. These can also underestimate the aggressive nature of the disease and cut short even the most conservative approximation. They buried Cynthia next to her mother and father under the name Cynthia Baxter, in the town of her youth, twelve months later. Rick asked that three words be engraved under her name: honesty, integrity, and love.

Despite his many shortcomings, Rick's father did return twice in the last year of her life. Rick's mind built more meaning into these visits than perhaps actually existed, and, even before his mother's death, he had began feeling the pull of family. For the first time, he had to consider being alone, which allowed him to overlook his father's flaws. The only family he knew well was his father, and, understandably, he needed him close.

When his father left Killeen, he headed for Durango, Colorado, with the promise of a job in construction from an old army friend. He rented a small, one-bedroom apartment just off Main Street and strategically within striking distance of the bars. Two months before the start of Rick's senior year in high school, Dale got a roommate.

Dale vowed to be a better father than he ever had been, but, predictably, the alcohol never made any such promise. Rick's bedroom, the living room, frequently filled late in the evening with guests dropping in for a quick drink. Few certainties existed around Dale, but one was that a "quick drink" was never quick. Before school began, Rick realized that his senior year, marked by another new town and school, would define itself by coming to grips with the loss of his mother. He also knew that the less time he spent in his father's small apartment, the better.

The community of Durango has always been a warm place with good people. Rick's introduction to this came at the Durango Diner where Gary, the owner, gave him a job. Over the years, Gary became an expert at employing people who needed jobs more than the diner needed another worker. There was but one qualification: honesty.

The day he was hired, a group blocked the diner's entrance, waiting to be seated. He excused himself by each until he was through the front door and in front of the cashier. "Excuse me, are you hiring?"

The waitress, who doubled at the cash register, kept her eye on the tall boy, looking him over before yelling halfway back into the restaurant where Gary was cooking. "Gary, string-bean is looking for a job." The entire breakfast crowd was suddenly involved in the interview. Gary turned from the grill, wrapped in his white apron and holding a spatula. Looking over the young kid, he simply asked, "Are you honest?"

"Yes, sir."

Gary pointed the spatula unceremoniously at Rick, waiving him to the back of the restaurant. "Wash your hands and get an apron. You're with me."

A week into the job, his character brought him a frank conversation with Gary and his wife, Donna, where they learned of his situation. That conversation resulted in sanctuary from his father's life: flexible work hours, hot meals, and a key that transformed an old storage room into a bedroom, whenever necessary.

Durango sits in a bowl, surrounded by spectacular mountains and along both sides of the largest river in the area, the Animas. Its location is the result of the railroad's interest in servicing the gold and silver mines in and around Silverton. To reach this small mining town, the tracks had to follow the river and so Durango grew around the river.

In his life, Rick had never lived in such a place. He discovered the peace that comes from the water, mountains, and the lack of any systematic construction. He now had this river, a place where he could come, sit, lose himself in the majestic flow, and just think.

If the diner was the first bit of good luck to come his direction, the second arrived as he sat staring into the Animas on a hot afternoon before school started. "Great water, isn't it?"

He turned to find a kid who looked to be around his age. He was by himself and stood with a fishing rod in one hand.

"Peaceful," Rick replied.

"Do you live here?"

"I do now. Just moved from Texas. You?"

"Out on the mesa," he said, pointing southeast with the tip of his fishing rod. "What part of Texas?"

"Killeen," Rick responded.

"Killeen?" the boy asked, making sure he had heard correctly.

"Yea, Killeen."

"Huh. Never heard of it."

"Not too many people have," Rick noted. "How's the fishing?

"It's been okay; worked my way up here from the center of town.

Rick was curious. "Just here to fish?"

"To register at the high school, but yes, mostly to fish."

Rick guessed they were about the same age. "What year are you?"

"My last, a senior. You?"

"Me too. just registered today."

"It's a good school; you'll like it. I'm Mateo." Mateo stepped forward, and the two shook hands.

"Mateo?" Rick's pronunciation was slightly off.

"Mateo." Only a slight correction from Mateo.

"I've never heard that name before, but I like it."

"Its 100 percent Mexican, like me. It means 'the great one.'" Mateo had a good-natured look on his face and searched to see whether Rick could deal on the same level.

"I'm Rick, 100 percent white boy. But I know enough Spanish to call that bullshit."

Mateo delivered a big grin, and they both laughed. They talked for a while about the school, the town, and some of the high-level details about Rick's move from Texas. It was clear that the two fit in well with each other and a friendship was born.

"Want to try fishing, white boy? It's best learned from a Mexican like me."

"I'd like that."

Mateo, Huff's son, turned out to be the best friend Rick ever had at a time when Rick needed a good friend. Mateo already had respect in the community, in part because of his parents, but also because he was a good and honest kid. He was popular with most other students in the school, and a few simple words let Rick enjoy the easiest transition he had ever experienced.

The first fishing rod Rick ever owned came from Huff — a trade for a weekend of putting up hay set him up with fishing equipment and introduced him to Huff and Maria.

The friendship between Rick and Mateo grew strong and thick in the mountains, rivers, and streams in the area. They hiked, camped, and fished together whenever time allowed and far past the first snows of winter. The back door of the school opened to the Animas River, so minutes after the end of most days, they were in the water again.

Just before the school year began, a favor to Huff let Rick and Mateo hitch a free ride on the train to Silverton. Somewhere in the middle of the ride, they left the train and began a week hike over and through the Weminuche wilderness where they fished the many streams and rivers that fed the headwaters of the San Juan and Rio Grande.

On this trip, and in this place, Rick told Mateo about his mother — a conversation Mateo had been expecting. His friend's mother was conspicuously absent and he appeared troubled, all of them had noticed. Nonetheless, Mateo let this come to him at the right time; his father had told him Rick would share when he was ready. On the third night of their trip, under the full moon and stars and in the most spectacular of spectacular places, Rick let go. It was a night of tears about Cynthia Baxter's life, where Mateo's ear was far more important than his mouth. He listened until Rick had nothing left. Sleep came to both as they stared up into the flawless dark sky, considering a wonderful life of honesty, integrity, and most of all, love.

The one flaw of the Stanford Plan had to do with how much money it would actually take to attend college. The account had grown and by the end of Rick's senior year would have easily covered four years in any state college. However, Stanford was private and located in one of the most expensive places in the country. Estimates were that the savings would address the first year and half of second. Nevertheless, the death of Rick's mother changed the Stanford Plan to the Stanford Certainty. Rick understood this subtlety, realizing it was the one thing remaining that he could do for his mother.

He had already tested and been accepted into the university before arriving in Durango. A month after graduation, he set off for Palo Alto, California. He drove his inherited Ford Pinto without the slightest hesitation or trepidation toward his new life and coming surroundings. Stanford was in his sight, subject to his determination, and thus now nothing less than a certainty. He needed a good job, the right job, like he found in Durango, allowing school to be his priority. At first, he lived out of his car, keeping his expenses to a minimum.

At the end of his second week, his persistence paid off. Guessing that successful companies, growing companies, would be the ones building new offices, he concentrated on the up and coming business parks. At 8:00 on a Friday morning, he ran into a man unloading a computer and other office equipment in the parking lot of one such business park. An offer to help the man unload and carry in the equipment led to a conversation. That, in turn, led to a remedial clerk position in the small company.

~~~~~

Although college can be filled with many distractions, there were only two that might have interfered with The Plan: Rick had stopped growing in the middle of his last year in high school, finally allowing his weight to catch up to his height. This had a marked effect by the end of his first year, as he was randomly stopped by the opposite sex with invitations to parties, coffee, or almost anything.

The second distraction he faced came from the job he had taken. A year in, he was an integral part of staff meetings, and his opinion was being trusted and followed with amazing results. They wanted him full time and made a financial case for him to leave Stanford. Although tempted, he turned down the offer — as well as all other distractions — remembering his mother and their plan.

~~~~~

During his junior year, Rick's study habits took him to the campus library from noon until 3:00 each day. He developed a routine of getting his work out onto a desk before exiting the library to a small coffee stand just outside. He purchased one large cup of Pete's coffee each day for a slow dose of caffeine over next three hours.

Over the course of several weeks, he noticed a tall, blond girl who used similar library hours. One day, standing in front of Pete's, he thought to order two large cups instead of just one. When he returned, she was not in her seat, so he simply placed the coffee at her table along with several packets of sugar and creamer, with the intention of introducing himself when she returned. However, returning, her surprise led Rick in a different direction.

The next day he took up a table in a less conspicuous location, made the same trip to Pete's, and waited for her to take a break. Then he snuck over and delivered her coffee without notice. He observed her review of the room, making several random inquires before returning to doctor her coffee with exactly two packages of cream.

Rick was good at this game. The deliveries were soon more exact, with only the two required packages of cream. She would stand, search the room, and make a random gesture of thanks by slightly lifting the cup.

As he continued, she tried hiding in the hopes of catching her perpetrator. This too was thought out, and now Pete and one of the girls in the copy center were in on the mysterious deliveries, and sworn to secrecy. She tried having a friend come to the library; they entered separately, found a quiet seat, and watched in hopes of catching him. That day, there was no delivery.

This service went on for three weeks, until it finally ran its course one Thursday afternoon. This time, Pete's finest arrived as always, but without the packages of cream. Noticing this, she stood and extended both arms in the air as if there were a complaint ready to file with management. Then, believing it was a simple oversight, she sat down to her work. Rick approached her table, pulled out a chair, and sat down.

Since the game had begun, each person who approached her received the same look of inquiry. Again, her eyes lifted, this time at Rick, and she raised both eyebrows. Different from all other times, Rick's eyebrows rose back at her. She now stared longer, and he stared back. He reached to his bag, took out a book, and began reading to throw her off once again. Disappointed, she too returned to her studies. It was then that Rick took a single pack of creamer from his pocket, placed it on the table, and flicked it with his finger so that it spun across the table in a perfect full turn, coming to rest directly in front of her.

The secret of the coffee had become the subject of many dinners at her sorority house. Over the weeks, several of the sisters had participated in the futile attempt at discovery, most certain that the person behind the mystery would reveal himself in the near future. The fun had then become deciding exactly what her reaction should be when he did. Ideas flew until they had contrived the boldest of all responses. Of course, it was predicated on how, when, and who was behind the mystery.

Peering at him, there were suddenly two questions to answer before the next move: Did she have the nerve? Moreover, should she risk losing the "Oh my God," as she described him later, that now sat across the table?

With her decision made, Rick watched as she opened the package and poured the cream into her black coffee. She slowly packed her books without a word or crack in her demeanor. This began to worry him, and he wondered whether his little game had gone terribly wrong somewhere.

She stood, picked up her coffee, and walked over to Rick. Placing the coffee on the table, she bent down and put her lips firmly to his for the longest, most passionate kiss that had ever occurred inside the Stanford Library. Then she picked up her coffee and walked out without saying a word. Rick sat alone, paralyzed, and speechless as entertainment for everyone who had witnessed the kiss.

Back at the sorority, she recounted the story masterfully. Most of the girls were anticipating the encounter and followed the "coffee report" for weeks. A packed room listened intently as Samantha described every detail. Several girls recognized her description of Rick, concluding that "Oh my God" significantly undervalued his appearance.

Eventually, Rick did come to his senses, gathered himself, and drifted through the rest of his classes and work that day. In the middle of the night, his eyes popped open. He realized what he would do next.

The following afternoon, Samantha sat studying at the same table. Rick approached and took the same seat. This time he bent to his pack, fished around for a moment, and pulled out the largest can of processed creamer he could find at the grocery store. It hit the table with a thud; He rotated it so she could read the label clearly.

She could not help but smile. His message unmistakable: 'I want more, a lot more.

The end of the Stanford Plan came with the release of countless black caps into the air. Rick's uncle, Mateo, his first and current boss, and one Samantha Reeves, who had developed an affinity for Pete's coffee, attended.

In those five years, Rick's luck completely shifted, and he enjoyed the best times of his life. That same night, his boss pulled him aside, offered a full partnership, and asked to open the business' second branch. Following the party, he and Samantha returned to their home, climbed under the covers, and wrapped into each other's arms.

<u>Chapter 15</u>

Late into the night, as the hosts decided to head home, Huff told the staff that breakfast could start two hours later than normal. He had seen this exact night happen before, knowing breakfast would only get cold waiting for people to wake. Adding to this, the smell of rain had rolled down the valley and caught Huff's educated nose. A good rain and a good party were better than any prescription sleeping aid ever concocted.

A soft rain continued with the first filtered light of morning. Most of the guests were unaware of the moisture, lying still under their quilted covers. That was fine for Huff, knowing that the staff, like the guests, were not immune to the powers of a good time.

Rick was the only exception to the late risers. He closed the door gently, stepping out onto the porch to check the sky. The rain was too light to change the river, and the clouds did not threaten with the darkness of heavy moisture. He arrived at the lodge before anyone was awake, brewed and drank the first coffee, collected his gear, and disappeared into the river's fog.

Hours later, the lodge did begin to stir; unshaven faces and messy heads of hair crowded the couches, chairs, and rugs that covered the floor in the main room. Everyone held a warm cup of coffee, content to let the day define itself.

Greg was one of the last to arrive downstairs, finding Sarah tucked into the corner of a couch. Like a chameleon, he seemed to surprise everyone, appropriately engaging in their common topics and even traveling the room with the coffee pot, topping everyone's cup. Sarah watched Greg intently, reminded of how he had found his way into her heart.

Nancy was running late, her upbringing not allowing her to arrive without being made-up, at least partially, for any occasion. Downstairs, she found Sarah, drawn by her easy nature and their friendship launched during the drive from the airport. They decided to follow their coffee with a hike in the light rain, leaving the lodge well ahead of everyone else.

A suggestion by one of the guides led them along a trail toward the east rim of the valley. A mile up, it took them into a dense forest of Lodge Pole Pine. The trees stretched straight and tall to the sky; the thick, overhead canopy robbing much of the light from the ground. Morning clouds mingled in the treetops, appearing as though they supported the soft, white ceiling. The needles covering the ground were wet, like everything else around the two hikers, water dripping slowly but deliberately from every tree branch. Sarah took time to reflect on her coming day. She had not planned the wonderful hike that now occupied her time nor scheduled the rest of the day beyond Huff's invitation to ride horses. However, it was the ride, the old cabin, and another talk with her friend that would pace her day and make whatever she found in-between move along like molasses.

"Have you ever been to Oregon?" Nancy asked.

"No, never to Oregon."

"Several years ago, Ted and I went out for a wedding in Portland. When it was over, we drove down to Canon Beach, about two hours west. It's beautiful there, like this. The fog moves in and surrounds the trees. Beautifully eerie, that's how I would describe it. You really should see it sometime."

"I think I'd like that," Sarah replied, her arms suddenly stretching as she turned in a complete circle, taking in the cool, damp smell of the pine forest. Simply reacting to a feeling that had come over her, she was suddenly aware of the oddity of her movement. "I'm sorry; I must look like I'm a little nutty. It's just all so wonderful!"

"Don't ever apologize for enjoying yourself, dear. The opportunities are too rare." Nancy continued, dropping her head back and repeating the spin just performed by her companion. In turn, Sarah turned again, this time her head tilted back as she looked into the shifting fog overhead. She let out a shriek of joy.

This time Nancy stood for a moment, observing Sarah's last exercise. As she came to a halt, Sarah encouraged Nancy, a large, provoking grin growing on her face. Nancy's head flew back, and she turned, screaming into their little paradise. Coming to a stop, the smile slowly left Nancy's face. "Are you okay, Sarah?"

"Yeah," the word dragging out from her lips; she left the trail focused on something deeper into the forest. Immune to the delicate arms of the floor's vegetation brushing against her legs, her curiosity drove her on. Briefly closing her eyes, Sarah again saw the beautiful color of hazel dancing around one of the thousand of ferns scattered over the floor. A few more steps and she dropped to her knees.

Nancy had followed each step, stopping as Sarah cupped her hands and extend them forward. As she touched the leaves of the plant, hundreds of beautiful red ladybugs crawled into her hands. Among the many, only this one plant contained so many of the delightful insects that the leaves appeared red. Nancy took a knee, extending her hand as the perfectly shaped shells began exposing the creature's delicate wings. Looking back to the trail where they had been, she realized there was no way to have distinguished this plant among hundreds. "How did you know this was here?"

Still transfixed on the beautiful bugs, Sarah responded, "I don't know … I have never known." The two stood, lifting their hands in the same motion as the speckled insects slowly took flight. "Not since I was a child has this happened," Sarah mouthed.

A smile, a wonderful, delightful smile, again came to Nancy. She turned beneath the cloud-covered treetops. "Me too. I was a child when I felt like this."

~~~~~

Around the middle of the morning, the overcast sky began breaking into singular cloudbanks floating gently over the valley. The rain had further cleansed the already pure air, and the smell of pine was now stronger, as if released by the showers. The sun's rays, intense as they passed to the ground, were quickly warming the humid air. This change compelled groups to form and plans to materialize.

Greg had only been fly-fishing one other time, in upstate New York. It was a marginally acceptable experience, he had concluded. Nevertheless, Ted's persistence convinced him to try it again. They were shuttled down the main road, entering the lower section of the river to share a day of fishing and of being experts on whichever subject they decided to choose.

Andrew and the best man made similar plans on a different section of river. However, they were both aware of their limitations, reserving one of the guides to assure their success.

Rachael and the other girls were not so quick to set a plan, deciding that their indecision was, in itself, a good decision. They remained wrapped in oversized pajamas, talking about the wedding as the others disappeared into the day. Once the tight-knit group of girls was finally alone, there was another subject to their liking: Where had Kelly spent the night?

Entering the lodge, Kelly faced the girls, all knowing her too well to let a detailed accounting of her night escape. The image of a friendly firing squad, dressed in colorful pajamas, briefly ran through her mind. Without hesitation, she delivered a tale of Harlequin Romance — the name Rick Wheeler forever etched on the minds of every woman in the group.

~~~~~

When they were young, and before Sarah knew others did not see the colors, she would speak to Rachael as if she understood. However, Rachael never had the gift and so could only listen and wonder. From that time, she understood that within each of Sarah's colors there were many shades, each meaning something distinct and different. Even though it was impossible to feel the colors as her sister did, she had learned that the color of blue always meant something good.

Rachael, listening quietly as the other girls egged Kelly on, almost fell over when she heard Rick's name. As they danced last night, Rachael had witnessed something inside Sarah. It was exciting and good and Rachael wanted it desperately for her sister, after everything she had gone through with their parents, Greg, and then her job. Rachael was unexpectedly angry with Rick, deliberately leading Sarah to her colors and then preparing to rip them away as if trivial or without consequence. He was going to hurt her.

Rachael made a decision, asking Kelly and the others to hold the story close, her excuse focused on painting the right picture for her future in-laws.

~~~~~

Returning from the hike, Sarah joined the others in volleyball and several hotly contested rounds of horseshoes. Individuals came and went from the games to enjoy naps and books inside the lodge. Despite her best efforts, the day did drag in anticipation of the ride. Around 3:30 in the afternoon, Sarah slipped on a pair of jeans and walked the lane down to Huff's cabin. As she neared, she found him preparing two horses for the ride.

"Good afternoon, Huff."

"Hello, Sarah. How has your day been?"

"Fantastic again, but I have been looking forward to this most of all."

"Good. I have too." He assessed the sky. "I'm hoping the weather won't get us. Did it bother you today?"

"Not one bit. It was refreshing, I thought. Nancy and I managed ·a great hike high into the forest. The clouds came down just above the treetops; it was very beautiful. We got caught in a big rain on the way back, but even that was fun."

Again, Huff observed the northern sky. "Let's hope the heavy stuff holds for us."

"Aw, heck, Huff, what's a little rain?"

"'A little' won't be a problem. How was everyone moving after last night?"

"Definitely moving slow in the morning, but then we put our game faces on." Sarah smiled. "The dinner was fantastic. Everyone's been talking about the food, and compliments have been flying around all day. By the way, is Maria here?"

"She went home around noon, headed down to Albuquerque in the morning, back toward the end of the week."

"She was lovely last night, Huff. You're a lucky man."

"I count my blessings every day Sarah ... every day."

Huff had a smaller horse saddled and was now ready to work on the larger paint that stood ready. "This is Maggie Jean; she's Maria's horse. Come say hi," Huff said, offering the saddled horse.

Sarah had not ridden a horse since she was a little girl. In the summer, her father would take the two girls to a farm that had a series of flat trails and rental horses. For a few dollars, they would ride around in circles until it was time to get ice cream. Ice cream was always tough competition for the horses.

Sarah stepped over to Maggie, and they said hello to each other. She greeted her by stroking just above the shoulders and on the side of her face. Maggie blew air through her mouth until her lips shuddered, then picked her head up slightly in approval, leaving little question that she was gentle. This, and her confidence in Huff, eased Sarah's anxiety about climbing aboard an animal she might not be able to handle. Maggie felt like a good fit.

Strapping the saddle onto the larger horse, Huff made the introduction, "This is Akilah."

"Akilah. What an interesting and pretty name. What's it mean?"

"Akilah — it's Arabic for wise and bright."

Sarah looked toward Akilah, and Akilah at Sarah, both trying to read the other. "He does look wise, Huff. I think it's a good name."

Akilah moved his weight onto his hind legs preparing to lift. His front legs came off the ground about an inch and his head came up a bit, all while keeping his left eye focused on Sarah. She was not sure whether this should scare her, but she followed Huff's lead and did not flinch at all.

"Okay, boy, soon enough," Huff said, rubbing the side of the animal. He glanced at Sarah, "He knows we're going."

Akilah responded with a whinny. Huff understood the horse, and Akilah understood Huff. "I found him and his mother at an auction. She came off some public lands up north when the herd outgrew some sort of management limit. See his ears?"

Sarah could see one was slightly different from the other. "Yes; one is a little bigger than the other."

"Exactly, his mother is the same way. People were passing on them for that little thing. It caused them to miss the gem of the bunch. His father was an Akhal-Teke. He broke a fence to meet the mother, they told me."

Sarah did not know what an Akhal-Teke was but assumed they were prized. She was sure that is what gave Akilah his size and structure.

"How did you know he would be a good horse?"

Huff thought for a moment. He remembered looking into the mother's eye and then into Akilah's, remembering seeing that they both had "It." "They told me," he replied.

"They told you?"

"Look at him, into his eye. Do you see?"

Sarah saw that the horse that had not turned his head from her. Akilah whinnied again and took his head away before bringing it back. "He knows we're talking about him?"

"Yes, I'm certain of that. Remember he is wise. He is Akilah," Huff said.

Akilah was growing impatient, knowing they were about to leave; he was ready to ride, look, go, and just experience everything. "Okay, boy. Let's go." He turned the horse to the north, pointing him up the field, and then he turned toward Sarah, "Mind if I give him a quick run to get a little out of him before we start? If I don't, he will be begging to run for the rest of the day. Believe me; the three of us will be much happier if he runs now."

"No. Please do."

Sarah thought over Huff's words, finding that he included Maggie in his count of three. She glanced at Maggie and the horse back at her. "Yeah, run him. Boys will be boys," the horse seemed to say.

As he turned the horse, the limitations of Huff's right leg were on display, his forward movement being awkward, yet efficient. In contrast, when he needed to change directions, things did not work nearly as well. His left hand took the horn of the saddle, and he balanced on his bad leg while the other foot found the stirrup. Akilah waited for the single move that lifted Huff into the saddle and brought his right leg over the other side. Then his right hand coaxed his bad leg into the stirrup.

As they began trotting, Sarah recognized a man transformed. Any awkwardness on the ground washed away when he and Akilah became one. Huff's body seemed to move precisely with every change made by the horse. He carried years of a good life around his midsection, but on the horse, those disappeared. He was skilled, secure, confident, and in control of everything. Akilah felt this too, knowing who was in charge, just as he knew when he could be the boss.

In the saddle, Huff brought himself forward and aligned with Akilah's withers, whispering something in the horse's right ear. The animal's ears lowered and came in line with Huff, who held close. Then, all power shifted to Akilah's hind legs and an impressive outline of muscles, tendons, and veins protruded at the same moment Huff said, "Let's go, boy."

Like a rocket, horse and rider shot up the field. Together as one, they elongated as their speed increased, the strides lengthening with the acceleration. Akilah's hind legs moved in unison, as did the front, his hooves digging to propel the machine forward. Sarah watched as his front legs stretched past his rear, looking for new ground to conquer and gobbling up the field in seconds. Moments earlier, the field appeared to be an expanse worthy of exercising the animal. However, Sarah now wondered whether the distant fence they approached was even an obstacle. In a cloud of dust, Akilah pulled up as Huff lifted from the saddle. Guiding the magnificent animal to the left, the cloud drifting by them, and they again accelerated to repeat the run south. Seconds into full gallop, Huff slowed the animal, pulling up before turning west toward the mountain.

Akilah loved to climb, welcoming the small task in front of him. He shifted back onto his powerful rear legs, and Huff pulled in close to help. The force from the huge muscles in his legs pushed them up into each step. The incline presented neither an obstacle nor a test; the two quickly disappeared over the ridge. A minute later, they were back, this time displaying the horse's skill moving downhill. Reaching down, Huff stroked Akilah's side, again whispering something into his ear.

"What are you telling him?"

"I told him he was a good boy," Huff thought for a moment. "but I told him in a way that would make him feel like a champion."

"He looks like a champion. Heck, you look like one too."

The joy in Sarah's face struck Huff; a dead giveaway to a beautiful heart. "Akilah's a fantastic creature."

The sky was a concern. Huff wondered whether the clouds that had drifted by all day would once again gather their strength. He turned to look over his shoulder to the north, into the mountains. It was not dark yet, but he did not want to waste too much time as a thunderstorm could come together in minutes.

"Are you ready to give Maggie Jean a try?"

"I'm ready." She was much less certain than her tone indicated. However, Maggie was a gentle horse, patiently waiting for Sarah to pull herself up.

"Okay. Let's go."

Akilah took the lead, knowing the proper pace and route. Riding Huff's favorite trail several times a week, this was an old and well-practiced experience. As they climbed away from the lodge, the trail narrowed and Maggie naturally followed behind Akilah. She did the work, leaving Sarah to keep her balance and the comfort of remembering the rides with her father. She could not get enough of what she saw. Years of erosion had cut paths down the mountain for the rain and snow to escape to the river. This process was slow, trees and brush crowding in except where the active channel took each year's rain and snowmelt. The trail they followed repeatedly moved down and out of these channels.

The scattered clouds brought shifting areas of sun and shade. Climbing from the valley floor, another beautiful perspective came to Sarah — the sun driving through the thinner clouds, its rays filtered and displayed as they traveled across the mountainside. The differing light seemed to change the exact same forest, field, or mountain. Sarah took it all in, each time staring long enough for the shadows to make sense against the varying terrain. The wind would come and go across the top of the trees, offering the smell of a distant rain blended with the pine. Here, Sarah shut her eyes to give her other senses their full turn. Then it happened, just as it had when she was a child. The colors began dancing across her vision.

"How are you doing back there?"

She pulled her eyes open, the flutter in her chest delaying the response. "Great, Huff. It's absolutely awesome. Thank you so much." Huff said nothing, turning forward again.

They moved through the forest for close to an hour. The river would reveal itself periodically, but always offered only a small glimpse through the teasing green of tree limbs. Sarah noticed Akilah look back, just as Maggie's pace increased. The trail had widened, and he was telling her to come up. Both horses and riders were walking slowly next to each other now. "You'll get a good look at the river in a few minutes."

"It's all so wonderful. Can you ride here in the winter?"

"It depends on the year. On a dry year, you can come clear into November, but you won't want to ride any part of this trail after the first snowfall. You will be convinced of that in another mile or so."

As their outing continued, so too did the conversation, returning to the comfortable level they had found during their morning tea. Huff's life, "the hunter," interested Sarah greatly as did the unique people he had met. Huff was curious about her childhood, laughing at stories and finding Sarah clever in their telling. He also got a feel for her passion as a teacher, convinced that all schools would be lucky if there were more like her. Letting her go was another consequence of a confused world, he thought.

Huff would dismount Akilah whenever he spotted something of interest. On several occasions, he found some of the plants used to make his tea. He had a particular interest in showing Sarah these, talking about how he had found each one and what it took to make it the perfect drink.

The horses would ride in line, coming together when the trail allowed. It was easy to talk with Huff because he never judged. To Sarah, he felt like a warm, safe, wise, and trusted grandfather. Huff also felt this role — a fantastic friendship was growing rapidly. He would listen, think, and then offer an opinion or nothing more than an ear. Relaxed in these surroundings and confident on Maggie, Sarah's let her guard down.

The trees opened to offer the most spectacular view of the entire valley. The river was so far below that the movements of the water appeared undetectable. Areas of white marked the most turbulent rapids, this continually infusing oxygen into the water. Huff and Sarah now stood just below a cliff. Over time, massive boulders had released, crashing down to their final resting place far below. She was somewhat anxious, approaching the precarious edge for a better look, peering over to see the largest of these boulders lying in the river as giants. These oddly held large piles of debris, far above the water's surface; the river's gentle flow now a contrast to the force that deposited these when the raging waters of spring subsided.

It was here, off their horses and fixated on the Tres Piedras, that Sarah allowed her most guarded secret slip, "I see and feel the world in colors." As it came from her mouth, she awoke from the hypnotic state, catching herself too late, "Oh, no. Did I just say that?" she quickly asked herself, turning to see how her secret landed on her companion.

She revealed this important part of herself to almost no one; lessons of childhood taught her that silence should protect her oddity. It was Sarah's to deal with and understand, interpret, and value. Of course, Rachael and her parents had to know and so, too, was Greg entrusted. Nevertheless, it had never been a topic of a visit or phone call.

Huff heard each word clearly, but looked at Sarah for a long moment, waiting for them to sink in. As he stood, the look on his face caused her concern. She wondered whether her new friend, a man she already respected, might think she was certifiably nuts. She was considering her options to pull back and recover from the silly words. Then, to her amazement, something remarkable came from Huff's lips. "When you close your eyes, you can see in color sometimes."

What caught her off guard was the way Huff said it, knowing it happened with her eyes closed. His response was not a question, rather, a statement of someone who understood. He continued, "Sometimes it is black or gray but often it's color, too. Those colors mean something, don't they? You feel them. Good, bad, hot, cold, pretty — even smells have their colors. More than that, feelings have colors too. You can feel when the colors are going to come. You need to close your eyes, see, and feel. That's right, Sarah, isn't it?"

Now it was Sarah's turn to stand in silence, her mouth partially open and frozen. Huff had just described her colors as well as she could ever have described them herself.

"It's a blessing, Sarah. It is nothing short of a blessing."

"How do you know about my colors? Do you ... I mean, have ... do you have the colors too?"

"No, Sarah. I am not that lucky, but you have met someone who does."

It came to her in seconds, the dresses and the ease at which their bond had formed no longer a mystery. "Maria?"

Huff smiled. "Yes, Sarah. Maria sees the colors too."

Growing up, Sarah had decided to tuck her gift away behind the realities of life. That was easier than seeking to understand something that could only emphasize her oddity. However, for the second time in months, she discovered that she was not alone. This time, unlike with the encounter with the homeless man, there was a person to help her understand. Energized beyond the Internet searches, library visits, and medical journals that had offered very little, Sarah now carried a need beyond curiosity, "When will she be back?"

"At the end of the week. It looks like the two of you will have something more to talk about."

In the last several minutes, Sarah Field had revealed a guarded secret to someone who, days earlier, had been no more than complete stranger. In a blink of an eye, Huff had taken her odd little quirk and made it a perfectly normal part of their conversation. This was Huff's way. He sensed the concern in Sarah's face and instantly knew exactly how fragile was the gift she presented, so he handled it with care.

"When I was a little girl, the colors were always with me. I could make them come whenever I wanted, or they were just there with everything: people, objects, emotions. They all had their colors. I felt as if I had some control over them. But, that changed as I grew up. I even lost them for a time. Then I discovered them again teaching — the children brought them back."

He was thoughtful. "You and Maria need to talk. Long ago, they had left her too. She had just lost her husband, lost her colors, and it took years for them to return." Huff settled, bringing his hand to his chin as her remembered, "I was there to watch them come back. They'll come back, Sarah. Trust me on that one."

"I didn't know Maria had been married before."

"Yes, I met her not too long after his death. She and Mateo had moved back to Durango to be with her parents." Huff was thoughtful, "It's strange how it all works out, Sarah."

Reflective, Sarah considered her recent problems trivial to Maria's loss. "Have they returned, the way they were before his death?"

"Yes. They came back. At times they are even stronger than when she was a child, but they come and go with life. I suppose it makes sense; it's easier for the colors when you're a child. Not too many things sitting heavy on your mind."

"My colors are returning here, at the ranch. It's the strangest thing, even riding a short time ago. They were just there. And, this morning hiking with Nancy, they told me that there was something to be seen in the forest. For a long time, they have only come with the children, but somehow … in this place …" She quickly debated telling Huff about the sunset with Rick and how there was something new to her sense. Rick worked for the ranch. Not certain how Huff would perceive their little outing, she held her tongue.

"Has your life changed recently?" he asked.

A chuckle jumped from her lips. "You could say that."

"Well then, are you leading a better life? I don't mean by a religious definition … or any definition but your own."

What an odd question, Sarah thought. A minute passed as she considered everything that had happened recently. "I'm struggling more than I have for years. I have to consider every penny I spend and what I do most days. I've replaced shopping sprees with walks in the park and expensive dinners by cooking at home, but, strangely, yes! I think I am leading a better life … by my definition." Her words both answered his question and told Sarah something about herself.

Huff smiled, knowing the magic of the colors was returning at Tres Piedras. "What better place to find yourself?"

She thought about his last words, deciding he was right. *The colors are who I am.*

Both turned as if they knew their time in that spot was finished. They walked the horses as the conversation about colors continued. A more serious cloud drifted overhead, causing Huff to look up. The smell of rain was now close, threatening their journey to the top of the ranch, the old cabin, and the graves of Mary and Thomas Williams.

Continuing along the trail, they passed its highest point along the eastern mountain before descending down toward the water again. At a narrow neck in the trail, Huff stopped short, seeing something that caused him to look closely into the river below. He turned back to Sarah and said something she could not understand before leading Akilah down to where the trail again flattened. They left the horses to graze in the thick grass along the path before edging their way down the bank, settling on a level ridge just above the water.

Huff pointed down river. There, standing perfectly still at the edge of the water was a tall man in a hat, instantly piquing Sarah's interest.

"Have you ever been fly fishing?"

"Never."

Sarah wanted to tell Huff about the plans she had made with Rick for the next day. Then again, she was not certain whether those were just her plans or whether Rick had forgotten them shortly after validating her outburst. This thought reminded her to clarify this before the morning.

"Watch him; I think you will enjoy it."

Rick stood without moving his body, his right hand holding a fishing rod. Slow movements of his head allowed him to observe the expanse of river.

"He seems to be taking his time," Sarah offered.

"He's setting up for this section of river, looking for the holes and how to approach the water. If he goes about it the wrong way, he'll spook some of the fish and turn off their feeding."

"How does he know they are feeding?"

"Unless he ruins the hole, there are always some fish feeding. He's figuring out how they are eating, watching for a fish to break the surface or for a flash underneath. The fish follow the insect hatches that go on throughout the day. Those hatches usually dictate their activity, somewhere between the surface and the bottom of the river. It's easy to see them rise, but those feeding on the bottom are much more challenging. It takes a good eye." Huff's words faded as he focused on Rick, "He's just getting a feel for everything."

Rick allowed his line to run out straight behind him in the current. With the smallest movement in his right forearm, the line sailed through the air, unfolding magically so that his fly dropped onto the surface of the water as gently as the real thing.

As the current brought the line back to him, he took up the slack with his left hand, pulling line through the fingers of his right. Suddenly, the water exploded. Reacting, his fingers clamped onto the line and the rod tip rose, hooking the fish.

It fought until it was exhausted, and the futility was apparent. Rick knelt into the water, coaxing the fish close with the rod. Without ever bringing out, he grabbed the end of the fly and turned it up, allowing the fish to slip off uninjured. He then glanced at the fly, dropped it into the water, and began the process again. The result of the second cast was identical to that of the first. Sarah turned with a question, "He doesn't lift the fish out of the water?"

"It's easier on them; he's trying to make sure they aren't injured. When he needs to handle them, he'll wet his hands to protect their skin.

A cloud drifted overhead and removed the sunlight from the river where Rick now stood. He and Huff reviewed the sky simultaneously, both certain a more substantial storm was developing. It was the first time his eyes had come off the water since Sarah had started watching him. Noticing the same thing, both Huff and Sarah independently hoped to stay hidden, an effort to protect Rick's privacy. He moved into the river without concern for the clouds, making his way between two defined currents.

"Do you see the fast water on either side of him?"

A large boulder sat in the water directly upstream from where Rick now stood. The river's current was breaking around each side to create a long eddy directly behind it.

"Yes, just on the other side of the bubbles."

"Exactly. The fish like the bubble line because it is calm, relative to the current next to it. They can sit there without using too much energy, keeping an eye on the current bringing the food down."

The next cast put a fly behind the rock and he patiently waited for it to drift back toward him. Periodically he would raise the tip of his rod and flip the line over in the water. "He's mending the line so the fly looks more natural."

"Mending?"

"The different currents will pull the line and drag the fly. The trick is to let it drift without being pulled by the line; he's turning the line out of the currents."

Rick suddenly lifted his rod and another fish broke the surface. This one had more size and immediately ran downstream, turning into the swift water to help its battle. He let it fight, knowing that it was older and smarter than the others he had just brought in. The fish settled, recovered its energy, and made another run.

"That's a smart fish," Huff said, enjoying the battle. "He's changing angles and finding different currents to help him pull. Watch Rick; he has to keep tension on the line or the fish will spit the hook out."

The fish eventually tired, allowing him to go to his knee for the release. This time, his hand met the fish under water and held it into the current.

"What's he doing now?"

"Letting the fish recover. He has its nose pointed into the flow to let oxygen into the gills. When it's ready, it will simply swim from his hand."

While he was waiting, a light rain started. Sarah was amazed that the adjacent hill was still drenched in sun; it was an unexpected and beautiful contrast. The rain was now steady, warm, and enjoyable as it struck her arms. Huff stood and moved under an overhang of rocks. She followed, lowering her head to fit further into the shelter. "It seems so peaceful," Sarah said, after watching Rick a while longer.

"There's a saying that goes something like this: 'I had a great day of fishing, even caught a fish.' The best thing about fly-fishing is that it offers an escape. I think that's why it's so popular now. You see, there is some real mind work going on out there. The water depth, the water temperature, time of year, the water's color, bug hatch, and where fish are feeding are just a few of the things to be considered. Then you must be careful and deliberate as you approach the water. You get all this right, and still the fish don't bite. Then you must think some more. Is it technique or how the fly is being presented? Should I be fishing on the surface, subsurface, or on the bottom of the river? Then back to the fly again. You might have the right fly but the wrong size. Then you get it right and begin catching fish only to have them turn off again. Then the puzzle needs solving again. That's fly-fishing.

During that, a person can escape. There's enough to think about and concentrate on to keep your mind busy, and think — this escape is done in one of the most beautiful places in the world. That's pretty hard to beat. Maybe the closest that most of us will ever be to the colors you see."

Sarah looked away from Huff and back to the river as she wondered what Rick was escaping from. Then it struck her, he was alone today, without a client. Had anyone fished with him yet? Sarah knew of no one, but that was not unusual, noting that other guides had slipped off on their own when they could.

The clouds eventually drifted past, allowing the sun to land back onto the river, but the rain continued. The light now reflected from each falling drop, illuminating everything to an unexpected brilliance. Rick noticed this too, pulling up his line and climbing onto a large, flat rock in the middle of the river. Placing the fishing rod at his feet, he removed his vest, setting it down too. Water now saturated and dripped from his hat.

In the sun, the rain actually picked up its pace. Rick's shorts dripped from the river's water and his shirt from the rain, until his clothing hung tight against his body. To the surprise of both Huff and Sarah, he lifted both arms and extended them straight out to each side. Both palms turned upward to accept the coming rain and beautiful rays from the sun. His head tilted back so his face could feel everything, too, holding for the water to run down and drip from his chin.

Sarah did not know how to react, feeling as though she were watching something not meant for her, Huff, or anyone. Strangely, it was not odd to her either. She understood to savor the energy from the rain and light. She watched, because she could not take her eyes away.

She then felt something else, recognizing it immediately, when the first surge shot through her body. She knew the colors were coming, because of the electricity, and she knew that these would be blue. Again, there was something different and so much stronger than ever before. Impossible to ignore, stop, or even slow, Sarah felt powerless as they built. Here, with her new and suddenly trusted friend, Huff, Sarah closed her eyes and let the colors flood in so she could feel everything.

Huff took his eyes off Rick and looked at Sarah. She was huddled near him, her legs crossed, and her hands tucked in close. On her face, he thought he saw something magical happening, something familiar, yet he was not able to be certain. Like when he first met his wife, Huff knew to let it happen, because it was so special, and so good.

As he sat, Huff focused away from both Rick and Sarah, understanding that he had stumbled on something private for both of them. He knew exactly where Rick must have gone, and in that same moment, Sarah's trust allowed the colors to manifest in his presence.

He waited patiently until she returned, and then it was time to go, the weather making the top of the ranch wait for another day.

The Colors of Blue

Chapter 16

Rick climbed out of the river a half mile past where Huff and Sarah had watched him fishing. The light had moved off the valley floor an hour earlier and the sun was now in another struggle to stay above the eastern rim of the valley.

The first time he noticed the chill to his body was when he reached the main trail leading to his cabin. The clouds and rain opened up with their best efforts of the day shortly after he started back. Earlier, the rain and river had fully saturated his clothing, so now the fabric hugged him tight, pulling the heat from his body. Shivering, he walked quickly to reach the cabin's protection. The thunder and lightning began just after he reached the back deck.

Under the cover of the roof, Rick hung his fishing gear and stripped naked. He dropped his clothes over the railing; he would deal with them in the morning. Inside, he headed directly for the bathroom, turning on the water for a hot shower.

The plumbing was from the 1940s, just like everything else in the small structure. The first few minutes in the shower chilled him further as he waited for the hot water to make its way through the old pipes. He stood under the water until the steam hung thick and he once again felt comfortable. After drying off, he threw on a thick pair of sweat pants, a t-shirt, and some Nike flip-flops before making his way to the kitchen. Periodic flashes of lightning illuminated both the valley and the inside of the cabin. The rain that now teased at every window would keep Rick from a much better dinner at the lodge tonight.

The furniture, pictures, appliances, and overall décor of the cabin were dated. A low constant buzz from the old electricity accompanied the kitchen's light. Rick stood at the entrance, briefly recalling the shopping trip he had taken before arriving at the ranch. He considered the possibilities for dinner.

Inside the vintage refrigerator, four bottles of Corona remained unopened. Their only neighbors were a pack of lunchmeat and four apples in a thin plastic bag. The offerings inside were bleak but not dissuasive. He removed one beer and the package of ham, setting them on the counter. To his left was the paper grocery sack with the name of the small store where he had stopped.

Except for the meat, beer, and apples, the bag remained unpacked. He pulled on one side, peeking in to confirm he had not forgotten anything that belonged in the refrigerator. He had not. A loaf of wheat bread, a jar of dill pickles, and a small jar of peanut butter all sat in the bag, unopened. Returning to the refrigerator, he confirmed that during his shopping spree he had forgotten all condiments necessary for a decent sandwich.

From the bag, he pulled out a long white receipt, the bottom showing a total of seventeen dollars and eleven cents. A funny look came over his face, as he tried to remember which account tied to the black card that he had simply swiped to pay for the groceries. He could not recall. Then he wondered whether the people monitoring his accounts ever laughed at a bill like this. For some reason this occupied him, and he stood perfectly still until he concluded that it made no difference. Seventeen dollars and eleven cents would be subtracted from at least $10 million, in one of the many accounts he could no longer remember.

He opened the bread; placing two slices into an old toaster that he was certain would either burn the bread or start the cabin on fire, if not monitored closely. While he waited, he pulled an apple from the plastic bag and dispensed of it in five bites. At what seemed the right moment, he forced up the toaster's lever, extracting the slices. Three slices of ham, accompanied by nothing, sat between two pieces of slightly burnt toast. He used a vintage bottle opener, rust included, to open his Corona.

Rick took his sandwich and beer to the table, sitting in the only chair he had taken down when he arrived. The other chair legs stood upright on the table, providing his only company again. His first sip of beer followed the disappearance of the sandwich. After placing his plate in the sink, he sat down on the couch that had provided the previous night's entertainment.

Halfway through the bottle, he dozed, caught himself, and placed the bottle on the floor. As he pulled a blanket over his legs, he was already looking forward to dreaming, knowing that his most vivid dreams happened when he was exhausted. He was thinking about this when his eyes closed again.

Samantha walked toward him on the white beach of Belize. She was naked except for a large beautiful green hat that sat perfectly on top of her long, tan body. On the couch, a smile crept over Rick's lips. A minute later, he was startled awake by the crack of thunder, and she was gone. He sat up, searching around the room to understand why he awoke. Listening, he heard nothing but the rain and wind. He relaxed again, falling asleep within seconds.

Rick was now looking over a bed, immediately recognizing the hotel room in San Francisco. As in so many of his dreams now, he was simply an observer.

Sam was tangled in the bed's covers and in no jeopardy of waking. He sat on the edge of the bed, just watching her breathe. He loved everything about her, now simply sitting and watching as he did countless other times. However, this day had a schedule, so he kissed his fingers and held them gently against her cheek. His eyes transfixed on the bed, he eased toward the door before stepped into the hallway. He took the elevator down to the lobby. By the time the door opened, his cell phone was against his ear, and he walked directly to the coffee bar.

"Hello, this is Mary."

"Mary, it's Rick. Is everything set?"

"Rick. Yes, everything is great. It's all so great." The words coming from Mary Robin were quiet and loving.

"Good, see you in a few hours then." He recalled all the work she had done. "And Mary, thank you."

"Don't say it again. Drive safe, okay?"

"Of course. We'll see you soon."

He poured himself a cup of hot coffee and made his way to one of the couches. Before he caught up on the San Francisco news, he took a moment and reviewed the lobby. The ceiling above him stretched for several stories, detailed with the turn of the century style retained, renovation after renovation.

The first time they stayed here, it was a gift from her parents. Celebrating the couple's engagement, they had provided for several nights at this hotel and several more at an inn in Napa. They loved this trip, repeating it each of the next nine years that followed.

Back upstairs, the door to the room opened as quietly as it had closed, but Samantha was now awake. He stepped into the bathroom to the sound of the shower. "Good morning, baby," he said. Sam's head reached around the curtain and they kissed. "How did you sleep?" he asked, placing her coffee on the sink.

"Good. Always good here. You?"

"Not bad last night." Rick stretched the truth.

Sam did not miss the little lie. "Was your mind working again?"

"Something like that."

"I'll be ready in a few minutes. I promise."

"No hurry," he responded, taking the opportunity to check his watch after Sam tucked her head back into the shower. They were on a schedule for the first time in the nine years of this trip.

~~~~~

As he settled into the cabin's couch, Rick turned over and briefly lost the morning in San Francisco with Sam. Quickly comfortable again, the dream was back: Now they were climbing away from the Golden Gate Bridge in their rental car. The fog had crept into the bay as the city slept.

Sam turned over her shoulder, rewarded with a postcard scene of the city. A thick blanket of white clouds surrounded all but the top of the towers. The red cables seemed to rise out of the white ground, climbing gently to the top of their support before sloping down and away into the shifting fog. For nine years, the trip was always the same; always the same, because it was perfect the first time. They traveled on the same dates, stayed at the same hotels, and ate at the same restaurants.

On their third trip, they met a couple in a Napa restaurant. Neither had been seated, so they happened to be waiting in the bar at the same time. A random conversation led to a single table with four seats. Both couples were on vacation, and they all had a beautiful time. That was it, until the next year in the same restaurant, on the exact same weekend, where they happened across each other again. They again had a beautiful time at the same table. This time Sam and Rick exchanged contacts with Bob and Sandi Jenkins and promised to communicate and get together during the coming months. However, life got in the way and they did not, until the following year's surprise on the exact same weekend, at the same restaurant. Every year since, without a phone call, e-mail, or letter, they had a date that they all anticipated.

~~~~~~

Rick's eyes opened. He did not want them to open, but when the dreams came by themselves, like tonight, he often awoke. Without cause, his eyelids would slowly lift, and everything would be gone. Sometimes he could fall asleep again, and Sam would come back where they left off, but not often. He hoped she would come back tonight.

Twisting, he sat up and walked to the bathroom to brush his teeth. On a small table just inside the cabin's door, he located his wallet next to a small clock. As he unfolded the wallet, he saw that he had been asleep for almost two hours. His finger searched the card slots until he felt the coiled metal. As he removed the chain necklace, it stretched straight, dangling motionless in the small room. Wrapping it in and out of his fingers, he walked through the room. A heavy click removed the last of the cabin's unnatural light as well as the accompanying electrical buzz. Rick felt his way to the couch, relaxing again with the chain now tight around his right hand, desperately trying to remember.

Outside, the rain had stopped. The pine trees that towered all around the cabin were now slowly shedding large drops of water onto the wooden deck, the sound of their impact cutting through the night's cool air. He pulled the blanket to his neck and rolled over on his side. His eyes searched through the darkness, trying to make out the details of the stone fireplace in front of him. He wondered about the men who had built it decades ago as he rolled the chain between his thumb and forefinger. These thoughts served the intended purpose, his lids creeping down, until he was asleep again.

~~~~~

At first, the dream was confusing because the figures did not make sense to him. Then he recognized the shape of Sam's hand resting on the center console of the car. Under her hand was his, the size and strength in marked contrast. Even deep in this dream, Rick knew what was wrong. The details of her hand had faded, like so many other things he once knew.

Her fingers slowly searched, exploring every contour of his hand, before turning it over to intertwine their fingers and squeezing tight. She divided her time between watching this and looking through her window at the passing scenery. She loved this trip and loved her husband so much.

They were in the car traveling through the tidal flats of one of the bay's reaches. A million years of gravity's pull had lifted and settled sediment in the brackish water. Reeds had grown up thick and tall in these rich deposits. They stood, subjects to the gentle push and pull of a weak ocean breeze. It was a peaceful and uneventful landscape, offering the perfect scene to quietly drive, think, and love.

Rick recognized this place. They had turned east in Novato, heading toward Napa. He glanced at their hands and quickly to his watch, checking their schedule without her noticing. The car turned from the flats into the low rolling hills where the land began to transform into wine country. They drove a narrow, two-lane road lined with tall cypress trees, planted so long ago no one would remember who had done it, or why. Just beyond the trees ran long, open fields that terminated into fences or shallow ravines. More trees had found these low areas, following the most consistent water each year.

Rick knew Sam would begin searching here, because she always looked here. Her hand slipped away from his as she sat up in her seat. At every rise in the road, she lifted her eyes to see whether it would be the one to reveal the church. She remembered almost every detail of the church, but never exactly, where it would appear. Out of the corner of his eye, Rick watched how each lift and turn in the road brought her anticipation.

"Let's stop today," he said.

"Oh, it's okay. Just slow down so I can have a good look."

"Let's stop," he said again. "We have all day."

Samantha studied her husband. "Okay, let's stop. It won't take long, I promise."

Each trip was the same. He would slow the car, and she would stretch tall in her seat the moment the church came into view. Then she would follow it with her eyes until it disappeared in the car's rear window. Settling back in her seat, her only assessment would be, "It's magnificent."

The road lifted the car again, this time revealing the tiled roof of the bell tower that ascended to the sky above the main structure. The red tile contrasted with the simple, bright white stucco construction. At the top of the tower, four identical windows opened out each of the four sides. A small bell that marked the beginning of each Mass hung motionless in the center. Crosses, symbolizing the ultimate sacrifice, clung to each side of the tower.

Soon after the church came into view, so too did the cars. The gravel parking lot was full, as were both sides of the lane that led to the church. On the main road there were more, each challenging the slope that ran down into the ditches along each side. They had seen this before as it was a popular place and usually busy on weekends. The sight of so many cars changed Sam's mind. "Just drive by, honey. We can see it another time." She spoke without thinking, briefly shaking Rick.

They were quiet again, Rick ignoring her last words as he composed himself. "We can just look outside. No one will notice us." He pulled the car up as far as he could and turned off the engine. Captivated again, Sam studied every detail of the old church, opening the door without removing her eyes. She stood outside with her head stretching up toward the tower.

Great care was given to every detail of the building; the crosses brought down, stripped, and stained well ahead of need. The stucco remained an unblemished white because of a similar vigilance. The style and construction reminded parishioners, guests, and tourists of the area's Spanish heritage.

Three black iron railings directed people to the two heavy, dark oak doors at the front of the church. The wood of their construction never thirsted for stain, standing strong against the persistent elements. The bottoms and sides of every window were straight, the tops all rounded into beautiful arches.

Sam and Rick wandered around the side of the surprisingly quiet church. The ground was covered by a freshly cut lawn that suffered from the shade of mature cottonwood trees. Tables had been set up on the grass, standing with beautiful white covers, apparently ready for the people inside. She turned to Rick, "It looks like a wedding."

Rick felt a confused ache shoot through his body, "Yes. I'm sure of that."

"We should go before they come outside," Sam said.

The fog in the city had completely burned off earlier in their drive. They walked to the car under a cloudless northern California day. Sam turned one last time to look at the front of the church before they left. She was following the details of the cross above the entrance when the noise of an opening door startled her. Ready to apologize, she was immediately speechless.

Again, she looked at the man, closer this time, and could still not find words. Then her eyes darted back to Rick who stood, waiting. Then back again to the man on the steps, "Daddy?"

Samantha was in her early thirties and a partner in a successful law firm in Seattle. She had not called her father daddy for many years, but in her shock, all society afflictions were lost and the core of who he was to her was put front and center.

It was her father, and the distance from Chicago let her know his appearance was no accident. She turned back to her husband, looking for words. "Whaa? How?" The magnitude of the surprise causing confused words, "I don't … I mean … I didn't know."

Rick always had a certain look when he knew much more than he was letting on. His head would turn slightly to the side, one eyebrow holding a slightly perplexed expression. When Sam saw this, she knew he had planned everything or at least knew what was going on.

She glanced, without saying a word, back and forth between the two of them until she recognized something else. Her father wore a three-piece suit and shoes polished until they were almost mirrors. It hit her; he was dressed in the exact outfit worn at their wedding.

"Hi, Bee," her father said, choking up.

Now it was her father's turn to be stripped down to the rawest and most vulnerable part of himself. When Sam was a little girl, he began calling her Bee. It had come to be how he always thought of his little girl and how he would always think of her. There was no degree, job, husband, or age where she would not be his little Bee.

Her father had been waiting in the church, in and out of tears, since the early morning. Just beyond the old oak doors, the sound of the car was almost too much to take. He sat and waited until moments ago, when it was time.

Bee climbed the steps leading to her father. He wrapped his arms around his only daughter when she reached him. Holding her tight, there was no reason to fight the tears, so they came again. It was impossible to hold emotions back from a father who loved so much, holding her and hoping to never let go.

Sam did not want to let go of her father either, wanting to be his Bee for as long as she could.

During their hug, Rick snuck up the stairs. Sam finally turned from her dad, closed her fist, and pounded it on Rick's chest as she fell in for his turn. "I love you," she said, and then again. "I love you." On this step, in front of a beautiful white church, and under the cross of Jesus Christ, stood Samantha Wheeler with the only two men she had ever truly loved.

The sound of another door opening broke the brief silence. This time it was her mother, coming to Sam for a similar greeting. Sam hugged her tight and held her away with both arms to look at a strangely familiar outfit; it, too, had been worn when Rick and Sam were married. The doors were now open, her mother ushering Sam inside the church.

It was dark and her eyes needed a moment to adjust. Focusing, she now stood facing a line of women, each with a bouquet of flowers. Here again, there was a huge surprise, each one of her original bridesmaids standing side by side. The fabric and style of their dresses were identical to the original, altered only to account for nine years of life.

Mary Robins stood at the front. She was Sam's best friend from Stanford and the one who had suggested the first kiss in the library. Sam stepped forward to greet Mary and each of her good friends. While they hugged and kissed, she saw the church filled to overflowing. They were watching every step she took and every reaction on her face. No one was able to fight off the emotion.

The church was Rick's idea. He had thought about it for many weeks before making a single call to Mary. It was no simple call, because of everything else that needed consideration. He wanted help with his idea. Soon after that call, he flew to Chicago and talked with her father and mother. At their home, they discussed the idea on the same patio where he first asked for her hand. This time, it was the smile and words of Sam's mother Janice that set everything in motion. Leaving their house, Janice hugged him, speaking softly into his ear, "It's a beautiful way, Rick. She will love it as much as she loves you."

In the church, to the far right of the entrance, stood a mannequin with a delicate white dress draped over it. As she came to the end of her line of bridesmaids, Sam faced her original wedding gown. Before arriving at this spot, everything was clear, but seeing this brought the purpose of the day to the forefront of her realization.

Rick had come into the church quietly, behind his wife. He had not seen most of the people inside for a long time. Mary was responsible for everything; her first calls spreading like the best chain letter, the idea striking everyone the same way. Business trips and family vacations all cancelled for something much more important. In the crowd were friends and family from every corner of the United States. There were two couples from Switzerland, another from France, and an old friend Singapore. Everyone who should have been in the church was there, including Mateo.

The sight of Mateo brought the enormity of everything to bear its full weight on Rick. Mateo was one of two people in the world who knew Rick at his core. He had been the one who helped him in Durango and through the most difficult time in his life. Mateo stood steady and moved his head ever so slightly up and down to let Rick know that this was right and the best it could be.

Rick knelt down because the time was right. He felt heavy, confused between the joy and the reality of the moment. It was the right time because Sam had just seen the dress. She now turned, surprised to find him on his knee.

The audience had anticipated this moment, any remaining noise in the already quiet church ceasing. A dropped pin would surely echo through the high Catholic ceiling, "Will you marry me again?"

It was a simple question with a simple answer. She walked forward, wrapped her arms around the back of his head, and pulled him tight. The only possible answer arrived quietly. "Yes."

It was now that Samantha began managing the mood of every one at the church. She recognized early in the surprise that the day would be a delicate balance, and she, most of all, would control the mood. She announced to Rick, but more for the rest of the crowd to hear. "Quite a little surprise you had up your sleeve, Mr. Wheeler." Then, looking at her best friend, Mary, she shook her finger. "And you. You and I will talk later. But now I'm ready for a wedding."

Sam did it, removing the tension that could not help but slip in. After she spoke, everyone's spirits lifted and the mood swung to celebration. Her words brought laughs and delight and now the confusion between tears of sadness and those of joy.

Like nine years before, the girls attended to the bride. Before ever arriving at the church, they had the dress masterfully altered to address

Sam's loss of weight. Experts for hair, makeup, nails, and anything else were also ready, in case Sam felt the necessity.

Rick and Mateo found another empty room where his suit was ready. Alone with his best friend, Rick let down. Mateo held almost all Rick's weight as they embraced, the tears running down the back of his best friend's jacket. It was in the San Juan Mountains where Mateo and Rick became best friends, and there where they came to understand each other. When they fished together, each would take a side of the river, the noise of flowing water often preventing any conversation. Communication became a slight lift, or dip, of the chin, somehow both asking and answering questions.

In the small room, Rick moved away from Mateo, their emotion leaving neither one in any shape to speak. Mateo lifted his chin, asking Rick if he was okay. In response, Rick closed his eyes and dipped his chin slightly before bringing it up again. Then they got back to the business of the wedding.

~~~~~

Rick stood at the front of the church with Father Manual Ramirez. He too had given up the day's responsibility at his parish to repeat some work he had completed nine years earlier. Rick's only request was that there be one omission in the vows: "as long as we both shall live."

Like everything else, the procession down the aisle was remarkably familiar. The same groomsmen walked the same bridesmaids, and the same relatives took the same seats. They found the spirit of the original wedding.

When Samantha appeared at the back of the church with her father, everything stopped, as it should. Rick had not anticipated this sight, not because he had not considered it, but rather because he never thought she could be any more beautiful. He stood at the altar, looking to the back of the church, amazed once again. He thought back to the wedding pictures at home, considering just how much of her beauty had escaped the camera. He was breathless and could not take his eyes off her. Sam's hair was up, but several strands had come down to tease at her cheekbones. She flicked these back with her hand just as the guests stood.

Music came from the loft, and Sam and her father began down the aisle. She was strong. Sam was always strong. She walked without conflict and found the joy in having this once again, with the man she loved, the parents she loved, and the people she loved.

Struck in a moment of weakness, Rick took his eyes off Sam, slowing the rush of emotion. He looked down and then focused on her father. He had shined and reshined his shoes to reflect the importance of this day. The cuffs of his pants were pressed so that they lay perfectly on top of each shoe. With each step, his shin would catch the front of his pant and carry it forward until his foot settled. The momentum took the fabric past his shoe until it caught on his calf. Then it returned, settling perfectly over his shoe again before the next step.

Rick watched this movement in slow motion repeatedly. The movement settled for the last time, and there were no more steps to take. It was here that Rick, Sam's father and mother, and everyone else felt the same pain. Sam hugged and held onto her father. Everyone waited patiently, and the world became perfectly still. They moved apart until only their hands met, then, continuing ever so slowly, until it was only their fingertips. Then, that was gone. Rick watched this, along with everyone else. For it was here, this very moment, that brought so many questions to him, and a fear that he was doing the wrong thing by creating this day. The great church was perfectly quiet as a father gave away his only daughter, for the second time, so terribly near a time when he and everyone else would lose her forever.

~~~~~

This thought woke Rick again. He always woke up here because it was just too much to bear. He turned and sat up with both elbows on his knees. His head dipped forward, waiting for his eyes to focus on his feet. He slid both hands over his face until his fingers reached his head, running them through his hair to recover.

He now consciously thought about that day and how Sam had understood the conflict that held heavy in the church's air. They had come because of their great love, known for more than nine years. They celebrated this love on the same day they celebrated her good life. It was also a day, for many who came, to say goodbye for the last time.

He stood to clear his head, edging his way back to the kitchen and taking a long drink of water. Stepping out onto the deck, his heavy breath shot far into the night's cool air. He rested both hands on the railing, dipping his head before looking up and peering into the darkness.

The last surprise of that day came from Sam, just before they fell asleep. In the same hotel room they stayed on every trip, she handed Rick a small wooden box. He sat up, returning a similar look that had greeted him earlier in the day. "What's this?"

"Open it," she said, motioning to the box. "You're not the only one who can keep a secret."

Rick lifted the lid cautiously, peering inside before removing a roll of paper. Around the outside of the paper, a simple gold chain held its shape. He slipped it off, looking again at his wife as he stretched the paper open. He had recognized it immediately as an ownership deed. At the top, there were three words: The Tres Piedras.

"It's near Durango," Sam said. "Mateo helped me."

Rick was silent. He simply asked, "Huff?"

"Yes, he helped too. He's a nice man."

Rick now opened his palm to see the coiled chain, looking at it curiously. That night, Sam had taken his hand and closed it around the metal. "Just keep it with you, please." Without releasing his hand, she had something else to say. "I've come to terms with leaving, but I'm scared for you. He could say nothing, only nodding his head as the tears rolled down his face, pooling onto the Tres Piedras deed.

The following night, in Napa, Rick and Samantha went to the same restaurant at the same time. In the bar, they met their friends, Bob and Sandi Jenkins, again having a wonderful time. Barb noticed the weight loss, but Sam chose to just cover this with an excuse, rather than affect one of so few remaining good times.

The following year, there was a different route into Napa. With the dinner as his only purpose, Rick's plane landed around midday. That night, there were only three at the table. He told his friends about Sam, their life together, and how everything important to him disappeared when she died.

Chapter 17

As the dinner wore on, it became increasingly clear to Sarah that Rick would not join the group. His absence removed the excitement of possibility, leaving her with only the persistent pressure of Greg's stare. Greg wanted to talk with her and was becoming increasingly irritated that she had not yet given him any time. He had traveled to Colorado for only one purpose: Sarah. She felt the pressure but was simply not ready yet.

Sometime before bed, Sarah considered the other question at hand. Was Rick actually planning to take her fishing in the morning, or had he just dismissed her outburst as something necessary to deal with Greg?

As she said good night, Rachael saw that her sister had something on her mind. She asked, and, in confidence, Sarah had told her about Rick and the coming morning's dilemma. "If he shows, he shows," was Rachael's advice. After Sarah was gone, Rachael quickly pulled her fiancé aside, letting him know what she thought of Rick. Andrew knew better than to do anything other than just listen.

In Rachael's mind, the character of Rick Wheeler had taken a significant hit after his indulgence with Kelly Rogers. She did not usually care about Kelly's proven methods, or about the men that enjoyed the benefit, but when one of those same men also reached the heart of her only sister, it mattered greatly. This was exactly what she thought had happened, because she had never seen Sarah so interested in anyone before, even Greg.

~~~~~

The Colors of Blue

In the morning, Sarah sat awake and alone, ahead of the sun, waiting, hoping, and anticipating. Her first sip of coffee brought a little satisfaction, feeling that the haphazard measurements that fed the coffee machine had actually produced a satisfactory drink. However, this was no substitute for the anxiety over the potential disappointment ahead. She wished she had asked Rick whether they were really going.

The second person downstairs was Rachael — well ahead of her normal schedule. Hearing something, Sarah turned over her shoulder. "Hey, why are you awake?" she asked suspiciously.

"Just woke up for some reason," Rachael responded as she poured her own cup.

"Go back to bed. If he doesn't come, I'm going to crawl back in bed myself. I just wanted to be ready in case he shows up."

Rachael felt her sister's anxiety, and changed the subject, "How's Greg?"

"He's fine. Persistent, I guess. We're going to talk things over at some point."

The boiling of Rachael's blood shook the sleep off quickly, "You're not going to go back to him, are you?" Rachael caught herself before she inadvertently delivered a more graphic message.

"We are just going to talk. I have some things to say, and I want him to listen."

They both took long drinks of coffee to add silence, time, and thought to a dangerous, difficult subject. "After the accident…when they were gone, he was very good to me, Rachael," Sarah began. "You and I

210

both needed people in our life; you had Andrew and Greg was there for me. I needed him and he was good to me. I can't forget that."

"But Sarah, he cheated!"

"I know Rachael, I know. If I can never forgive someone, what kind of person does that make me?"

"Sarah..."

"No, Rachael, I know. This thing is not black and white, nor is it easy to wrap my arms around." Both were quiet in reflection before Sarah continued, "Forgiveness is easier if you love each other; it may be impossible if you don't." She considered her time with Huff, "I just need to understand if we love each other or not." Again, they both sat, sipped their coffee, and thought. "See, it's easy, right?"

Rachael's eyebrow raised, understanding the magnitude of Sarah's struggle, "Easy," she replied and they both laughed.

Rachael studied her sister; she was the most strikingly beautiful of all beautiful people. Her mother's genetics delivered lightly bronzed skin that offered a unique contrast when her curly black hair danced against it. People always spoke of the eyes of her father's mother. These did not find their way to her father or any of his siblings, but somehow they reappeared in Sarah. Her green eyes were the reason most people stared at Sarah. Her beauty brought many opportunities to her doorstep. Most people wanted more, but for some reason Sarah had not, until Greg. Rachael had always suspected the colors ultimately stopped most of Sarah's relationships from developing, but she was not sure. She also suspected it was something else that let Greg penetrate her life. Was it simply that she needed someone when her parents died? On the other hand, perhaps she mistrusted her instincts and took a chance, one that even now tore at her deeply. The one serious relationship Sarah had ever had ended in a disaster. Now, armed with Kelly Rogers' secret, Rachael sat waiting to protect her sister against another unsavory character. She was just uncertain of exactly how she was going to do such a thing.

The first second that passed the hour was the heaviest for Sarah, because Rick was now late. This was when both girls began to lie to each other. "It's no big deal, Rachael. I just didn't want him to show up and not be ready."

"We're still going to have an awesome day, sis. If you want, we can go into town and explore Durango."

"That would be fun," Sarah replied with forced enthusiasm. Both knew they would wait and see whether he was coming. Nevertheless, it was better to have an up-side surprise rather than a huge disappointment. Therefore, they hedged their bets with excuses.

At fifteen minutes past the hour, he was nowhere in sight. Sarah concluded he was not coming and curled into a ball on the couch. Rachael unfolded a knitted blanket and laid it over her. She was asleep in minutes. Rachael wanted to finish her coffee, so she picked up a magazine and got cozy in one of the oversized chairs hidden in the corner of the room. Occasionally, she would glance at the clock, wondering whether, he still might show. She sat, read, and watched over her sleeping sister. Each minute that passed brought a sense of relief from the distance it put between Sarah and Rick. However, she also knew that each minute whittled away at her sister's excitement and her confidence.

Rachael had just settled into her magazine when a sound came from the stairs. She turned just as Greg landed at the bottom. At first, he saw neither girl, moving slowly until he found Sarah curled on the couch. Thinking they were alone, he glanced at the clock before mumbling just loud enough for Rachael to hear, "He stiffed you, huh."

Rachael wanted to wipe the smug look from his face. "What do you want?"

Surprised, he found her in the corner, "Nothing. Just checking on Sarah."

"Yeah, you're such a good guy. I'm sure you're very concerned for her health."

His upper lip lifted, "What do you have against me?"

"It's not against you in particular; it's just that all cheating assholes disgust me!"

Somehow, Greg had convinced himself that Sarah had not told her sister the specifics of their problem. "Why don't you let us figure this out?"

Just as Rachael was about to fire back, she caught Rick ambling down the lane through the window next to her. She was suddenly anxious, wondering how Greg would react when he walked in the door. His purpose would be obvious.

Rachael let out a long breath, reflecting the impossible position faced by her sister: Greg offered the slow, methodical strangulation of a python. Next would enter the other snake, one that could kill with a sudden bite, a pool of venom arising from a night with Kelly. One method fast and the other slow. The results would be identical. Still, she imagined the confrontation would be worse.

With the building pressure of Rick's eminent arrival, Rachael was unsure of where to take the conversation, so she stated the apparent. "You're down here because you knew she was planning on fishing with him. Are you afraid she might enjoy someone else?"

The juvenile treatment had its effect. Greg glanced at the clock and then back to Sarah. "Looks like she'll need to make some other plans," he responded. Rachael quickly glanced out the window again, seeing that Rick would make the steps in less than a minute.

Delivering a sneer to his adversary, Greg turned and loafed toward the stairs. Simultaneously, when Greg reached the second floor, Rachael sat back in her seat, and Rick landed on the deck outside.

Rachael tried to look natural, burying herself in an article about Caribbean vacations. She watched as he entered the room, almost standing to protest, but then realizing he had not seen her. She thought differently, deciding to sink slightly lower within the shelter of the large chair.

He immediately noticed Sarah curled underneath the blanket. As he approached, he saw she was sleeping and became very careful and deliberate with each step. Should he leave her to the peace she had found?

Rachael studied him intently, assessing how he would handle her sister. She was cynical and ready to come to her Sarah's aid. Suddenly, Rachael saw Rick's face change. It was subtle at first and then unmistakably certain. Did he care?

He might have found her shoulder and rapidly urged her from the tranquility of sleep. This is not what he did. Instead, he took a knee next to her and whispered her name gently, so she would comfortably float back to the surface. "Sarah," he waited for her. "Sarah," he whispered, patient again.

Rachael saw it before Rick knew it happened; Sarah caught him, or rather, her beauty had caught him. This time her name did not whisper from his lips. Instead, his hand found the curls of the magnificent black hair that lay just above the brow of her eye. He lost his sense of time and purpose and the restrictions of "proper" as he followed the curls that now intertwined his fingers. He could not help himself. The pressure of his palm was gentle against her skin, giving just enough to bring her slowly to him.

Sarah's eyes were beautiful even when closed. Her lashes were long and dark and seemed to hint of the innocence that lay just beyond. He called her to him again, "Sarah."

This time she heard him. Just as her eyes began to open, he started to take his hand away. Instinctively she caught it before it moved, pulling it closer until his hand rested on the cup of her neck. Sarah's hand held Rick's from moving from her skin. He did not resist, because he simply could not. The short nap had brought warmth to Sarah's body. Rick now felt this, and it caused him to look at his hand, as if it were receiving some priceless jewel.

The brilliant green of Sarah Field's eyes flickered open and struggled to focus, abruptly bringing Rick from his trance. How was he here? How was it that he now knelt in front of her, his hand consuming her warmth and laced within her beautiful hair? He worried that he had taken something that was not his.

He began to pull away, but she would not let him. She did not let him because there was no surprise when her eyes opened. As it turns out,

Rick was with her the minute she had fallen asleep. The anticipation of the day and the desire brought him to her as she lay sleeping. When she awoke, and he was there; it made more sense than if she were alone.

It was now Rachael's turn to have a strange feeling: remorse. She was witnessing a care so natural that it should be theirs alone. She saw, felt, and knew it before either one of them understood. Rachael wished she could magically vanish and leave this, whatever it was, to just the two of them.

Sarah held Rick's hand as she sat up, leaving the dream of Rick Wheeler for the reality of Rick Wheeler. Her mind was clear enough to feel that both were damn good.

Although they both felt the energy in their hands, there was awkwardness in how they had come together. Space came between them, and they settled into a distance that properly set the day's expectations.

"I'm sorry I was late. I left and realized I forgot lunch."

"No, it's fine. It looks like I needed a little more sleep anyway," she said, trying to sound casual and cover the pounding of her heart.

"Are you ready to go?" he asked.

Sarah stood up, folded the blanket, and placed it over the back of the couch. "Let's do it. Do I need anything?"

"You should have a light jacket for the morning. You won't need it in another hour."

Sarah was dressed in a pair of shorts and a pullover sport shirt. Rick noticed her sandals. "Do you have an old pair of sneakers? We will be in and out of the river, and those won't last long."

"I do, on the front walkway. I'll get them on our way out."

Rick led Sarah toward the door. On her way, she remembered Rachael, curious as to where she had gone. She turned, her eyes passing over the old chair one time without noticing anything. She searched once again, this time discovering the two eyes and forehead of her slumping sister.

"Shit," Rachael thought to herself, hoping to escape undetected. Now caught, she could think of nothing to do except lift her right hand and offer a meek wave good-bye.

Sarah wrinkled her forehead, and the question was clear: What in the Hell are you doing over there, hiding?

Sarah turned back to Rick who was holding the door. Another look back at her sister revealed a clear message, "I'm so happy that I'm about to pee my pants." Turning at just the right moment, Sarah's eyes led Rick to Rachael. When it was clear that he was now looking directly at her, she raised her hand and repeated the same weak wave. Wrinkles came to the sides of both his eyes in the same instant Rachael saw the beautiful white teeth behind his smile. When the door closed, Rachael slid to the floor, trying to hide from herself.

~~~~~

"Are you interested in going up river today?" he asked, now some distance away from the lodge.

She thought, "I'm pretty much interested in going anywhere with you." However, the words she chose were tempered, "Sure. That sounds fantastic."

Rick carried a small pack on his back and a fishing rod in one hand. They followed the dirt road until it was gone, and the same trail from

Sarah's horse ride began to lead their way. "Have you lived around her a long time?"

Rick realized how little they knew about each other, "I moved here when I was in High School."

"Is that when you learned to fly fish?"

"Something like that. Mateo, Huff's son, and I became very close. We hiked and fished all around these mountains."

"Is that when you knew you wanted to be a fishing guide?"

Rick stopped, looked over his shoulder at the same moment he understood her confusion, "Yes...around then."

"I had tea with Huff the other morning and saw a picture of Mateo."

"Huff trapped you in the cabin and forced you to drink his home brews?"

Sarah laughed, "He's good company."

"That he is!"

Rick was curious, "So where's home?"

"New York."

"City or state?"

"Both," Sarah responded.

"Did you grow up in the city?"

"No, moved there for college and it kinda stuck. I'm a teacher...an unemployed one."

"We need good teachers," he responded as he methodically marched them toward the river. "You're looking for work then?"

"I have been, yes. Not much luck, yet. If it gets really hard I'm going to run away and teach overseas."

"Wow, that's ambitious! You should go to England, if you speak the language?"

Sarah laughed, "I've studied hard and think I've about got it down."

"Let me know if you need any help; I'm fluent."

Laughing, she replied, "I'll keep that in mind. You are so very helpful!"

"I do what I can for the little people." Their interaction was easy, light, and enjoyable; a simple pleasure, they both recognized.

"Seriously, I'd love to spend some time teaching in Paris. When I was in High School, I spent ten days there with my French class. I've always wanted to go back. Maybe this is my opportunity?"

"You enjoyed it?"

"Oh God, yes. The Eiffel Tower, Louvre, Notre Dame, I could spend a month at each one.

Rick gave this some thought, "I love the lights on the Tower at night."

This statement shocked Sarah, having molded her impression of Rick by Huff's original description of the guides. "Most worked part-time in the surrounding communities and guided on the side to support their other jobs," Huff had said.

"You've been to Paris?"

"Yes, many times. I like to get away from the tourists, find what other countries, cultures, and people are really like." Rick was afraid of two subjects on this day. One, of course, was Samantha. This was not because he cared that people knew or that he had trouble speaking about it. Rather it was because the subject usually changed how people saw him. He knew people would respond with sympathy in their voice and by treating him differently, so he kept the burden to himself. The other subject was his work. For many of the same reasons, it was a burden. When people found out about his money or who he was, it changed things. It changed how they thought of him or saw him. He suddenly became "sir" or another formal title, so he usually stayed away from the subject.

In the effortless conversation with Sarah, his experience in Paris simply came out. He felt careless, leading her into topics he had hoped to avoid. The first one arrived, "What do you do for a living? I mean ... besides fishing."

Cynthia Wheeler, Rick's mother, had a funny saying she would use when things were tough or when she had a difficult question to answer. "What would a pirate do here?" This funny little reference had jokingly infiltrated many days shared by Rick and his mother. It was now the first thing that popped into his head to answer Sarah's question. "I'm a pirate."

A serious expression marking Rick's face, Sarah stopped walking and considered every legitimate possibility. She could think of none. "A pirate? Like 'Walk the plank,' pirate?"

"Yes, well, more of a swashbuckler with a purpose. Those other pirates give us a bad name."

Sarah wanted to laugh aloud. Instead, she joined the game. "Isn't that job a little difficult around here? I mean, there's not an ocean, I'm pretty certain."

"It does have its challenges, I'll admit that."

"Where's your patch?"

"I thought it might scare you."

"Your parrot?" she asked.

"Same thing. If the bird doesn't like you, then...sckkkkkkkk." He made a funny sound as he drug his right index finger across his throat.

"Yes," she said. "I've heard of the killer parrots from Mandgoli." She invented the name to fit the ridiculous dialog.

"Well, I'm just warning you, okay?" he said, still holding firm.

"Thanks. What do they call you anyway?"

Rick only hesitated briefly. "One Eye."

"One Eye? One Eye the Pirate?" She smiled, "That's all you got?"

"Yes, One Eye. Got a problem with that?" He worked hard to keep a straight face.

She was ready. "Shouldn't One Eye have ... well ... one eye?" she responded, raising her brow.

To this, he made sure they were looking directly into each other's eyes, then, slowly, he simply closed his right eye. Finally, they both left their little improvisation and began laughing with each other. Sarah's hand reached out to Rick's shoulder, pushing him with all her strength. He moved away only slightly as they continued to laugh.

They continued their walk, now more relaxed and delighted than ever. They passed the place where Huff and Sarah had watched him fishing, continuing until Rick stepped off the trail and began heading to the water. Sarah held for a minute. He turned back to her and urged her on with a motion from his chin. "One Eye says this way." Sarah smiled, stepped off the trail, and followed her favorite pirate.

Rick stopped up just as they reached the water. A large rapid tailed out into a long run of calm. They now stood on the shore at the end of the slow water. "Let's see what they are up to."

"How do we do that?"

"Pretty much just watch. I'm looking to see if any are on the surface yet." They stood and watched the water, Sarah's eyes following his as he searched the river and the bank.

"See anything interesting?"

He pointed to a bug flying over the surface of the water, "See the insect hatch?"

Sarah had not noticed the bugs flying over the river. After he pointed the first one out, she now saw hundreds of the tiny insects hovering two feet above the surface. "The fish have not turned onto them yet. It will come fast, about the time the sun reaches the water," he explained.

They had walked into the sun just as they reached the river. It brought the temperature up so quickly that her light top was already too much. The day would be very hot.

"Do you have room for this in your pack?" Sarah peeled off her jacket. Rick had taken off the pack and was now sorting through flies to match the hatch. He took Sarah's jacket, folded it tightly, and put it in the bottom.

"The water is off a little from the rain last night. It might take a few hours for them to really get interested."

Sarah was feeling feisty, "Excuses, excuses. I want a heap of fish today. So get to it."

"A heap? I thought you were a teacher?"

"You heard me right. I want a heap. For that matter, I want a gigantic heap of fish today."

Rick, on his knee digging into the flies, grinned at her playful energy.

"You got it. Let's get us a 'heap of fish.'"

They had already reached a fun banter and both were warming to the personality of the other. She swaggered in her playful demands for fish. Secretly, she knew she would panic if she even had to touch one.

Shortly after stepping into the water, the first fish came to the top. Sarah did not see it because it barely disturbed the surface when it took the floundering bug.

The immediate lesson was about how to cast a fly rod. It appeared simple enough when Sarah had watched him the previous day. That proved to be very deceiving. Rick stood upstream and handed her the rod, then pointed to a rock in the middle of the river. "Just cast at that rock. I want to see what I have to work with here." She smiled back at his smile. Then she threw the end of the rod in the direction of the rock. The line coiled and tangled in mid air before landing in a mess just in front of Rick's feet. He intentionally stared at the coiled line for a moment. "Now, that's a heap." She punched him in the arm.

Rick quickly untangled and straightened the line before handing the rod back to Sarah. "Let's give it another try. This time let the line drift down stream until it's tight."

She watched the line come straight in the water below her. "Now pick up the tip of the rod so only the last part of the line and the fly are in the water. Then keep your wrist straight and be slower in the cast." This time the line flew upstream perfectly, but the fly landed too close to the shore.

"Great," he cheered her.

The current brought the line back quickly, and it wound around their legs. Once again, Rick fixed it and set her up again. "This time, get it farther out in the river," he encouraged.

She complied and a fishable cast resulted. "Perfect. Take up the slack as it comes back at you," he commanded, raising his voice with excitement. Sarah pulled at the line as it drifted back, trying to remove the slack.

He enjoyed every effort she made, seeing that Sarah was a determined student, listening and working on each instruction.

Sarah's next cast caught the first pine tree of the day. It would not be the last. He patiently resolved the problem, finding a long stick on the bank and using it to work the fly out.

Around her tenth cast, she landed the fly masterfully in the bubble line. Rick knew this would produce. "Good. This is good. Slow now, bring in the slack. Not too much, don't pull on the fly, let it drift naturally." Then the fly suddenly disappeared under the surface. It was so fast that she missed it at first.

"Lift," he urged.

Sarah raised the rod tip but let the line go at the same time. With the sudden slack, the fish spit the fly and was gone. Her first fish was safe with only the curiosity about an energetic fly to ponder. Rick was proud of his student. "Good one. That was great. You almost had him." The fish was gone but Sarah's sudden burst of adrenaline was not. It was so fast. The tug on the rod demanded her action, and it scared her. It also excited her, so she began again.

The river was off color from the sediment that had risen with the night's rain. It slowed the action but also gave Rick time to teach. They fished for an hour and a half with three more fish showing interest, but caught none.

Above the second rapid, they crossed the river. By then, the water was refreshing against the intensity of the Colorado sun. They approached the next run of water, and Sarah prepared her first cast. It landed perfectly again, and she handled the line like an expert. The fish that exploded from the water had been waiting for the exact bug that she presented. This time she held the slack and lifted the rod until the hook had set perfectly. It was small enough that the flaws in her technique were covered. It ran and pulled at the line before leaping from the water. Sarah's enthusiasm urged her on, the fish tiring as she brought the rod tip to Rick. He grabbed the line and followed it into the river. The fish was tired and came to him without any more fight. He knelt and made sure his hands were wet before touching the beautiful colors of the trout. Before unhooking it, he gave Sarah a better view. She knelt to inspect the beautiful colors of her first fish.

"Do you know what it is?" he asked.

Sarah had seen the many pictures of trout — cutthroat, brook, rainbow, and German brown — on the walls and in the many magazines strewn about the lodge. Still, she was not sure what she had caught. "No. What is it?"

Rick turned to her with a very serious look on his face, "It's a fish."

She responded in the least intelligent voice she could muster, "That's a fish?"

"Yes, you can tell from the fins and how it lives under water."

She was ready, "Oh, like a whale?"

"Yes, like a whale, only these can get bigger." Rick easily slid the hook from the colorful whale, releasing it to swim back home.

Delighted with her first fish and everything else, Rick received a huge hug when he stood. However, the intention of the hug quickly fell victim to something much stronger between the two of them. Both felt it seconds into their embrace. It led to an awkward moment where neither wanted to let go or could explain the reason a fish might necessitate such an embrace. Their hearts pumped when they realized what was happening and what they were feeling. Their energy was confused; neither was certain of the other's feelings.

Sarah had looked for and found the ring shortly after they left the lodge. It was there, always there, never hidden, and never removed. She had mixed feelings, knowing how Rick made her feel. Just his presence brought her something new, something she had never felt or seen before. However, she knew he was special most of all because of the colors.

She would never take something that was not hers, so it held them apart. Sarah caught herself each time she realized she was taking from him and each time she felt him taking from her. She was cautious of his intentions and even more cautious of her own. She wondered if she was taking by simply enjoying herself, the question itself cautioning her.

Rick also felt this distance. He had been surprised to find Sarah inside the invisible barrier he carried after Sam. In addition, there was the man on the deck, Greg, who felt he had some claim on Sarah. "Just enjoy the day," he told himself.

The day was to be enjoyed not simply for the company, but because the river and mountains were spectacular and full of possibilities. Each turn of the river brought something new. Each hour brought a different angle of the sun's rays on everything natural. There were new colors, smells, and sounds that came in the peace of these mountains. Both recognized it to be one of the best places and best days they had had.

They would fish one side of the river until the bank ran out before crossing to begin again. Each time they crossed the river, Rick held Sarah's hand. When the current was strong, he walked just slightly upstream of Sarah so the water broke against him before reaching her. Nevertheless, Sarah was ready for a rest when he suggested lunch.

When the heavy rains came, the mountains would shed water through a series of arroyos. Where these reached the water, deposits of soil flattened the land just beyond the bank. Grasses and other vegetation flourished in these places, making them ideal areas to rest. They sat on the soft grass that emerged from the sandy soil. Rick opened the pack and began to dig, first pulling two beers out, their temperature not lost on him, "Warm beer for you?"

Sarah came to her elbows to look at the offering, "Love one," she replied, feeling the bottle as he handed it to her. "Is this as warm as you can get it?"

He smiled, his eyes not immediately leaving her. She was smart and silly, and he loved her personality as she playfully harassed him.

The contents within the backpack were unloaded as he continued his disorganized search for lunch. Three fly boxes, two apples, and various other items covered the ground before he reached the sandwiches. Sarah spotted something else that caught her curiosity—a plastic Ziploc bag held Rick's wallet and a small, blue, soft-cover book. Because of the wallet, she was careful. "May I?" she asked, picking it up and holding it for his approval. Without care, he nodded approval. She removed the book; its cover was plain blue, tattered and faded with a simple title, *Poems, Rhymes, and Other Curious Things.*

There were single long stems of old grass that marked different pages in the book. At some point, water had found the bottom third of the book. She guessed it was why it now traveled in a plastic bag. The pages curled slightly, but the words were still clear. She opened and read one to herself:

The Colors of Blue

Hope Is the Thing with Feathers

By Emily Dickinson

"Hope" is the thing with feathers
That perches in the soul
And sings the tune without the words
And never stops at all,
And sweetest in the gale is heard;
And sore must be the storm
That could abash the little bird
That kept so many warm.
I've heard it in the chilliest land
And on the strangest sea,
Yet never, in extremity,
It asked a crumb of me.

Rick watched her read out of the corner of his eye. When she finished, she closed the book and sat thinking. He read this book the same way: first, the slow read, then the book closes, and then thought. "Did you find one you liked?"

"I did. By Emily Dickinson."

Rick saw that Sarah enjoyed the thought it brought to her, "Can I read you one?"

This surprised and thrilled her. "Yes … please …I would like that very much." She handed him the book. He exchanged it for a flattened sandwich wrapped tightly in plastic.

"Sorry about the sandwich. Looks like the beer and apples got on top somehow." She searched for the edge of the plastic that would reveal her lunch. Rick crossed his legs and sat upright. He took a drink of beer before he began to thumb the book for something to read.

Sarah peeled the two pieces of bread apart to have a look. There was peanut butter on top and peanut butter on the bottom. "Did you make the sandwich?"

Rick could not answer because he had taken the first bite of his. It was dry and not easily shifted for conversation. He nodded his head, knowing she was taking a crack at the lunch. Rick got his first bite down before exclaiming, "Everybody loves peanut butter. There's nothing wrong with you right?"

"Oh, no. I've just heard that in foreign lands they combine things with the peanut butter, such as jelly or honey or …"

Rick jumped into Sarah's jabbing, "Or potatoes?"

She laughed aloud, "Yes. A peanut butter and potato sandwich — that's what I was craving."

"Sorry. I didn't have any potatoes," he added with a very large smile. Then he got serious for a second. "Is it okay? I forgot to buy jelly."

She felt that she had taken it too far, "Yes. Gosh, yes—it's great. I was just kidding with you."

"Good. Eat your sandwich."

Sarah smiled as she took her first bite. She helped the search, reaching to the book and picking the only page that was marked by three stems of grass. This had drawn her curiosity. She wanted to hear it — from his lips. He glanced at the title and closed the book, looking Sarah in the eyes and perfectly reciting the page:

The Hope of Loving

By Meister Eckhart

What keeps us alive, what allows us to endure?

I think it is the hope of loving,

or being loved.

I heard a fable once about the sun going on a journey

to find its source, and how the moon wept

without her lover's

warm gaze.

We weep when light does not reach our hearts. We wither

like fields if someone close

does not rain their

kindness

upon

us.

Sarah loved it. She loved it because he had memorized every word and because she felt every word. Her eyes closed, and she just asked, "One more time, please?"

As he repeated it, the words came more slowly than before, and Sarah listened intently. Lying back onto the river grass, she closed her eyes and searched. However, this time she was confident. For the first time since she was a little girl, she knew how to bring the colors. When he finished, they both held silent under the prominent sound of the river. "Can we endure with only hope, or do we need love?" she asked.

Again, he liked her question. "Maybe we can endure with only the hope? But to thrive, I think we need love ... and we need to be loved."

They were both now sitting up, interested and intrigued by the other's questions and thoughts. The dry sandwiches, helped a little by the warm beer, were now being enjoyed immensely. The morning had produced an easy dynamic between the two of them. They both moved in and out of ridiculousness and thoughtful dialogue, picking up where the other had left off. Rick, like Sarah, had looked forward to the day. As their time together moved on, they were both surprised by how easily the energy came. The attraction was hard to ignore.

The day was dry, warm, and windless. The sun was now directly overhead, and the smell of pine permeated the air. Rick was again thumbing through the book in his lap, working the last of his lunch down. Sarah found herself just looking at him. He was handsome, funny, and bright. Laying her head back to feel the sun, a funny thought arrived, This was the best, and worst, sandwich I have ever eaten.

As lunch ended, Sarah launched a little surprise. Seeing Rick occupied tying on a new fly, she took it upon herself to clean up, stuffing the pack with everything she could find. Plastic wrappers from their lunch, two empty beer bottles, sunscreen, fly boxes, some small rocks for fun, the plastic bag with Rick's wallet, the book of poems, and miscellaneous other fishing equipment were all crammed inside.

Without him noticing, she slowly tied one of the straps around a small root that was exposed above the ground. She then covered the knot and the open zipper, properly disguising her trap.

When the fly was ready, she took the rod, surprising Rick with her enthusiasm to begin fishing again, almost tearing it from his hands in her zeal to start. Rick smiled, standing while he spoke, "Okay, then," he said, reaching for the pack so he could catch up. Her plan worked to perfection. Rick pulled to lift the pack and scattered its contents over the ground.

There was a moment of shock, as he stood still and observed the mess while trying to understand exactly what had just happened. When he spotted the knot, it immediately caused him to search for the perpetrator.

She had walked about ten feet before turning back to witness the event. It worked exactly as she had planned. Sarah waited for Rick to understand and for him to turn toward her. She was ready, hunching over slightly and covering one eye with her right hand. A wonderfully bright look of success raced across her face just before she delivered the only response possible. "Arrrrgggggghhhh." Rick grinned as he laughed, finding the dimples that formed with her smile impossible to ignore. She turned, bouncing upstream to catch another tree.

Chapter 18

"So I have it figured that you got your hand caught in the cookie jar?" Greg was neither surprised nor shocked by the question, knowing Ted had a forward personality like his own. They stood side-by-side in the river, Ted feeling that this was the perfect place to dig into such a thing.

Greg, neither ashamed nor concerned, considered the question only shortly. "I've always appreciated beautiful women," He replied without emotion.

Together, Ted and Greg's father had speculated on the rift between Sarah and Greg, noting that she had moved out of their home, and that Greg had said it would only be temporary. His father suggested that the problem between them had to do with Sarah, suspicious of her offbeat nature and guessing it had somehow taken a toll on the relationship. However, Ted had a different idea, guessing that their problem had more to do with Greg's prowess with women. Until moments ago, he had kept this thought to himself.

"You old dog. I'd like to get a good look at the one that ruffled Sarah's feathers. Bet she was something?"

Greg's eyebrows lifted, and a smirk grew across his face, "Maybe you already have. Like I said, I appreciate the beautiful ones."

"What are you going to do with Sarah?"

Greg's expression went blank, "I'm here, aren't I? I'm doing my part to smooth this thing out." He spoke with an edge to his voice, annoyed that he was standing in this godforsaken place. "In the end, this will be good for her. She'll get some time alone and an appreciation of the life she left to be an unemployed teacher." A smile emerged with the thought.

"She'll come around. In my younger days, I had a few problems just like yours. They always come back." Ted now laughed, doing his best to relate to Greg, whose life he admired.

Greg turned toward his companion, a slight lift in his lip and nod of his head acknowledging the comment. He could not believe the two ever had any similarities, certainly not with women. It was time for the subject to change. "She's out with that asshole today."

Ted was competent with a fly rod, casting toward the hole they had waded out to reach. He responded just as the fly landed on the water. "Don't worry about that. She's just rattling your cage a little. What's she going to do, move to Colorado and live with a poor river rat?"

"Yeah, that's about what I thought. She's playing a little game because I'm here." Greg watched Ted cast again, standing next to him with no interest in fishing. Since leaving the lodge earlier, it was no secret that he was uninterested in fishing. He only came along because of Ted's prodding. "Listen, I'm going to head back to the lodge, Ted."

Ted was ready to get serious about fishing, "Sounds good. I'll catch up to you later for a beer or two."

Greg lumbered out of the river, fought through the foliage that covered the bank, and reached the lodge after a long walk. He sat down beneath the stairs that led to the deck to remove his wet fishing boots. Above him, he could hear the voices of several people.

~~~~~

Sharon Davis had finally found a time where she could pull Kelly aside. They moved to the edge of the deck, unaware they were just above where Greg was now sitting. Sharon searched, assuring they were alone. "Okay. I've been dying to hear all the dirty little details."

Kelly thought a little twist in the story couldn't hurt. Seeing that Sharon was going to keep this under wraps, she straightened her posture and took on a more arrogant demeanor, "Oh, you're talking about my roll in the hay with Rick?"

Greg's eyes opened wide, and he froze, holding perfectly still as he listened. The removal of his gear would wait. "Hell yeah, I'm talking about that. I've been trying to get you alone since you came strolling in like the cat that just ate the canary."

Always loving an audience, Kelly improvised further, "Let's just say I have a new appreciation for Colorado men. Sharon, you've gotten a good look at him right?" her question was rhetorical. "Well, it gets a lot better when his clothes are off."

"God, I want to be you." Sharon responded, as they both laughed. "Did he say anything about his ring?"

"Not a word. Guess he had something more important on his mind at the time."

Sharon shook her head from side to side very slowly. "It seems you made the best of your week." She was thinking about something else, "Did he say anything about Sarah? I mean…she doesn't know, right?"

Kelly's mood cracked, letting out a sigh and wanting to make something very clear, "No offense to Sarah, but he's a little more 'man' than she could handle."

There was more to their conversation, but Greg had heard everything he needed. What Kelly had done made no difference. However, this guy, Rick, had stepped over the line the other night, and now there was no doubt about Sarah's interest. A gun, with every chamber loaded, had just found its way into Greg's hand.

Chapter 19

The best times of the day were simply the result of being together and alone. Teaching, Rick would stand behind Sarah, her arms and hands mimicking his every motion. As they moved together, her technique was lost, the simple sight of his hand delivering the energy to make her heart race. Pressed against his chest, she fell in love with fishing for nothing more than the feeling it brought her. He felt this too, his lesson failing with each breath, his face settling down onto her neck. A silence came to the river and the small world they were sharing.

She had not been this far up river the entire week. Like other places on the ranch, it was beautiful. Here cliffs rose up from the west bank of the river to tower over the top of them. A single tree had somehow found a grip on the fractured rock face and had thrived for decades. The branches now provided the perfect perch for two large, black birds. They watched Sarah and Rick climb out of the opposite bank and into a long open field, coming to the remnants of an old home.

The cabin's old logs of were black with decay, and only two connecting walls remained upright. Most of the roof and other structure had long since returned to the earth. Sarah realized where they now were. "This is the original home on the ranch, the Williamses', right?" she asked, remembering the letters from Huff.

"Yes, the Williamses'. Did Huff show you the letters?" he inquired.

"He did. The morning we had tea."

Sarah became curious, wondering where the fence had been. She walked around the walls, trying to see the angle and how the camera had been set. "Where do you think the front door was?"

"Right here. Did you see the pictures in the lodge? They were looking directly up the field."

She moved around to Rick's perspective. "Yes, I see it now."

She stood where the camera must have been placed, trying to imagine the fence and the garden so many years ago. The house sat in the narrowest part of the valley, the long field and river occupying the only flat ground. Sheer cliff walls defined the view to the west, and a more gradual slope came down to the cabin from the east.

"How long have you worked for Huff?"

Rick did not find it necessary to correct her, so he responded truthfully, "I've known Huff since I was in high school."

Sarah said nothing, still looking at the old cabin.

"Come here, I want to show you something," he said

Sarah followed Rick around the back of the cabin and up the field about fifty yards. An old tree stood away from the mountain's slope and, oddly, in the field where there were no others. All other trees hugged tight to the eastern edge, where the field met the rise of the hill. As they approached, she saw two headstones resting under the shade of the old pine. "It must have been planted when they were buried," she thought.

Time had worn away at the chisel marks; the message faded but was still clear. The branches of the tree protected the final resting place of Thomas Williams and his wife, Mary. Sarah saw that the ground was clear of all sticks, needles, and weeds, "Huff?" she asked.

"Yes, I think he rides up several times a week just to tend to them."

Sarah's heart could not have cared any more for Huff than at that very moment. Teaching children and dealing with their parents gave one of her strongest beliefs: the true nature of a person is found within their motivations.

Granite stones, tilted slightly by time, marked each grave. Cut square, the edges of the solid blocks were rough with the faces polished smooth. Sarah wondered about their lives and how they had come to rest here. Had someone planted this tree for them, many years ago? Who would have done such a thing? They had a child, Clayton; what became of him? Did he bury his parents here? Sarah knelt between the two stones and ran her hands over the dates. "Mary died two years after Thomas."

"Yes, I saw that too."

"Do you know how they died?"

"No, but they lived into their seventies, so they must have died naturally. That must have been a long life then." Something in Rick's voice had changed, each progressive word coming slower and carrying him deeper into thought.

Sarah too, was quiet, thoughtful, and cautious. Her parent's death would not be a subject for this day, or with this man, but she was curious, "I knew a woman who died shortly after her husband. I've always wondered if she gave up hope after he was gone; if the void in her life was too great to continue." Both stood without looking at each other, eyes transfixed on the stones. "A broken heart; do you think that's possible?" she asked pensively.

Rick did not expect this question; it immediately brought him thoughts of Samantha. Her death had left him unsure about what to do or how to act. After nine years together, his life revolved around the two of them, and he did not know it any other way. The first year, he had missed her so much that his energy was gone, and even simple foods brought uncomfortable aches to his stomach. He lost a great deal of weight and the joy that had so naturally been part of his personality. Alone, he experienced the most basic of all struggles; this led him to answer Sarah's question with certainty, "Yes. The loss of such a love can take a great toll on a person ... even to the point of threatening their survival."

Sarah felt something in his voice and turned from the graves to find him. She wondered what it was. He knelt to the ground, filling his right hand with dirt before standing again. Opening his hand, he studied it before letting it sift through his fingers. He wanted to move on.

At the end of the field, the river was wide, and the trees set back far from the bank. It seemed like it would provide the perfect place for both Sarah's fishing and a new topic of conversation. "Come on. At the top of the bend, there's a good spot."

They hugged the tree line at the edge of the field as they walked. After ten minutes, they came to a creek that ran off the eastern ridge. Rick pointed the rod tip just past the creek, "It's just up there, past Cascade Creek."

The name was familiar; she remembered. "The letters. They both spoke about swimming in the Cascade."

Sarah peered over the creek, interested in contrasting the pool against the image she had built in her head. She saw nothing that would suggest such a spot. The creek dropped rapidly over hundreds of rocks, and the water broke white as it struck them. Rick understood what she was thinking. She looked perplexed as she searched. The first time he had looked for it, he had stood here and with the same look on his face. "It's up there," he said.

Sarah followed the end of his finger into the eastern mountain, where Cascade Creek originated. "How far?" she asked.

"Not far. Maybe fifteen minutes. But there is no trail, so it's a little rough."

"I'm game. Are you?"

Rick nodded his head and began following the stream toward the mountain. The creek appeared from inside thick vegetation just before it emerged to cut across the field. He stopped, removed the pack, and set it down with his fishing rod. "We need to get in the water and walk up the creek." Sarah could see there was no other way. The constant rush of water over the rocks created a mist that fed the soil around the creek. This microenvironment allowed a diversity of plants and trees that tangled with each other along the steep bank; this dissuaded any thought of following along side of the creek. "After I read the letters, I came here to look for the swimming hole. I gave up at first, thinking a landslide or something else had changed the creek. I came back the next summer and went exploring. That's when I found it. Outside of Huff, I don't think anyone knows it's here."

The water was slightly cooler than that of the river. Sarah saw that the hike would be the most challenging of the day. She was glad she had followed Rick's instruction and brought a good pair of shoes. The water was not deep, but it was stronger and more turbulent than the river. Rick led the way, offering a hand for her balance whenever necessary. The bank of the creek was infrequently available because the limbs had bowed over into the water. However, these same obstacles provided compensation by acting as handholds.

The noise from the cascading water and the rigor of the hike eliminated their conversation. A leaf fluttering in the windless air caught her attention. She studied it before closing her eyes and finding its color. She was a child again, becoming confident and in control of her sense. Sarah began to toy with her colors. "Huff was right. This is a magical place," she thought.

They walked in silence until the creek's water suddenly slowed. Rick turned, "We're almost there." Sarah saw nothing out of the ordinary. However, she could feel that the force of the water against her legs had eased. The larger rocks that defined the early part of the creek gave way to much smaller stones. Then they entered an opening that changed everything dramatically.

A nearly perfect pool of clear water sat hidden in a basin of the mountain. The water dropped over a large stone deposit before falling directly into the pool. This drop, along with the tremendous amount of water from the melting snow, trenched the bottom. This same force pushed pebbles and other small stones to the pool's exit. They now stood looking at the exact oasis enjoyed by Thomas and Mary Williams more than a hundred years earlier.

"It's fantastic! How deep?"

"Right now? I bet it's twenty feet deep under the falls," he speculated. "You can perform most Olympic dives, if you're so inclined." He pointed to the solid mass of rock that began to their right and climbed around to surround the pool. Near the top, she saw it flattened to the perfect sundeck and diving platform. Summer's lower water exposed a sand bar to their left.

Sarah walked to the sand and began working at the knots in her shoes laces. She had never seen such a perfect place to swim. The best magazine photos could not pull at her like this place. It was one of the most beautiful places she had ever seen, but also special because of the Williamses. She would ask Huff to read the letters again, knowing this place and thus the Williamses better.

"Thanks for showing me. I can't tell you how it makes me feel." Sarah finally got both shoes off. She held them over the dry sand, hesitating as the excitement of the setting reached her soul. The next, and boldest, game of Sarah and Rick's day began. "How about a swim?" she said, facing him. It was a simple question, but it was not asked simply. Her voice was playfully seductive, asking just as she dropped both shoes to the ground. The challenge was unmistakable.

Rick was a cool customer. He kept his eyes focused directly into hers, hypnotically accepting. He reached down, unhooked the Velcro that secured his fishing sandals, and held both in his hands for a long moment. Then he dropped them to the ground, tilting his head to the side without losing eye contact.

"Shit," Sarah thought to herself. She was so zealous and excited that she had started a game of chicken and her first move was met head on. On top of that, she would have trouble swimming naked in the middle of the day even if she were the last person on earth. She was inherently shy and weighed her next step against her personality.

A thousand thoughts shot through her head: she was with a man she barely knew, in a very isolated place, and he was married. She tried to evaluate all of this in the short time she had before her next move was expected. She left the last thought alone for the moment, focusing on her shirt, the payment for a bit more time.

Sarah loosened the white t-shirt from her shorts, delivering the best look of confidence and defiance she could muster. She pulled it off, the shirt pulling her curly black hair back as it lost its last grip around her head. She emerged with her eyes closed, shaking her hair, and holding the shirt over her shoes for another extended period. As the shirt dropped through the air, she shifted her weight to one hip, again finding his eyes.

Adrenaline pumped into her bloodstream, released by the confused reactions of sheer excitement and pure terror. Her heart's pounding verified that she had never been anywhere close to this place before, but the outward result was only a slight rush of each breath. She stood completely scared, her posture bluffing defiance and challenge.

As Rick's beautiful smile grew, Sarah knew he would call her little bluff. His shirt was off in seconds, but, as part of the game, he held it for a long time in his fingers before releasing it to the ground.

More questions shot through Sarah's head. Was she ready to give in the match she had started? The next step was clear, but it too brought a more practical question. What underwear had she put on this morning? She scolded herself, "Shit, of all days to pick a thong."

She peered deeper into his eyes, affirming that he wanted to continue. Rick read this perfectly, his face challenging her without saying a word. The fingers of both hands slipped between her shorts and underwear.

Her eyes left his for the first time as they followed her shorts to her ankles. She stepped out of them, again holding them for the required time before gravity pulled them to the sand. As they fell, her confidence slipped. She glanced down to make sure her underwear was cute. A small pink bow sat in front and perfectly emphasized the small triangular patch of black fabric—a gift to herself a week after Greg had decided another woman was somehow better. The day she picked them out, her only purpose was to feel pretty.

Math was never Sarah's favorite subject growing up, but here Sarah performed a crucial calculation with exact results. They both stood with only two articles of clothing. His turn meant that he would need to bare all before she would. On the other hand, her top would come next. Her heart jumped again. From the first moment they met, there was a fantastic comfort between them, never spoken about or scrutinized by either one. It was just there, and it came with trust. It was that trust that ultimately led to their day of fishing and to the Cascade pool. However, it had also been trust that led her to disappointment with Greg, so she could not fully rely on that feeling alone. She was very aware of the ring, and it was not within her to just dismiss it or disregard what it meant. Although she trusted Rick, that alone was not enough to let her share this or any other intimate moment with someone else's husband. However, there was something else about him that she had become aware of. She felt it several times throughout the day, the last when they were at the gravesite. It was not hers to ask about, yet it, along with her trust, allowed her to be here.

Rick kept his eyes forward, but the pink bow was clear in his peripheral vision. He stepped up the game, "Nice bow," he said slyly.

Breaking the silence helped the pounding of both hearts. He was not nervous. Rather, he was concerned for Sarah because she was much more vulnerable in this situation. He knew that she was safe with him but also knew that she could not be certain of that. He hesitated to give her every opportunity to stop, thinking the comment he made might let her find an excuse to end their enjoyable charade. To his surprise, she did not take the out; instead, lifting her eyebrows, she delivered a clear message; it was his turn.

Rick slipped his shorts off, waited, and dropped them onto the building pile. He stood in only his underwear, and Sarah stood in her underwear and bra. She knew the best opportunity to call his bluff would come only if she challenged his last piece of clothing. However, to do this, she had to remove her bra and stand in full sunlight. The weight of this decision took its proportional amount of time. Rick could see it was not an easy decision. Then, her hands reached around to unclasp the bra. As she pulled it from her body, she desperately wanted to fold her arms over her chest. The preposterous confidence she had played from the beginning would not allow this happen. Both hands found her hips, and she shifted her weight, moments after the bra fell through the air.

There was no decision remaining. Rick's underwear came off, and he held them again before his final contribution to the pile. He stood in full confidence in front of her, and her eyes fought to stay above his waist. He saw this and grinned.

Sarah slipped her panties off. This time, rather than dropping them, she gingerly placed them on the very top. He thought he saw a dent in her confidence, so he kept his eyes clearly on hers to make it easier.

Rick offered his hand, "Come on," he exclaimed, before turning to lead Sarah to the rock wall. As they were undressing, she had considered the moment when they would be naked, thinking it would be uncomfortable. Now, under the intensity of the sun's rays, and in this fantastic place, she discovered an ease and exhilaration.

They moved across the bottom of the pool to a point where they could climb up the rocks. In front of her, Sarah saw the most exquisite body she had ever seen. His legs were defined and muscular and left no question where one feature ended and the other began. Her eyes traveled from his calves to his shoulders, spending an inordinate amount of time on his rear end. She tried to be cautious in her use of expletives, even when speaking to herself. However, this view caused her to forget all caution. "Jesus," she thought.

Rick turned to offer a hand as they climbed. The rock flattened at the top, allowing for another different, yet perfect view. They both took it in briefly before Rick launched a flawless dive into the deep water. He emerged shaking the water from his hair. Drifting to the end of the pool, he stood and urged her on.

Sarah's entry into the pool won no awards, her right hand plugging her nose as she dropped feet first with both eyes closed. She came up without effort, but the water shot her toward the pool's exit before her feet caught the bottom. Rick grabbed her arm as she drifted past him. He lifted her until her legs steadied against the current. The water was cool and felt magical against her body. She had never done anything like this before, running her fingers through her hair. Her eyes opened and the water ran off her face. The feeling brought a joyful laughter and huge smile, considering what she had just done. She followed him out of the water to try it again.

They jumped, dove, and laughed, until the fact that they were fully exposed was completely lost to both of them. When they tired, they sat on the warm flat stone above the falls. Side by side, and naked, they spoke of music, books, and other things they both found meaningful and interesting. Sarah learned about his mother, her death, how this led him to Durango and Mateo, and his love for the mountains. "This is a magical place, Sarah," he said, and she knew that he was right.

Rick avoided the most obvious subject: naked except for the gold band on the second finger. Something told Sarah not to ask. She accepted earlier that he should bring it to her.

She turned and stretched out onto her stomach, resting her head onto her folded arms. Rick took this position too, no more than two feet away. Drawn to Sarah's hand, he noticed a mark between her thumb and forefinger, the top and bottom of the hourglass oddly symmetrical and unnatural. It was obvious it had caught his attention, "Yours since birth?"

"That's what my parents tell me. My dad says it's there to keep me on time."

"Oh, always a few minutes late, huh?"

"Not since I was little."

"It's pretty. Do you have any others I should see?"

"How much money do you have?"

Rick wanted to laugh aloud, but a smile was his only answer. They exchanged a long, searching gaze; her beautiful green eyes trapped him. She felt it too, and if not for something even more powerful, her eyes would not have closed. Like at the sunset, and on the horse ride, she could feel the energy. However, here, it was so much stronger. The warm surge she felt deep within came just as the colors began to release and race across her soul. She was unable to stop watching but was acutely aware of her company. It would just have to happened, she knew, before returning to the colors of blue.

For his part, Rick was curious, as he had found himself a hundred times throughout the day. Something was happening — the contortions of her face and rapid movement behind her closed eyes were apparent. He knew the face of joy, and this was simply enough to delight him. He was patient as time passed, and then she was back. There was nothing to say about what he had just witnessed, because he felt it too — something as mysterious as the energy from looking into her eyes. Rick noted the sun, "We should go. It's getting late."

Preparing for her last jump, Sarah stood with her back to Rick, feeling beautiful, confident, and aware he was watching. She sensed him following every detail of her body, so she waited, because she wanted to give this to him. Both hands fingered through the curly damp hair that hung over her right shoulder, her head turning to the right and displaying an approving smile.

~~~~~

They reached the field with enough sunlight left to make it back to the lodge. He chose a slightly different way home, following the creek until it reached the river. They turned south and came out of the creek into the lower part of the field.

Sarah noticed a single purple flower, standing by itself at the beginning of the field. Dark purple veins shot up from the yellow core, existing to carry the nutrients to the delicate, lighter colored fabric of each leaf. She picked it, bringing the beautiful smell to her nose. Glancing forward, she now saw that the entire field stretching in front of them had thousands of these fragile jewels. Rick followed her thoughts, "The rain brought them out. I was here two days ago, and there was not one in bloom." She turned because his words came slowly once again but sounding different from earlier. The flower still to her nose, she noticed he had a measured look on his face. He was struggling with a question and seemed uncertain of exactly how to ask. Sarah took the flower slowly away from her nose, patiently waiting for him, as they walked forward into the beautiful sea of purple. The short distance they walked gave him enough time to find the right way to ask the question. He too picked a flower, handing it to Sarah because it would cause their fingers to touch. In this motion, he took them and squeezed tight so that she knew he wanted to hold her hand. It immediately took her back to his face, where she saw this request came from a place of necessity, rather than one of a simple want.

The question was unmistakable but without a simple answer. She felt it was something so much greater than anything yet shared. Rick and Sarah had spent a good part of the afternoon stripped naked, exposed in front of each other, but this was so much more. The thoughts of his wife led her eyes to their hands. He followed this, seeing her focus now on his ring. There was a quiet hesitation, as he immediately understood her concern. Rick let go of her fingers, walked to her other side, and offered his right hand. He now stood vulnerable, hoping, and realizing he needed her desperately. As if in slow motion, the fingers on Sarah's left hand opened and moved toward his. When they met, the energy came immediately, both almost feeling weak as it pulsed through their hearts. They began the walk home. Sarah closed her eyes periodically, searching for what she had found at the Cascade.

A few minutes into their walk, Rick noticed Sarah pushing and pulling his hand in different directions. He saw that she was aiming their hands so that the beautiful little flowers would run into them as they passed. Curiously, as each the purple blossoms brushed her skin, there seemed to be a warmth that he felt through her touch. Was he imaging this? This struck a perfect place within him, and he now assisted her efforts so that they missed none.

They walked more slowly through the long field, both hoping to extend a time that neither wanted to end.

Chapter 20

An awkward moment arrived when they realized the walk was ending. They both wondered when they should stop holding hands. Each recognized it had to end, for if neither could explain to themselves how they had walked for miles with their fingers intertwined, how would anyone else understand? The lodge was close, the roof now visible just over the treetops below them. That meant people would be around.

"Do you know your way from here? I'll cut off to my cabin," he said, motioning toward a narrow road obscured by undergrowth. "The lodge is around the next corner," he offered, pointing down the road.

Nodding, she acknowledged her familiarity with the trail. Reluctantly, their hands released. Sarah used her other hand to rub her fingers and he opened and closed his slowly. They shared a strange feeling that something important was suddenly missing.

"I see the roof," she confirmed.

There were further questions each wanted to ask. Sarah was curious about his wife, especially because their walk home felt so right and so good. She questioned how it could really be okay. How could he hold her hand if he was married?

Rick, feeling something for the first time in years, just knew he was not ready for Sarah to leave. He wanted more — but more of what and how? These questions, so clear in thought, felt awkward, complicated, and impossible to put into words. Rick tried first. "I ... I ...had. I mean ... today ... today, I had ... it was ...today was ... well, today ...thank you... thank you." Normally articulate and clear spoken, he found himself tongue-tied and fumbling.

Then it was Sarah's turn to try, "No, thank you. Thank you — it was the most beautiful day I have had all week." Sarah's words were steadier, but they too felt awkward and insufficient. If she were able, she would have told Rick it was the most fantastic day she had had in her entire life. She simply could not account for everything experienced, knowing that the colors and the feelings they brought her were new, different, and nothing short of amazing.

"Are you coming down for dinner tonight?" she asked, trying to determine their next time together.

Rick read his watch, getting his bearings before he answered. "I am. I'll grab a shower and walk down. I assume I will see you there?"

"With bells on," came from Sarah naturally. Then the two faced exactly how to part company. Their minds raced through the same thoughts: Wave. Hug. Shake hands. Nothing seemed quite right, as neither understood exactly how the other was feeling.

"Okay. Well, I will see you in a little while then?" Sarah offered.

"Yes, in about an hour."

Each turned in their respective direction. Then, at the same time, they both glanced back to catch one last look at the best part of their day. Awkward again, they both smiled and turned home.

She took three more steps before remembering her responsibility as a guest of the ranch. When they had first arrived at the lodge, Huff had informed them that their host, Ted, graciously paid for the guide services. However, there was also the matter of the customary tip. This was the responsibility of the guest, and thus Sarah's responsibility today, at least in her mind.

"Rick."

He turned toward her, "Yeah?"

"Can I put your tip on the bill at the end of the week?"

He was briefly confused. Then it hit him; she still believed he was one of the guides. He kicked a small twig on the ground, watching it tumble to a stop as he responded. "That would be okay. How much do I get?"

Sarah had hoped for the opportunity to consult Andrew or Huff, or someone who might give her some idea how to answer this exact question, but without doing that, she was unsure of what to say.

"Uh, I don't know. What's normal?"

Rick had her exactly where he wanted, looking at the sky and then back to his watch as if making some exact calculation, "A thousand dollars."

Sarah was shocked. She repeated the amount as her eyes widened.

"Yes. Well guiding services … plus …you know … asking me to go swimming without my clothes on." A smile arrived on Sarah's face, her head tilting to the side as she realized he was at it again.

She jumped right in. "Yeah, I calculated that. I was thinking more like fifteen dollars …all in."

Her smile was infectious, and he had caught it. "I think we are on the same page here. Fifteen dollars for guiding and … you know … giving you a look and all. Then …let's see … Nine hundred and eighty-five dollars for having … well, to look at …" Rick's eyes traveled from Sarah's head to her toes.

Their little match just landed her a huge insult, yet she found it so funny that both eyebrows lifted and she began laughing aloud. "That bad, huh?"

"I'm just saying a thousand dollars looks about right to me."

"I'll tell you what, I'll surprise you and just leave it with Huff, okay?"

Rick loved it, wanting to be there to see Huff scratch his head trying to understand why Sarah was trying to give him a tip. "That would be great."

She turned back toward the lodge wearing a smile so wide it made her cheeks hurt. She was just about out of sight when he stopped her again, "Sarah." He was walking toward her after setting down the fishing gear. "I ... wanted ... to talk." He was having trouble getting everything out. Sarah studied his face and saw that this time it was a more serious conversation. "My wife, Samantha," he held before trying again. "I was ... or I just wanted to tell ..."

"A little late, don't you think? It will be dark soon and some people were wondering where you've been." Greg Watkins had found them.

Sarah turned to find him marching toward her, "Are you serious, Greg? I'm sure everyone knows I'm fine," she said, irritated at the interruption. Greg had always had selective hearing, choosing to ignore any words that did not serve his purpose.

She returned to Rick, but with Greg near, it was not the right time to tell her about Samantha. Rick saw that his time alone with Sarah was gone. "I'll catch you at dinner, all right?" His chin lifted slightly as he recognized her company. Sarah brought both shoulders slightly up and down, sorry that they had been interrupted, but also knowing that Greg could be trouble.

~~~~~

The sight of Greg and Sarah arriving at the lodge together surprised Rachael, "Hey, how was fishing?" she asked, consciously tempering her question but looking directly at Greg as the words came out. In his absence, Sarah would have replied by hauling Rachael off to a hidden spot and telling her about a day she could never before have imagined.

As it was, the day was, "Fun," Sarah replied.

Rachael knew better, waiting for Greg to turn before making eye contact with her sister and receiving the best, "Oh my God," that a slow, exaggerated movement of facial muscle could deliver. She was immediately excited and wanted nothing less than every single detail. The current circumstances would force her to wait.

"You were worried about me?" Sarah asked Rachael.

"Hell no. Why?" Sarah shot a glance at Greg who, conveniently, did not hear her last question.

~~~~~

Rick arrived at his cabin to find a note tacked to the door. He opened it and saw it was in Huff's handwriting. Aside from being almost impossible to decipher, it was short and to the point: "Dan Baker from San Diego called this morning. Call him as soon as you can."

Rick showered, changed, and walked down to Huff's home. Huff's cabin purposely contained the only phone at the ranch. On the way, he ran into Huff and Maria who were on their way to dinner. Maria spotted Rick first, "Ricky!"

"Looks like you're once again setting the standard for the evening," he replied, greeting her with a kiss to the cheek.

"You should take a lesson from this young man," she said, gently elbowing Huff.

"Yeah. Straighten your act up," Rick teased. "You took a call from San Diego today?"

"I did, early this morning, about 7:30. It was Daniel something-or-other; sounded a bit agitated that he could not reach you immediately. He wondered why your cell phone didn't work here." Huff thought for a second before adding, "I told him you might stop by the phone booth in the middle of the river." Rick thought that regardless of the reason, it must be urgent, noting that the call came at 6:30 AM San Diego time.

He had employed Dan Baker for more than six years as the director of the Southern California branch of Wheeler & Kline Ventures. He was competent and skilled in his position, but any actions before 8:00 AM not associated with either sleep or coffee represented a serious intrusion on his time.

"I was coming down to use your phone."

"The door is open. Are you coming to dinner?"

"I am. I'll be there soon."

"Do you want us to hold dinner until you're done?"

"No. I'm not sure how long this will take. I'll just jump in when I get there. Thanks, though."

Maria changed the subject, the absence of both Sarah and Rick today not lost on her. "What did you do today, Ricky?" she asked, playfully dragging the words out.

He responded with an answer so ridiculous it would let her know he was on to her, "You know that cute little girl with the beautiful, curly black hair?"

"Yes. Sarah, I believe?"

"We went swimming in Cascade Creek buck naked."

So absurd was the answer, Maria was very certain he was jabbing at her. She giggled at the thought. "You're silly." Rick turned toward the cabin, thinking about the Cascade and chuckling to himself.

~~~~~

The cooks had worked extra hard during the day, not only fixing dinner, but also readying the setting. Inspired by Maria's ideas, Ben decided tonight's meal would be served on the grass plateau overlooking the river, just north of the lodge.

The decision to flatten this area had come when the Tres Piedras Ranch began hosting guests. It was always a popular spot in the day, the horseshoe pit hosting the most intense and competitive games on the ranch. In the center, surrounded by flagstone, a pit built from river rock contained the fires that would burn late into most evenings, drawing people through the darkness. This week, most of the guests became familiar with this area because of a white fabric massage tent, erected on one end of the lawn. The idea to hire a masseuse was Nancy's and, if measured by attendance, was one of the week's better ideas. A constant stream of people moved in and out of the tent throughout the day.

For dinner tonight, the fabric walls of the tent were rolled up tight so people could enter from every side. Long rectangular tables now sat underneath and held a multitude of dishes. Tables and chairs were set up just beyond the tent and electric cords ran from the lodge to add light to each corner of the grass. Bamboo sticks with white candles were then set in the ground to outline the perimeter of the outdoor dining room. The smell of burning cedar drifted through the setting, both welcoming the guests and providing a natural barrier to the insects.

~~~~~

Around noon, it had been clear to most of the girls that Sarah was missing. The possibility that she was fishing with Rick became the accepted explanation sometime in the early afternoon.

A bridesmaid recognized the problem Rachael was contending with, asking, "Are you going to tell your sister that he slept with Kelly?" This had been tearing at Rachael since she had watched Rick approach her sleeping sister, and was the reason why she had kept their outing to herself. There was something between them, and the burden of worry was heavy. He had much more than a passing interest in Sarah, and Sarah did not just like him — there was more, much more. It had surprised and confused Rachael. How could it have developed so quickly? Rachael debated when and how to deliver the news, certain that there was no good way. She wondered whether it would it be worse to tell her immediately or to let it go and see whether anything developed. There was a risk either way.

There was something else, Rachael considered. She liked Rick. Although they had only had a few interactions, she could not dismiss how genuine he seemed to be. What had happened between him and Kelly? Nevertheless, she had seen more than one chameleon in her time, each focused on his skill in the art of getting exactly what he wants. Beyond that, there was the biggest potential problem of all — a question that circulated through the group of girls. Is he married?

Rachael was not a nosey sister, but she was protective. For this reason, she thought a small seating arrangement at dinner might help clarify things; she enlisted Andrew to keep the chair between Sarah and her empty and available for the river guide.

~~~~~

Once again, accounts of the day were bringing energy into the crowd as the evening began. The lines between the guests and employees thinned as the week wore on, and the atmosphere now more akin to a large party with close friends and family. However, Greg was not comfortable with such confused interplay. He liked people to understand their proper place and did not accept inviting the "help" into the fray.

Dinner began with one conspicuous absence. Sarah hoped to see Rick before Huff started the procession to the buffet line. Rachael also kept an eye open so she could direct him toward the open seat. She repeatedly insisted that others take their turns at the buffet as she waited, strategically positioning herself to have a few minutes of Rick's time and to direct his seating.

When he finally appeared, most everyone had already filled their plates and taken a seat. Rachael put on her best act, "Oh, hi. Rick ... right?"

"Yes. You're Rachael, Sarah's sister?"

"That's right. I don't think we have officially met." Rachael extended her free hand, and he shook it lightly.

"We haven't met, but Sarah and I spoke about you quite a bit today. I know this is all about your wedding. Congratulations. That's exciting."

"Thank you. I hope my little sister had good things to say about me?"

"Well, I gotta tell you, it was a little sketchy at first." He spoke as he filled his plate. "I told her it wasn't okay to talk about you like that, so she cleaned it up." His eyes lifted, and he smiled. "She loves you." Until now, Rachael was not certain she should approach Rick or ignore him. With a few well-placed words, the two quickly established a pleasant rapport.

"I thought it was brave of Sarah to try fishing. How'd she do?" Before he could answer, Rachael asked another question. "Actually, I guess I should ask how you did, since it was work for you?"

He answered both questions, "It was fine. Not too much trouble, other than a tangle or two. She actually caught on pretty fast."

Rachael had another very simple, yet more telling question, "Did you have a good time?"

He leaned toward Rachael, so that it felt as if it were just the two of them. "She's amazing. She's beautiful, smart, and funny. I hope her day was as good as mine." Rick brought each word out, delivering them so Rachael could feel their importance.

"Would you sit at our table tonight?" she asked, turning to point out their table and the conveniently open seat. As she motioned, she witnessed the last futile attempt by her fiancé to keep Greg from occupying the seat. Andrew offered the most helpless expression he could muster.

"I would love to, but it looks a little tight over there. Maybe we can talk after dinner?"

Rachael's frustration was apparent but could not be resolved easily. Greg made her careful planning and meticulous timing futile. He possessed a shameless sense of entitlement; this characteristic alone made Rachael wish he would simply disappear. Making her way to the table, she shot Andrew the deadly look he was expecting, and let out a long audible exhale as she took her seat.

Rick had a place at another table waiting, taking the seat next to Maria and Huff. Huff greeted him, "How'd the call go?"

"It could have gone better. I've got to be in San Diego tomorrow."

"An emergency," Huff asked through one side of his mouth — the other side filled with the better part of a homemade roll.

"Nothing that can't be handled, but it does need to be handled."

Now Maria was interested, "When will you be back?"

"As soon as I can. Three weeks … maybe a month. I need to be in Zurich in ten days. That should take a week or two by itself. Soon after that, I hope."

"When are you leaving?"

"They're bringing the plane into Durango in the morning."

"Do you need a ride to the airport? I need to go into town anyway," Maria offered.

"Thanks, but I have a car that I need to return."

Since he began coming to Tres Piedras, Rick had frequently just shown up when time permitted and left when work demanded. He exercised far fewer rights than might be expected by any other owner in his position. One of his few requests was that his cabin was always open, in case an unexpected gap in his schedule presented the opportunity to come. Huff and Maria had become familiar with these visits; the unexpected arrivals, sudden departures, or how a plane would seemingly appear in Durango all seemed normal.

~~~~~

Sarah was disappointed Rick would not eat at her table but oblivious to Rachael's plan, Andrew's attempts to preserve the seat, and Greg's efforts that totally dismissed those as insignificant. The first look Sarah and Rick shared was intentional, both searching for the other. The second was too, both pulled by the opportunity as they sipped their wine. "She's magnificent," he thought to himself, the conversation around him relegated to the background. Her spectacular green eyes pulled at him, warming the space between their tables.

The two pulled at each other, becoming bolder throughout dinner because they simply could not resist. The evening's main course was Rocky Mountain trout, providing Rick with ammunition to play with her again. Glancing toward him again, he inconspicuously motioned toward his plate, lifting it just slightly, "Fish," he mouthed. The continuation of the day's education caused her smile to grow, her white teeth cutting through the dim light.

She responded by bringing both arms over her head in a poor attempt to fake a stretch. With her arms wide apart, she used her hands to shape the return message, "Whale." Their covert exchanges continued. "Fork," he said, clearly pointing at a spoon. She responded with "beer," as everyone stood with an expensive glass of red wine during one of Ted's toasts.

Huff and Maria had both noticed their exchanges; unfortunately, so did Greg. He was infuriated. Sarah had not given him the time he had

The Colors of Blue

expected all week, which fed an anger that had been building since he recognized why Andrew was protecting the seat. Sarah was his, even now, and he felt Rick had overstepped his menial position.

He had been sharpening the dagger since he had overheard Kelly's story earlier in the day. At the time, it was a perfect bit of news, but now it was priceless. There was never a doubt that he would use it to stagger Sarah, even if what he had seen between her and the guide was only a mild attraction. Spurred on by his anger, the only thing left was to calculate the best way to unsheathe the weapon and deliver the blow.

Greg picked up the glass of wine and took a long drag, drawing Sarah's attention in time for her to watch him finish swallowing. He motioned with his head so that there was no question of whom he was speaking, "You see your little boyfriend over there?" he asked, loud enough for Sarah, Rachael, Andrew, and others to hear. Sarah's eyes once again were on Rick, but this time it was different from the others. "He fucked Kelly the other night." He let this sink in before adding, "I bet it was a real good ride for the both of them." The words he picked were intentionally crude and jagged, making the act all that much more repulsive. Greg circled his glass to implicate the others at the table, "Ask any of them, they all know."

Sarah searched the table but found that each person was unable to look at her. She realized Greg was right, and they all knew. She quickly turned toward her sister. Rachael did not drop her eyes, instead trying to explain the unexplainable. This just confirmed everything; Rachael knew. They all knew. Sarah felt like a fool.

Greg was not done, because there was still some twisting of the dagger that remained. "Oh, and why don't you ask him about his wife? Or did you miss the ring?"

This was the final straw. Sarah could take no more, wanting desperately to pretend it did not matter. She stood and politely excused herself before giving one last, long look toward the one person who, until that moment, had held all of her trust. Rachael simply shrugged, feeling terrible. Calmly and sternly, Sarah set a schedule to talk with Greg. "I'll see you outside the lodge at 8:00 in the morning."

Leaving the table, Rachael had something to say to Greg too, "Hypocritical asshole. You're a true asshole." She caught Sarah as she entered the lodge, following her upstairs into the bedroom. "Sarah, please."

"Greg's right," Sarah responded.

"What do you mean? No one has the right to say things like that, and in those words. His point was to upset and embarrass you. It's how he controls."

"Rachael, I'm so stupid. My judgment has been so poor, first with Greg, and now with him."

Rachael did not know everything that had gone on, "Did he hurt you?" she asked.

"Who?"

"Rick."

A pathetic laugh broke through the flood of tears. Both now sitting on the small bed, Rachael found a tissue on the nightstand. Sarah dabbed at her eyes, "No. God, no. He treated me fine. He would never hurt me."

"I'm sorry I didn't say something about Kelly."

"You should have told me! I'm so stupid."

"Stop saying that."

"It's just that I haven't had many relationships. I can count them on one hand and have fingers left over. It's not normal. I mean look at you..." She stopped herself, a laugh cutting the emotion. She tried again. "Greg was my first serious relationship, and I can see it was huge mistake."

"Sarah. You knew that it wasn't right. Do you remember our talks? You weren't happy, it just took what he did to bring it into focus. You can't feel bad about the mistakes either. Everyone has a bad relationship or two; those just provide perspective for the good ones."

Sarah wiped her nose, her voice cracking, "I just hope that someday I will find someone good."

Rachael gave this some thought, "You may have."

"What do you mean?"

"Rick." Rachael stopped abruptly before starting again, "I made a mistake when I found out about Kelly. I should have told you, but I saw some things that I didn't want to ruin. The way you felt about him, I could see it."

"Yes, so, I was a fool."

"No, Sarah. It was more than just you. This morning, when you were asleep, I watched him wake you up. On my life, I swear that he felt something. At dinner, he told me you were amazing, beautiful, smart, and funny..."

"So now you're falling for his lines?"

"No. It's not that he said it; It's how he said it."

Sarah settled, taking several deep breaths, "I went back to the car, after the accident."

A perplexed expression came across Rachael's face, looking at her sister and tilting her head, trying to understand.

"The police let me into the lot. Chaos, that's the best way to describe it; the roof was collapsed, seats twisted, torn, and glass everywhere. You and I were lucky; the accident could have killed us too." Sarah wiped her eyes, "In the middle of the mess I found the blue shoe box, as perfect as it was when I took it out of the store." Again she hesitated, cleaning her face as Rachael tried to understand what this all meant. "It survived everything without a scratch… intact, and undamaged." Considering all of this ridiculous, a low laugh came from Sarah, "The stupid little box means hope to me; that somehow I'm not damaged or that I can be whole again. Maybe that's why Greg is so important; I needed a perfect life to be whole."

Rachael leaned over, wrapped her arms around her only sister and let her tears come too. "He told me he had a great day with you."

Sarah was quiet; considering the last part of their walk. "He tried to tell me something today, but Greg interrupted."

"Like what?"

"I think he was trying to tell me about his wife."

Concern molded Rachael's face. "I don't know, Sarah."

Chapter 21

The next morning, Greg Watkins was ready for Sarah at 8:00 sharp. He had never heard the tone in her voice that came out just before she left dinner. He knew that his comments had crossed the line but was also certain she would forgive him. It was time for the experiment to end and for her to get back on board with his plans.

Sarah found Greg in the downstairs, seated alone, anxiously awaiting her arrival. She fixed a cup of coffee without saying a word to him. "Come on, let's go for a walk," she demanded, wanting this conversation to be on her terms. Her expression confirmed what he had heard in her voice.

Sarah had no plans for where she wanted to go, randomly choosing a path toward the fire pit. The chair she had sat in reminded her of everything he had said, and everything she had felt. Taking one final drink of her coffee, she placed the cup on one of the tables, and began heading north, along the river. Greg followed, walking faster than was comfortable just to keep pace. Their walk was silent and cold.

Several hundred yards up, she traveled to the river's edge, removed her sandals, and waded out to two flat rocks that faced each other. In a different position, Greg would have objected to entering the cool water. It would have been yet another objection, just to object, or perhaps, to exercise control. However, here, he knew things were different, so he followed without a word.

Taking the opposite rock, he peered over her shoulders toward the lodge before dropping his eyes to Sarah. Toes buried in a deposit of river sand, she stared into the shifting water. "You had no right to talk to me that way. You used words that were meant to hurt me," she started, without ever looking at him.

Greg anticipated beginning here, "I'm sorry. I was out of line. I saw you and that tall assh ..." He caught himself before the entirety of the word came out. If not for her sensitivity, he would have delivered the same word infused with acid. He continued, "You and that guy were playing around, and it set me off. He's not a good guy Sarah. He's slept with Kell ..."

Sarah cut him off, "Stop. Stop. That's not the point. This is not your business. That ended with your affair. It ended with what you did."

They had reached the purpose of their talk. It was another chance to get it on the table and finally resolved. Greg still felt it was just a temporary nuisance, one to forgive and put behind them. "Look, I screwed up all right. I have told you that before, but I will tell you that as many times as you need. It was a mistake, but I'm here for you. I want it to be us again."

Sarah continued to look at her feet as she listened. She lifted her head, "Greg, until I moved in with you, I had never lived with another man. You know that. I've thought about what you did a million times since I found out." Sarah stopped herself, wanting to stay focused. "Do you know why you were the first one I lived with?" She did not wait for him to answer, "I hadn't taken that chance because I had never trusted anyone enough. I trusted you."

~~~~~

For the first time all week, Rick had both a schedule and an agenda that rushed him. The rental jeep pulled out of the cabin's drive at 8:25 AM.

He would be at the airport no later than 10:00 and in San Diego by 11:30 local time. There was an important stop to make before leaving the ranch.

He had hoped to spend time with Sarah last night, wanting to find a way to see her again. When neither she nor her sister returned, it was apparent that something had gone wrong. He tried to find her at the lodge but was unsuccessful, so he returned to his cabin for the night.

Rick eased his jeep up in front of the lodge, running into Kelly on the back deck, "Hi, Kelly."

"Rick, how are you?" she replied, a sharp edge hanging in each word.

"I'm fine, thanks." He was all business. "I'm looking for Sarah?" Kelly stood motionless, her eyes cutting a hole through his chest. He had come for Sarah.

Kelly had come onto the deck just in time to see Sarah and Greg walking away; their body language telling her the mood was serious. She was certain this would be the wrong time for Rick to speak with Sarah. "That way," she said, her finger pointing him up the river.

Rick checked his watch, thanked Kelly, and hurried off.

~~~~~

For the first time since he had met Sarah, Greg saw something he did not recognize. Her voice was steady, focused, and resolved; it concerned him. He could do nothing but listen. "I trusted you," she said. "I gave you everything. Why couldn't you see that?" Sarah waited briefly, but he said nothing. "If I didn't find out, would you have ever told me? Would you have ever stopped seeing her? Our bed, Greg? Do you know what that did to me?"

He tried to slow her down by injecting some emotion. "I told you I screwed up. What do you want me to do?"

Sarah remained level, as she had told herself to be. "It made me question everything. Was I pretty enough? Was I smart enough? Could I have done something better? Did you love her?"

He jumped in, "No, I didn't love her. She was just … a stupid fling."

The way he presented the words still made her wonder whether he understood. It reminded her of everything, how she had faced it alone. "During all this, you have had an advantage; you knew everything. Only you truly knew what she meant to you. And, it's only you who truly knows what I mean to you. There was no way, and is no way, for me to know these things without trust, and you took that away."

He tried to stop the slide. "Sarah, I do love you and …"

Her eyes shot up to cut him off. "No. No! That word is too important for you to use it here. Please do not!"

"But that's how I felt … how I feel."

Sarah was calm again. "Greg, without trust, that's only another word. What you did, it left me to answer everything on my own. It made me search for what I truly want and try to understand what I truly feel."

"Sarah ..." He tried to stop her again.

"Let me finish."

She had arrived at Tres Piedras with questions and uncertainties about Greg and everything that had happened. She knew she would find some time alone during the week, and believed that this would allow her to discover the right answers. In fact, her answer did come, but surprisingly not while she was alone. It came to her while she drank tea with Huff and it came from her colors. "You made me look inside myself, at who I am, and who I want to be ..." She paused, the brief silence assuring her next words, "I don't love you."

Greg now understood why she was so determined; this was the end. He took a more practical approach. "Let's just give it one more chance. Maybe it will work, maybe not, but we should give it a try. It makes sense, Sarah. You can live with me for free," he insisted, believing she must follow the same principles that drove his life.

"Greg, this isn't about money," she responded, her words powerful. However, her look told him his efforts were futile. Her decision was made; Greg had no influence on it. For the first time in his life, he had no control over what happened.

The opportunities of life had always presented an easier path away from self-reflection. However, here, Greg had no other choice but to evaluate himself and the core of what was important to him. He had changed after Sarah left, uncertain of how to act in a space he could not organize. He shuddered in the realization, finding that failure itself was intolerable, for that meant a crack in the foundation of everything he had ever built.

She thought anger would come next, but at the same moment Greg felt the surge, he spotted Rick emerging from a thick cover of trees. He knew Rick was here for Sarah but also that she had not yet seen him. Realizing he had lost her, he quickly focused his emotion on one thing, hurting their chances. "Can I have one last hug and kiss — friends? Perhaps we can talk sometime in a few months?"

This surprised Sarah, expecting that when she cut the last threads, Greg would respond with a great deal of emotion. After last night, she cared little how he took it, but never imagined it would be this easy. "Sure," she agreed, surprised by his maturity.

Standing, Greg shot a look at Rick, somehow causing him to watch a moment longer. He had set Rick up perfectly, approaching Sarah for their last embrace, but delivering it as if it meant something completely different. Sarah felt confused, the hug more impassioned than expected. The kiss left no guess that something was off, as Greg held the back of Sarah's head and pulled her into his lips. Her hands came to his chest as she pushed him away. "What are you doing?" she demanded.

Greg glanced up and saw that Rick was gone. The first smile of the day crept across his face. Then he easily answered her question, because she meant nothing to him. "Nothing. Just saying good-bye." He again felt the surge of control, exiting the water, gathering his shoes, and leaving Sarah to deal with the last few minutes by herself. "You're a fool, you will always be a fool," he said. "Just a fool who believes she can see colors."

~~~~~

If he had noticed them before walking into the opening, Rick would have turned back. As it was, he had inadvertently witnessed a private time between Sarah and Greg. He knew he should not be there, turning away as they kissed. The sting was unmistakable, delivered cleanly after he had dropped his guard. Since Samantha's illness, he had lived with the consequences of wanting and caring, and yet subject to the vulnerability of loss.

Walking back to the lodge, he was hard on himself, realizing how he had begun to care about Sarah. This mistake left his belly fully exposed, and it now gnawed within him. His judgment had slipped because of something he could not explain; the lapse caused him to miss that she was already involved. He had made an ass of himself too, walking into the two of them. It must have been clear that he was there for her. He wanted more, and she could not or would not.

In the rental car, his stomach and heart wracked with the familiar feeling of care and loss. Rick's breathing was markedly heavy, lifting and lowering his entire chest. He started the car and began driving, but a moment of clarity stopped him. Pulling his bag from the back seat, he opened it and found the object. After ten minutes, he had reached the spot, dropping to his knees to settle himself. Closing his eyes, he felt the warmth of two tears rolling down his face. He could not help but think of Samantha's death.

"Are you scared?" She had asked the obvious to move forward.

He recalled his answer, how it crept from his trembling lips. "Terrified."

"What is it ..." she had paused, gathering the energy to propel thought. "What scares you?"

He had held in silence, hoping that his wife would move on, but the answer was something she needed, so he opened his heart. "The first minute that I know I will never hear your voice again. I'm afraid of not holding you and of never again just watching while you sleep. How can I breathe if I can't see you, touch you, or smell you again?"

Fighting through the pain, Samantha had considered his answer. The morphine coursing through her body only provided a fleeting window where she could stay with him in thought. The conversation needed to be steered toward her purpose, but weakness was a formidable adversary.

Ahead of the effort, he had voiced a question that helped her cause. "What scares you now?"

With the most basic of all functions failing, he recalled how time passed as she searched for the moisture to propel her words. "That you will never find this again. That you will never love someone like you have loved me. I love you — I will always love you. I want you to know that I wish for you to have this again." Samantha had made her point.

Rick's eyes opened as his head tilted back, slow, heaving breaths shooting into the Colorado air. This was the one memory of Sam that was intolerable and had taken its toll. He forced himself to remember, perhaps as a payment for the foolishness that had just unfolded.

The room was sterile, stale, and dim. The important ones — Sam's parents, a few close friends, and those whose job it was to attend to death — waited just beyond the doors. The expensive machines made their noises, the curtains hung motionless, and the two of them clutched each other.

"I'm ready," staggered faintly from her mouth.

Chapter 22

Sarah needed some time alone, a chance to unwind after the morning spent with Greg. Leaving the rock, she climbed the bank and turned right to continue up the river. She was unaware that Rick had come to find her. Her walk was slow, methodical, and thoughtful. There was no place she had to be, at least none more important than where she was now, allowing her to gain perspective in solitude. She thought about Greg and Rick, trying to reconcile the greatest contrast the last several days had brought to her. It was her last day, and so much had come to her this week, yet so much was left undiscovered.

Around one in the afternoon, she knelt at the Williamses' gravesite, diligently brushing away the few needles that had fallen down overnight. It seemed right to tend to this place, just as Huff did whenever he was in proximity. Following yesterday's route, she climbed up Cascade Creek toward the pool. Why were the colors gone today? She had not expected them after finishing with Greg, but here, she thought them certain to appear.

At the pool, Sarah again removed her clothes, climbed, and leaped into the cool water. Again, at the top, she stretched out onto the warm stone, resting her head on her folded arms. She wanted the colors, to confidently toy with them again, and she wanted the way they made her feel. Why had they come to her so easy yesterday? Why were the colors of blue staying away?

The sun had dried and warmed her body. She stood, hesitating briefly, before plunging into the pool for the final time. On her way back to the lodge, Sarah knocked on the door of Rick's cabin. It was 5:15 PM. There was no answer, and the car she had noticed yesterday was now gone. Reaching the lodge she ran into Andrew, who had not seen Rick either. She started toward Huff's cabin, before seeing he was coming down the lane toward her.

"How's the beautiful Ms. Sarah today?"

"I'm great Huff. I've been hiking for most of the day."

"Were you coming down to use the phone?"

"No. You know we leave tomorrow, I guess. I was just coming down to let you know how much I enjoyed this place and to express my thanks to both you and Maria for everything. You, Huffy, are a wonderful man who made my stay much better. Thank you again."

"You're welcome, honey," he replied as they exchanged a hug. "Maria will be at dinner tonight, but she's hoping to see you before that. Something about colors ..." he played.

Sarah smiled. "I can't pass that up, can I?"

"You better not. She's down at the cabin," he said, pointing south.

"Okay, I'm going now," Sarah replied, before turning toward the cabin. After one-step, she turned back, "You haven't seen Rick have you? I owe him some money for the day he took me fishing."

Huff had just learned two things: Rick had left without telling Sarah, and she believed he was one of the ranch's guides. "Sarah, Rick left this morning. He had business in San Diego."

Huff watched her sink, suddenly quiet and perplexed. Her body language clear, she tried to recover, "I owe him some money." Huff looked at her curiously.

"Some money?"

"Yes. For his tip."

"His tip?" Huff needed to confirm what he had heard.

"Yes. He took me fishing yesterday."

Huff was suddenly in tune; Rick set up a little prank. "Was it Rick who suggested you bring the money to me?" Huff hinted to Sarah.

"Well kind of, I guess. It just worked out that way."

Huff could see her confusion. "Yeah, Rick has a way of making funny little things like this 'work out.' Sarah, he is not one of the ranch's guides."

"I thought he worked for you?"

Huff's smile widened. "Do you have a minute?"

"Sure."

It had been calm all day. The smells of the trees and grasses saturated the air around them. They moved into the shade of a nearby tree. "Rick moved to Durango the summer before his senior year of high school. He had lived with his mother somewhere in Texas, until her death. He came here to live with his father, but that turned out poorly. He was alone and in a strange place, dealing with the loss of his mom." Sarah was listening intently. "He and Mateo, my son, met that summer. They got along well and have been best friends ever since. Mateo taught him to fly-fish, and they spent every free minute hiking, camping, and fishing around here. He had come here to be with his father, thinking family would help him with his mother's death. As it turns out, it wasn't his father that helped at all. It was these mountains."

Sarah stopped Huff for a moment, "That's when you met him too?"

"Yes, but we never saw too much of him them. Maria and I did what we could, provided a meal here or there, some clothes, and advice when he asked for it, that kind of thing. Rick had a focus about him that was different from other kids. I guess it had to be that way. At seventeen, he was providing for himself, working to get into college, and dealing with the loss of his mother. It was a significant load for anyone, let alone a kid.

"After high school, he attended Stanford University, in California. He did well there, graduating, finding a job, and eventually marrying Samantha."

"Samantha?"

"Yes." Huff looked up the valley as he spoke, tapping his memory to get the details right. "Mateo was Rick's best man, and Rick was his. Rick would come to Durango when he could, and Mateo would try to come home, too. They would disappear for days with their packs and fishing gear."

"Did Rick and his wife have children?"

"No, there were never any children." Huff stopped briefly, wondering if that was a good or a bad thing.

"I began working for Tres Piedras when it was owned by a family with the last name of Horton. They had run out of ideas about how to make money on this place. That's when they brought me in, and soon after that, we began hosting guests, like your party."

"I thought you and Maria owned the ranch?"

"Most think that, but I just run the place." Huff was searching again. "Mateo called me one day and asked if I thought the Hortons might sell this place. They were older, and I thought there might be an interest, so I passed along their number. I was sitting down at the cabin a few months later…" Huff's hand rubbed his chin. "Let's see, about three years ago I guess. One of those large black SUVs pulled up carrying Bob Horton and Samantha."

"Rick's wife?"

"Yes, his wife. She was very thin by then — did not look well at all. I'd been to their wedding and met her several other times before, but I didn't recognize her. She had lost so much weight. Bob sat in the car as we walked up to the lodge. She confirmed what I knew, telling me she was sick, and that it was just a matter of time." Huff reflected on the day, letting a minute drift off before continuing. "She had accepted it but still had some things she needed to take care of. That's why she came here.

She knew the mountains helped with his mother's death and was looking for a place where he could go and sort things out, a place that wasn't a part of the two of them. When we walked past the lodge, I remember asking if she wanted to look inside, but that was of no interest to her. She just looked at the mountains and asked how far Rick could go. Forever, I told her.

That was enough, I guess. A month later, they told me that the ranch had been sold. My job was to keep running until I heard differently. A few months after that, Mateo called us and said Samantha had died. I didn't see Rick for more than eighteen months. Paperwork arrived and accounts were set up, but nothing came from him.

"One day, I was working on the roof and saw a man walking up the road. Rick was much thinner than he is now, from dealing with Samantha's death, I'm sure. 'I guess I own this place?' were the first words from his mouth." Sarah watched as Huff began shaking his head slowly, remembering the encounter. "Our conversation was rather brief; he wanted to know about the fishing. I gave him some flies I had tied, and he was off. He stepped into the river at the bend," Huff's finger pointing to the spot.

Sarah was listening intently, feeling sorrow for everything Rick had gone through with the loss of both his mother and wife. Since seeing the ring on his finger, it had never been far from her mind. Now racing through their time together, she was thankful to have accepted holding his hand. Their walk home together meant more than she could have imagined.

"The sun went down that night, and he had not made it back. It was too dark to go looking for him, so I rode up at first light. Found him in the river two miles above Cascade Creek. He just waved, as if he had not just spent the night outside. I heard him on the porch that night, well past dark. It was all part of the fog he was living in. To this day, I'm not sure where he slept or how he managed to stay warm," Huff reflected. "Hell, even I think that would have been a little scary.

"Rick just wanted to talk about fishing. After downing a pot of spaghetti, he slept on the couch and woke up the next day around noon. I asked him what he was planning for Tres Piedras. 'It seems like a beautiful place that others should see; just keep running it the same way,' he said. That's how we got here."

Some birds were feeding on the small black berries near the fence. As they jumped between the limbs, their wings brushed against the plant's leaves. These, and the river, were the only sounds for several minutes. Sarah broke the silence. "I think he tried to tell me about Samantha yesterday."

This pleased Huff, feeling that it was significant. "He doesn't tell people about her death; at least, I've never heard him say anything, but I thought he might tell you."

"Me. Why?"

"Call it a hunch."

"He's a nice guy, Huff."

"He is, Sarah. One of the best you'll ever meet."

~~~~~

Sarah found Maria tending to a small garden near the cabin — the source of fresh vegetables and the flower arrangements each day was no longer a mystery. She stood up as Sarah approached, straightening her back and pushing the brim of her sun hat with the back of her hand. "Well now, there you are. I was beginning to worry we wouldn't have any time," Maria said, removing her gloves as she spoke.

Sarah hugged her. "Are you kidding? You have been on my mind since Huff told me about your colors."

Maria moved back, holding Sarah by the shoulders so she could look at her, "I knew you were special the first time I set eyes on you. At dinner, I could see your colors. You ask Huffy, he will tell you. I could feel them in you."

For the first time in her life, Sarah was speaking to someone who knew. "How do they come to you?"

"They're everywhere, Sarah. They come with feelings, and sometimes they lead the feelings. They are never far apart, first one then the other. The beautiful colors come when I don't expect them. I get a feeling that tells me they're coming. Then I close my eyes and just wait."

"Why? I mean, why do you think we have them?"

"Why do we see, smell, hear, taste, and feel Sarah? It tells us something about our world. That's what they are to us."

"I see that sometimes, Maria, but my colors are not always there. They seem to come and go."

Maria smiled, the experience of age providing perspective. "It's hard to trust them, isn't it? All this coming and going without any control," her grin producing a small laugh. "They are not like your other senses. Like a baby learning to walk, they can't help but to be awkward, until you learn how to use them."

"When I was a child, everything had colors," Sarah said. "The smell of cut grass, the way a bird moved its wings, everything had them, Maria. Then they went away, not suddenly, but over time. I found them again with children and, surprisingly, again this week."

"They were never gone, Sarah; they just didn't know how to come out. When I was young, I didn't understand them either; they would come and go, like yours do. My colors seemed to die when I lost my first husband. He was a wonderful man, and I couldn't imagine how I would ever enjoy life again."

"I'm sorry."

"Thank you, honey. It happened many years ago." Maria shifted, bending over to pick several flowers. "I met Huff after that, and they came back stronger than ever. They were always there; I just needed to find a way to use them."

"How's that? How do you use them now?"

"They're another sense, to be used with all others. When you're with friends at dinner, do you enjoy the wonderful smells that come from the kitchen? It makes you feel good, and that's good for you?"

"Yes, those are wonderful feelings."

"Your colors can be as simple as that." Maria lifted the flowers in her hand, "The colors that these beautiful flowers bring can build into feelings like that. We're lucky, Sarah; these feelings are more difficult for others to experience."

Sarah was nodding, understanding Maria's description. "I felt them yesterday at the Cascade. I watched a leaf fluttering on a tree and was surprised to find it had colors. It was strange because I was able to play with them a little bit, deciding when to let them come."

"That's it, Sarah. That's what I mean. You'll learn to use them like that, and much more."

"More?"

"Yes. Ahead of your other senses, they will tell you when something is good or bad, if it's to be embraced or avoided. When you learn to trust them, you will feel their power."

Sarah stood in thought; her time at Tres Piedras was far too short. "Would you mind if I sat with you and Huff at dinner tonight?"

"You would find my bad side if you sat anywhere else."

"Thank you. Both you and Huff have been so good to me." She held for a moment but had more to say, "Would it be okay if I wrote you once in awhile?"

"There's nothing that would make me happier, dear."

After Sarah mentioned the colors she had seen at the Cascade, Maria thought the subject of Rick was sure to follow. She sensed Sarah holding back and knew this was the most important of all topics color. "You had a nice day with Rick?"

The question was a surprise. "We had a wonderful day together," Sarah offered, wanting to ask something but not sure exactly what.

Maria felt this and helped, stating the obvious. "You two got along well?"

"We did. He's an easy person to be around."

"Did it scare you?"

Sarah's head tilted slightly, "What do you mean, 'scare me?'" she asked, curious about the question.

"Are you scared about how easy it was to be around him? Was it hard to trust him?"

Sarah realized Maria had found her dilemma; everything was so natural and easy with Rick that it was impossible to trust her feelings. "Yes," she admitted. "I don't know how to place it exactly; he's different from anyone I've ever known. It can't be that easy."

"Will you do something for me?" Maria asked.

"Of course, what is it?"

"Would you close your eyes for a minute?"

Sarah appeared confused, "Maria?"

"Just entertain an old woman, would you?"

A smile came to Sarah before closing both eyes. "Sure."

"Think about the time you spent with Rick this week."

Sarah's eyes opened briefly, taking a long look at Maria before closing them again. She thought about the first morning they had met and how he had surprised her when she came downstairs. Even his silhouette was attractive, she remembered; he was tall, strong, and pleasant to watch just sitting with his coffee. Then her thoughts drifted to when they had danced together, how she had pressed her head against his chest and forgotten about everything. Sarah reflected on their day, settling first on the memory of Rick reading to her as they ate lunch. She loved every inflection in his voice, attentively watching how his facial expressions seemed to tell the story along with his words. She felt herself smile, remembering the pirates, and the trap she had set.

Naturally, she came to the Cascade, perhaps the most spectacular place in the entire valley. They had sat above the falls and just talked, so easily sharing her thoughts without judgment or evaluation.

Maria watched Sarah, noticing when she relaxed. She guessed the thoughts of Rick were now flowing effortlessly.

Sarah's memory pulled her to the field, the beautiful flowers, and the moment Rick's hand first took hers. Her smile grew, and Maria was certain that the first colors of blue would be next. "I've been in love two times in my life; both times the colors told me first."

The first streak of blue raced across Sarah's vision. It was a very light tone at first, but became progressively darker and warmer as it traveled.

Maria watched her shoulders drop, knowing the reason she was relaxing. The colors of blue were coming. She continued. "The colors are what convinced me to trust what I had found."

Other tones now followed the earlier hints of blue. Sarah was aware that they were coming, yet was unable or unwilling to stop them. An indescribable flood of different shades now entered, somehow occupying her entire vision without hindering the image of holding Rick's hand. Like at the Cascade, the colors did not come alone. They were accompanied by soothing warmth. She relaxed further. The only distinguishable input beyond the colors was Maria's voice, and Sarah heard and understood every word. "There are no colors like those of love, Sarah. Trust the colors of blue that you see."

Sarah's eyes remained shut, waiting for the colors of blue to settle. In that time, Maria returned to the cabin, giving her space and time and hoping she would understand why the colors had found her again.

When her eyes opened, she thought, it can't be love, before realizing she still did not trust.

~~~~~~

Nancy was standing alone on the deck when Sarah arrived. Noticing her, Sarah stopped by the kitchen and collected two cold beers. Nancy did not turn immediately when Sarah approached and continued to look out into the river. "Isn't this a wonderful place, Sarah?"

Sarah was reflective. "I thought that Andrew was exaggerating, but it's even more beautiful than his description."

Sarah lifted the cold bottle, "Would you like a beer?"

"Thanks. How was your day, honey?"

"It was good. I walked up the river trail to the top of the ranch, hoping to see everything one more time. How was yours?"

"Very good. I talked your sister into going shopping with me in Durango. We looked for you but heard you had gone for a walk with Greg." Sarah said nothing. Nancy continued, "The downtown is very cute. Many of the original buildings are still standing, and the new ones are built to fit in with the turn-of-century architecture."

"Sounds fun — I bet Rachael loved it. Did you have any success shopping?"

"I picked up a few little things to remind me I was in the Wild West," she said with a sarcastic grin. "I think your sister had a good time," she continued. "Or maybe she just felt that she needed to accommodate an old bag like me. What do you think?"

Sarah laughed. "First, I don't think you're an 'old bag,' and second, I bet she had a great time. That sounds like something right up her alley; she loves places like that."

"It did seem like she was having a good time. We had lunch at one of the old hotels, The Strater. It was built in 1887, right on Main Street. Next door, there is a dinner theatre. We should all go the next time we come here."

Sarah said nothing, hoping there would be a next time. It reminded her that they would all leave early in the morning, and she had one last thing she wanted to see. They both took a sip of their beer.

Nancy turned back to look at the river. "I heard there was a bit of a blow up last night?"

Sarah wondered how much Rachael had shared but was comfortable with Nancy, "No, not a blow up. I just thought it better to leave dinner before something was made of it."

"Greg was jealous because of the tall, handsome fella?" Nancy inquired.

"It sounds as if you and Rachael did have a good talk today."

"Actually, she did a nice job avoiding the topic." Nancy lifted, again finding Sarah's eyes, "You'd be surprised how much an 'old bag' sees."

Sarah considered Nancy's angle. Ted certainly had his opinions. Was Nancy about to add some pressure too? she wondered. Then, without blinking an eye or lifting her head, Nancy offered her opinion, "Greg is a self-consumed asshole." Nancy lifted her beer for a toast. "Go for the hot one, I say. Life's too short to get stuck with someone like that." Nancy's brows lifted, letting Sarah know she was speaking from experience. Their bottles touched, and they both took a long drink. "I'll see you at dinner," Nancy said, already walking toward her bedroom.

~~~~~

As the last bit of her beer went down, Sarah noted the sun was already dangerously near the western rim of the valley. Early in the day, she had decided to trade a few minutes of dinner for one more sunset.

From the lodge, she took the trail she and Rick had followed earlier in the week. At the top of the incline, the large tree they had sat beneath stood even more prominent than she remembered. Approaching it, she noticed something leaning on the base of the large Ponderosa and recognized it almost immediately. Through the plastic bag, she read the cover: *Poems, Rhymes, and Other Curious Things.*

The sadness that Sarah had felt over Rick's departure suddenly turned to joy; he had left it for her, knowing she would come to this place one last time. Why didn't he just find me or leave a message? she thought. Had something happened?

Sarah took the book from the plastic bag, feeling how something resting in the pages wanted it to open. She let it, seeing that a beautiful purple flower marked the page. Her eyes savored each delicate pedal, remembering the field they had walked through and their day together. The page it marked held a single title: "The Perfect Day"

Sarah read:

Today, The Perfect Day, the rain came down in sheets until the rivers ran red with soil.

Today, The Perfect Day, the snow fell heavy and piled so that doors could not open.

Today, The Perfect Day, the sun so hot that feet could not possibly tolerate the scorched ground.

Today, The Perfect Day, the wind so strong that giant old trees fell as if cut free from their roots.

Today, The Perfect Day, the sleet came with such force that its impact against skin was intolerable.

Today, The Perfect Day, again spent with you.

Below this, scratched in his handwriting, was a note: "Thank you for the best day I have had in years. The Perfect Day."

Sarah closed the book and set it on her chest, watching the sun until the last rays fell below the ridge.

Chapter 23

When Sarah returned home, there were three messages on her answering machine. One was a wrong number, and the other two were from the same private school, twenty-three blocks from her apartment. Her first interview, exactly one week later, landed her the job. She had a one-year contract to teach a third-grade class, roughly half the size of the previous year's class. Unfortunately, the compensation was no better, but it was enough to make it an easy decision.

During the next three weeks, she contacted every parent to introduce herself, readied her classroom, and met some of the staff. The parental demographic was significantly different from that of her last school, most of them taking the opportunity to set up meetings over coffee and even lunch. The parents were more than happy to talk about their child and any surrounding concerns. Sarah would begin her new job with a good understanding of each of her students and with the full support of every parent.

She was thankful that concerns about her employment were not paramount during the weekend of Rachael's wedding. Descending the escalator at the airport, she expected to meet her sister, but no one was there. Waiting at the baggage carousel, she felt a light tap on her shoulder. She turned to find Kelly Rodgers. Completely surprised, Sarah let out a deep breath, as she said, "Kelly." Still confused, she leaned in for a hug, but Kelly was clearly cold and distant. "I didn't expect you. Where's Rachael?"

"I asked her if I could pick you up."

"Okay." Something was clearly off. "Listen, if this is about you and Rick, in Colorado, I've gotten over it."

"No, it's not about that … well it is, and it's not. There's something else, but this is not the place, okay?"

An awkward silence followed them to the car. The next words from Kelly arrived as they merged onto the freeway. "This is not easy for me," she began as her voice cracked. Sarah glanced over to find tears running down Kelly's face. "I've thought about this every day since we were in Colorado, and I need to get it out. You should be the first to know, before Rachael and the others."

Again, Sarah waited as Kelly composed herself. "When I was twelve years old, my body started to mature, ahead of the other girls. At fourteen, I looked like I was in college. In high school, there was a party every weekend, and I never missed one. My looks made me popular. I remember feeling so lucky."

Kelly wiped her face with the sleeve of her shirt before taking the wheel with both hands. "I've learned how to flirt. God, can I flirt," she laughed through the tears. "It's always been so easy."

The car sped along toward Nancy and Ted's home. Rachael, Andrew, and other wedding guests waited, ready to kick off the dinner celebration. Kelly's breath deepened as she searched. "I've been living in the city for about eight months," she blurted, waiting to see if Sarah understood.

"New York."

"Yes."

"Why didn't you contact ..." Sarah now realized why Kelly had picked her up. This was nothing less than a confession. She turned in her seat, a look of disbelief transforming Sarah's face. "How?"

"We exchanged numbers at Thanksgiving, almost two years ago. There were a few texts here or there. They seemed innocent enough ... but they were never innocent. I've had to admit that to myself, and I know what it makes me. After quitting my job in Baltimore, a few more exchanges with Greg, and I was convinced that New York would be a good move."

"Why him?"

This was perhaps the hardest question of all and one that had tested Kelly. "I started asking myself that in Colorado, searching. I am so sorry, Sarah. I just couldn't believe that anybody who was in love with you could be interested in me. I'm so dumb!"

Kelly pulled herself together, sitting up straight and fighting the emotion. "I'm sorry that I'm crying. I'm not looking for sympathy, and I know the consequences of what I've done ... my closest friends. You didn't deserve this and neither did Rachael."

Sarah had relaxed back into her seat to let the last ten minutes sink in. As she drifted back in time she uttered, "Greg never loved me."

Kelly heard this clearly. "Sarah, I was foolish enough to have thought that he had come to Colorado for me. Then, I watched him when you danced with Rick. That's when I realized I meant nothing to him ... that same night I went to Rick's cabin."

After exiting the interstate, Kelly realized she would reach their destination in a matter of minutes. She pulled over for more time. With the car stopped, she turned toward Sarah, "Rick didn't sleep with me. He showed me his ring and told me he couldn't."

"But ... Rachael said you didn't return that night."

"I was furious. First Greg's rejection, then Rick's too. So I left his cabin, ran into Billy, the young guide. I made up the entire story. I'm sorry!"

The ride from the airport had been unexpected, as was the amount of information Sarah was now trying to digest. She sat quietly and listened. "The last day in Colorado, when you and Greg left the lodge early ..."

"Yeah?" Sarah was again curious.

"Rick came looking for you. He didn't know you were with Greg ... I didn't tell him."

"I never knew," Sarah reflected, trying to wrap her mind around the repercussions.

"He came rushing back and left quickly. Something was obviously wrong with him. I guessed it had to do with Greg."

"I didn't know he was there."

"I'm sorry that I'm only telling you now, but I think it matters. I've spent so much time evaluating myself. I don't know what it takes to have a man love me." Kelly's tears started again. Sarah reached over and rubbed her shoulder. In return, Kelly lifted her eyes, surprised by the act. "Both of these men want you, but there is only one who deserves you. Don't let Rick go."

Over the last four weeks, Sarah had accepted that the week in Colorado was nothing more than just that. She had met a wonderful man, had a great time with him, and would never see him again. She had waited for the day when he would slip from her memory, the day she would forget the colors of blue. However, that was not happening, leaving her to question herself.

Am I nuts? How could I have fallen this hard over someone I was with for such a short time? It was a quiet battle she had contained within herself. Sarah remained lost in these recurring thoughts.

Kelly started the engine and pulled out for the final two blocks. "I've always believed that once I had someone in my life, love would be natural, that if I were attractive enough, it would happen. I've been wrong." The car settled in front of the home but remained running. "I don't know how to do things differently, but I do need to change. I'm going to work on that. I'm so sorry for what I've done to you and Rachael."

Sarah did not move; she just stared through Kelly. "I can't forgive you, not for a long time." A few moments passed before she realized that Kelly did not intended to park the car. "You need to come inside and stay."

"I don't deserve that. It wouldn't be right."

"Kelly, I don't want to pretend this will be easy or that you and I will suddenly be friends, but I do believe in forgiveness. You've been a part of Rachael's life for many years. I don't want that to end."

Kelly said nothing as tears now dripped from her chin. "Have you told anyone else?" Sarah asked.

"No. You needed to be first."

"Between you and me then?"

Kelly could not believe she had heard correctly, looking into Sarah's eyes in disbelief. "I need to tell Rachael. I've promised myself to change, so I need to do that."

"Fair enough, but after the weekend, okay?"

"Yes. Okay. Thank you. I don't deserve this."

Chapter 24

During his first year of college, Rick had stumbled into the office of Nelson & Kline, looking for some work to help him pay his bills. Fredrick Kline had made several million dollars by selling his stock options in a Palo Alto electronics company, his employer for almost two decades. He resigned, collaborating with David Nelson to start a business seeding startup companies. This proved to be a venture that needed much more capital and much better luck, than either of the two men seemed to possess. Nelson cut his losses, escaping with the shirt on his back and enough interest in the company to keep his name on the stationary. When Rick walked into their office, their little venture had already lost three-quarters of the founders' money and relocated to a much smaller office.

Hired to organize data and file some remedial paperwork, Rick became curious about the assessments his boss was utilizing to make investment decisions. He began spending late nights going over business plans, market estimates, and competitive analyses of companies they were considering.

A decisive point arrived when Rick convinced his boss to make the initial investment in a laser product used to predict wind shear. The seed was $350,000.00 and was too long of a shot for most "real firms" in the venture capital arena. Rick had done his homework, finding a military application he thought had significant synergy with the idea.

They produced the prototype in thirteen months, and the technology sold even before the company's infrastructure formed. For their investment,

Nelson & Kline received $7 million. Fred Kline immediately paid off every debt Rick had accumulated in college, wrote him a check for a quarter of a million dollars, and offered him a partnership once he graduated. The next four investments, guided by Rick, were all winners; the record of Wheeler Kline began catching the attention of people and corporations who had money to invest.

After Samantha graduated, they moved to Seattle to open the second arm of the company. Rick had a knack for picking winners and the humility to quickly accept defeat and deal with the ones that were not. Over time, their success brought further expansion. Three years after he began working for them, their firm had offices in San Diego, Seattle, Chicago, New York, and two locations overseas.

After the Seattle office was up and running, Rick signed up to open the Chicago branch. He and Samantha liked this idea because it was close to her parents. They purchased a stunning home in an up-and-coming area, lived in it the two years they called Chicago home, and held onto it for periodic visits after they left. It was intentionally within walking distance to the branch office.

~~~~~

After leaving the ranch, Rick spent more than a week fixing the problem in San Diego and another two in Zurich, before flying directly into Midway Airport. He stepped off the plane at 1:30 PM and went straight into the Chicago office.

It was important for him to spend some time in the office, but experience told him that jet lag would take a bigger toll the following day. The car reached the office at 2:45 PM and left with instructions to take his bags home. He spent an hour in a staff meeting getting an overview of each of the branch's projects. He was happy to find only a handful of problems and none that appeared significant.

At six in the evening, he declined an invitation for a drink and began his walk home. On his way, he stopped into a familiar corner grocery and picked up a handful of items. Near the exit, he grabbed the local weekly and located a simple moon phase chart in the back. He saw that tonight there would be a full moon.

At fifteen minutes before seven, Rick turned the last corner home. This led him onto a busy street full of restaurants and bars. The people around him set his pace down the sidewalk. He glanced into the windows of Jax restaurant as he passed; while Samantha was alive, they would eat there at least twice a week. It was still his favorite restaurant in the neighborhood, but tonight he was too tired. Perhaps he would try tomorrow.

The crowd in front of him began to slow until everyone was standing still. Rick quickly understood the problem — there was a show and the line had formed in front of him. He crossed the street and made it to the front of his building. The door attendant recognized Rick immediately, "Welcome back, Mr. Wheeler."

"Thanks, Earl. How have you been?"

"Good. You know, a few pounds here, a few there. That's about it."

Rick remembered Earl Washington's long suffering love for the Chicago Cubs, "How are the Cubbies shaping up?"

He returned a concerning look from under the brim of his hat. "Don't count on it this year, Mr. Wheeler."

Rick walked past him, adding another comment. "Earl, My name is Rick. Cut the Mr. Wheeler this and the Mr. Wheeler that shit."

Earl had worked at the building since the first unit sold. His job introduced him to every owner and most everything that went on in their lives. The occupants were all necessarily wealthy, but most also were too pretentious for Earl's liking. Rick and Sam had never fit that mold, making them the most enjoyable tenants in the building.

The day Samantha died, Earl decided to walk home after work. He traveled the seven miles in the dark, so no one would see his tears. Concerned, his wife was waiting at the door when he arrived. They hugged, cried about Samantha, Rick's loss, and the fragility of life. Earl Washington climbed to the second floor, collected his two young children from their beds, and tucked them in bed between him and his wife.

To Rick's comment, Earl replied. "You got it, Rick. No more Mr. Wheeler."

Rick took two more steps, "Did they bring my bags by earlier?"

"Yes, Mr. ...." A broad smile came across Earl's face before he tried again, "I put them inside your home, Rick."

"Thanks, Earl." Another thought. "Earl, if I came up with two tickets to the game tomorrow night, would you be interested?"

"Heck, yes."

"How about your wife and boys, would they come?"

Earl's eyes lit up. "They'd be all over it."

"Good, five tickets then. Let's eat at the ball park, huh?"

Earl's face told Rick everything. He pointed at Rick. "Thanks, Rick," Earl said. "The dogs and beer are on me, right?"

"You got it."

Rick entered his home and found his bags. He poured a drink and settled into the evening. The room was oddly long and narrow; each wall made of old brushed brick that blended well with the entire design of the home. He liked this room, because Samantha had liked it. They would just sit here together, watching as the moon would climb into the sky against the city's lights.

He found the remote, pressing a series of buttons until he decided John Mayer sounded right. It had been almost a month since Rick left the ranch. He thought of Sarah most days, sometimes just remembering what a pleasure she was.

The time change was catching up to him, and he was getting tired, hoping he could last long enough to see the moon. He knew he would see Sam tonight too, because he was back at one of the places they had shared together.

He took a drink, relaxed onto the familiar couch, and felt his exhaustion for the first time all day. His eyelids became heavy, struggling to stay awake just as the bright rim of the moon began its ascent. He dropped off to sleep without a fight.

Sam came to him almost immediately. At first, it was just her hand, and he took his time to study every detail. He saw his hand take hers, weaving their fingers before turning them over to study how they tangled together. However, here, something was different, something familiar, yet it did not make sense; he knew it, even in the dream.

There was something different about Sam's hand. He recognized the hourglass just as the flower brushed against their skin, remembering the dark purple veins and yellow core. He was at the top of the ranch and knew the hand, too. It was Sarah.

Exhausted, he struggled to wake and sit forward. He had already drifted into a deep sleep and now fought to understand why Sarah was there tonight. He sat motionless and uncertain of how he felt.

Downing the remainder of his drink, he made his way to the phone in the kitchen. Balancing against the granite counter top, he dialed by memory. It was a familiar voice. "Hello."

"Huff, it's Rick."

"How are you, stranger?"

His voice was slow and groggy. "I'm good. How are things in Colorado?"

"Same as when you were here, a little warmer maybe. There was a small fire north of the ranch about a week ago—lightning strike. They sent a Hot Shot crew in from Ignacio—had it put out a day later."

Whenever Rick called, Huff would immediately begin giving an update on everything going on at the ranch. Now he finished his download. "We had a real nice group of folks in last week. Two of them spent some time fishing and did real well." Maria shot a look to Huff from the couch. "Oh, and Maria says hi. She wants to know when you're coming back again." Huff was now thinking for her.

"I may get a chance to come this weekend. What does the guest log look like?"

"Well, this works out," Huff said. "The only visitors next week are Mateo, Janet, and the kids. Driving in sometime Saturday, I think. Huff began thinking about plans. "You really should make sure to visit while they're here," he said, knowing that a few days fishing with Mateo would tip the scales.

"That sounds real good. I'll call Mateo in the morning and see if we can coordinate.

"You come down here, Ricky," Maria shouted from her seat.

Rick smiled on the other end of the phone. "Tell her to control that Mexican blood, Huff."

"Now that's a good idea. You'll find me out sleeping with the dogs." They both laughed.

"Did you call to tell us you were already coming down?" Huff asked.

"Well, yeah. Something like that, but I was also wondering if you had the phone number for Sarah Field."

Minutes earlier, when Huff picked up the phone and realized it was Rick, he picked up a piece of paper from beside the phone. It contained what he was now asking for—a way to find Sarah. It had been waiting in that spot, for this exact call, since the time Rick last left the ranch.

Maria and Sarah had exchanged letters, the envelope providing Sarah's address in New York. From the guest registry, Huff had written down the only phone number from their group. Not wanting to be too conspicuous, Huff pretended he was searching for the information. "Let's see. Let me look in the log here. Oh yeah, here we go. Do you have some paper? I've got her address, but the number they registered under was the groom's father, Ted."

"That'll work, Huff." Rick wrote down the address and the phone number. At the bottom, he wrote down the name Ted Strickland before circling it. "Thanks," he said.

"No problem, Rick. Anything else I can do for you?"

"No, Huff. I've got it from here, thanks. How's Maria doing?"

"Oh, she's doing fine. I'll tell her you were asking."

"Yes. Please do that."

After they hung up, Huff turned toward the couch. Maria had rested the book she was reading, anticipating his report. His look told her everything, but she asked anyway, *"¿Es tratar de encontrar con ella?"* (He's trying to find her?)

"Si"

Huff's expression did not change, happy that Maria had guessed right. He sat down next to her again, opening his left hand to accept hers again. *"La énergia de la vida,"* she said. (The energy of life.)

Huff agreed, *"Si, la énergia de la vida."*

~~~~~

Ted Strickland's phone rang. Removing it from his blazer, he did not recognize the number. He answered just as Sarah and Kelly entered, "This is Ted Strickland."

"Yes, Ted, this is Rick Wheeler. I'm sorry to call you at this hour of the day. You and I met at the Tres Piedras Ranch, about a month ago, in Colorado."

Ted remembered him immediately, "Yes. What can I do for you, Mr. Wheeler?" he asked in a very stiff voice. In the past month, Greg's anger had overflowed to his father, and that, somehow, had entered their business relationship. Despite the knowledge of Greg's wrong doing, Ted still felt Sarah held the responsibility for their failed relationship. He had arrived at this perception from the lurid picture Greg had painted of Sarah and Rick's time together at the ranch.

"I was hoping you might be able to put me in contact with Sarah. Perhaps you have her phone number?"

Ted, ear to the phone, watched Sarah as she hugged her Nancy. "I'm sorry, Mr. Wheeler. I have no idea how to contact her. Please do not ever call this number again." Ted hung up.

~~~~~

As soon as the phone went dead, Rick dialed another number. "Hello, this is Bastiaan

"Bastiaan, it's Rick. How are things?"

Bastiaan was in the middle of reading a company report. He immediately placed it on his nightstand, a new energy picking up his evening. "Mr. Rick, what's up with you?"

"I need you to find someone for me."

Chapter 25

At 1:30 Monday afternoon, Sarah landed at JFK International Airport after anxiously bouncing through the turbulence of a broken layer of clouds. It was another warm and humid summer day in New York. She had expected to be tired after the wedding, but now she was completely exhausted and needed a long nap. Ninety-five minutes later, she had collected her luggage, caught the ETS from the airport, and stood at 116th and Broadway in front of the gates of Columbia University. The shuttle in had been surprisingly quiet, allowing for the deepest sleep she had gotten in the last four days.

During the cab ride to her apartment, Sarah reflected on the weekend. A smile came across her face as her thoughts focused on her sister, remembering their childhood and all the dreams they had shared. Three blocks from her apartment, Sarah began digging through her purse for the cab fare, causing her to miss the man sitting on her step as they pulled up.

Stepping from the car, she finally noticed the stranger straightening his clothing as he stood. He was dressed in a dark business suit without a tie. The man's skin was dark, and he wore his hair in short dreadlocks, well above his shoulders. Sarah paid the driver after he unloaded both bags, never taking her eyes off the man. The driver had just sped off when the man reached her. "Excuse me, Miss, Would you happen to be Sarah Field?" he asked in a thick Jamaican accent.

"Yeah," she replied, dragging the word and making sure there were no other surprises lurking. "Yes, I'm Sarah," she clarified.

He could see that she was a little anxious, so he got to the point. "My name is Bastiaan, and I am here on behalf of Mr. Rick Wheeler."

Sarah's heart jumped when she heard his name, but she allowed herself only a simple, curious reply. "Yes?"

"I'm to tell you that he has been trying to contact you," he hesitated, "without success until now, obviously." He's hoping that you will meet him in Colorado, at the Tres Piedras ranch."

At this, Sarah's mind began racing. She was excited that he was looking for her, thinking of the ranch, and trying to understand what she had just heard. "When?"

"He's there now and hopes that you would come as soon as you can. Perhaps tomorrow?" After saying this, he waited for a moment to see how she would react. She was silent in her contemplation, so he continued. "I've been trying to find you for several days. I'm sorry it's such short notice." He waited again for Sarah to say something, but then he remembered Rick's message. "If it's too late for Colorado, Mr. Wheeler said he would like to have dinner with you, here, in New York, whenever you can."

"How long?" she asked. Sarah saw that her question confused him, quickly clarifying. "How many days will I be in Colorado?"

"Until next weekend or as many days as you can," he answered, remembering his boss' schedule.

"No, I mean, it's just a little sudden, and I need to think through things," Sarah replied, thinking of everything that might stop her from just going. Then she considered the logistics. "I don't have a ticket," she simultaneously thought and said aloud. Sarah remained practical; she had used most of her airline miles to fly to the wedding, It will cost a fortune with almost no notice, she considered. She caught herself, thinking, Am I goofy? Ten minutes ago I would have sold one of my students for this same invitation. She said, "Yes ... I mean, yes, I would like to go to Colorado tomorrow. I just need to check on a ticket first."

Bastiaan's English was very formal. "Miss, please, do not worry about the transportation; it will be arranged."

"Thank you," she said instinctively.

"Would nine o'clock in the morning be okay for the car to arrive?"

"The car?" Reality hit with the first hint of a schedule.

"Yes, the car, to the airport."

She understood. "Nine in the morning would be perfect."

"Ms. Field, Rick has provided a telephone number, if you would like to speak to him in Colorado. His mobile telephone will not function in the mountains. This is the number for the home of Mr. Huff," he said, handing Sarah a white sheet of paper. She took the paper, relaxing and laughing lightly at the notion of "Mr. Huff."

"May I help you inside with your luggage, Miss?"

"No, thank you Bastiaan. I can manage."

"Okay, fine then, 9:00 AM. I have written my telephone number at the bottom of the same page, in case you need something or have any questions." Sarah glanced down, confirming what he had just said. She saw that it was a local area code.

He turned and began walking down the sidewalk. Sarah extended the handle on her suitcase and drifted to the foot of her steps, thinking about all that had just happened. Before she reached her door, she heard Bastiaan's voice again. "Excuse me, Miss Field."

"Yes?"

"Rick gave me something, in case you did not want to join him in Colorado. He called it the 'secret weapon.'"

"A 'secret weapon'?" Sarah's face held a very curious look.

"Yes, Miss, just in case."

"But I said I am going to go."

"Yes. Nevertheless, I think it would be a good idea for you to have it anyway."

"I see. Okay."

Bastiaan covered his right eye with his right hand, letting out a long, Jamaican- influenced, pirate's arrrggghhh. Bastiaan's smile was wide, bright, and joyful. They laughed together. "He would have begged, you know?"

"Bastiaan."

"Yes, Miss?"

"My name is Sarah. It's what my friends call me."

He gave her another beautiful, wide Caribbean smile. "Yes, Sarah. I will see you in the morning then."

At the top of her steps, Ethyl Schuler, the downstairs neighbor, greeted Sarah. Their two apartments shared a common entrance, and Sarah lived directly above the eighty-three-year-old. Her elder neighbor had lived there for decades, warming slowly to Sarah after she had moved in. Ethyl spent her days watching the street outside of her home for the slightest hint of wrongdoing. With Ethyl on the watch, Sarah was certain she could leave her door unlocked at any time.

"He sat on that step for three days, you know?" Ethyl was not shy.

"I'm sorry, Mrs. Schuler. I didn't know that," Sarah replied trying to be sympathetic.

"I called the police because he seemed a little suspicious, and you just don't sit on someone's step for such a long time." Sarah expected Ethyl to begin pointing and shaking her finger at any moment. "You can never be too careful around here," Ethyl admonished.

"And what did the police do?"

"They checked on him, asked him who he was and why he was just sitting there, of course."

"The police let him stay?" Sarah asked, wondering how this had all worked out.

"I told them he could stay."

This was shocking. "You let him stay?"

"Yes. Yes I did," Ethyl replied. "I heard him tell the officers why he was here, so I let him stay." She responded defiantly, yet proud of herself.

Sarah was now more curious than ever, "And what did he tell the police?"

Ethyl gave Sarah a look she had never seen from her neighbor, complete with a smile that told her she knew something Sarah did not. "He told them his boss was trying to find you."

"That's it? You let him stay because he was trying to find me?"

Ethyl had turned and walked to her door. "It was hot outside. I made him some lemonade every day," she said, opening her apartment door.

"Wait." Sarah yelled, walking after Ethyl. "You let him stay and made him lemonade because he told them his boss was looking for me?"

Ethyl had stepped inside her apartment, closing the door so that Sarah could only see her face. "No dear. Not because his boss is looking for you. Bastin was looking for you."

Sarah quickly forgave Ethyl's butchery of Bastiaan's name. "I don't understand, Mrs. Schuler."

Ethyl delivered another rare smile. "You see dear, his boss asked him to find you, but he did not wait for you because of that. He waited because he thinks very highly of his boss, so much so that he took it upon himself to find you, waiting in the hot sun on his own time. Bastin told the police that his boss is a very good man and that you must be very important to him or he would have never been looking for you. Sarah, he said it's the first time his boss has wanted anyone since he lost his wife. That's why I fixed Mr. Bastin the lemonade. He's a nice young man."

Sarah had just discovered that Ethyl Schuler had a heart. "Thank you, Mrs. Schuler," she said, picking up one bag and pulling the other up the first step leading to her apartment.

"Sarah," Ethyl called.

She turned. "Yes, Mrs. Schuler?"

"There's nothing like love. There's simply nothing like it."

Inside her apartment, Sarah was happy to find her roommate away. She set her bags on the floor, closed the door, and rested her back against it. In the last twenty minutes, her world had begun to spin so fast that she only now had a minute to consider everything. She had learned Rick was looking for her, had found her, and now she was going to Colorado. Only then did she consider every appointment, meeting, or other obligation coming in the days ahead. There were several, but with school out, none so important that it could not be rescheduled. She thought about her luggage, washing her clothes, and repacking. She remembered the book, not wanting to forget it, either.

Her hand searched her pocket, pulling out the single sheet of paper Bastiaan had provided. Opening it, she considered Huff's phone number, quickly deciding not to call because she would see Rick tomorrow, but even more because she was not certain of what to say. She felt herself become nervous, flattening the palms of each hand against the door to help her balance. There's nothing like love, Sarah thought, considering the words of her neighbor.

Downstairs, Ethyl Shuler occupied her favorite chair, which allowed her to peek through the curtains at the sidewalk. Just as she had settled, a very loud, yet unmistakable shriek of joy came from upstairs.

~~~~~~

At 6:00 PM, Rick set his gear down, removed his wet boots, and climbed the back stairs of the lodge. There were no paying guests at the ranch this week, so the guides and others took the opportunity to return to their own homes. Still, the deck was crowded. Huff, Maria, Mateo, Janet, and their two boys sat around the table.

Rick sensed something odd going on. The typical boisterous greetings from this family were missing. As he walked to the table, the group pretended not to recognize him. Mateo's two young boys were the first to crack, both of their large grins missing a few teeth. "Hi, Rick," they both said. The adults kept eating without looking at him or saying a word.

"Hello, boys. The two of you have such nice manners. What do you think is wrong with these funny adults?"

"They have a secret to tell you." This came from George, the older of the two.

"If they tell me, it won't be a secret any longer." Rick toyed. "Do you think it's worth it?"

"They want to tell you," Mathew chimed in. "My Papi says it will make you happy." The four adults stayed with the game but giggled under their breath.

Rick bent over, speaking only to the boys again, yet loud enough for the others to hear. "Which one of those scoundrels do you think will be first to break?"

Both boys immediately pointed at their grandfather, "Papi will break."

Rick turned his focus to Huff. "Watcha got, Papi?"

Huff was ready, lifting an ear of corn and looking it over before taking a bite. With his mouth full, he mumbled. "Bastiaan called."

Although Rick had not directly told Huff he was searching for Sarah, he had asked him for her number. Now there was Bastiaan's call—he could only be calling for one reason. Born from guilt over Samantha's death, Rick felt uncertain until the first time he held Sarah's hand. He had never once considered that he might become close with another woman. This led him to a difficult thought: How could he ever fall in love again, when he had never stopped loving Samantha?

Maria knew his conflict. Long ago, she had lost her husband, struggling with similar questions as she fell madly in love with Huff. She wanted to be careful with Rick, standing and taking his hand just as Huff mentioned the call. She walked him to the edge of the deck. Out of earshot, she turned Rick so that they faced the others, "Do you see the kids, Ricky?"

Rick nodded in acknowledgement.

"When Mathew was born, Mateo and Janet did not love little George any less; their love just grew." She waited a minute for this to sink in as her right hand began rubbing his back. "That's what's so special about love. It can just grow like that, without ever being taken away from someone else." Maria hesitated as she watched Rick close his eyes. "We all know how you love Samantha. There's nothing that will ever change or diminish that."

When Rick opened his eyes, he was looking down at the deck. "It's just that Sarah is such a gift — one that I'm not sure I deserve."

"Ricky. You did nothing less than love Samantha with everything you had. What happened ... happened to the both of you. You gave her nothing less than every part of who you are. Anyone would be thankful for such a thing."

"You and Huff have been very good to me."

There was certainly something behind Bastiaan's call. "Okay, what did he have to say?"

Mateo could not wait. "He found Sarah, and she's coming tomorrow," he blurted, thrilled for his best friend.

They all waited to see how Rick would react, watching as a playful grin slowly grew into a beautiful, excited smile. "She's coming," he said. The wrinkles on the sides of his eyes accompanied his smile and confirmed his excitement. "Sarah's coming," he repeated, trying to convince himself it was true.

~~~~~

Sarah had unpacked her bag, washed her clothes, rearranged a meeting with a friend and one with a parent from school, visited her bank, and finally repacked for the trip the following morning. She slept poorly, too excited and thinking of exactly what she would say when she saw him.

At 6:00 AM, Sarah entered Starbucks Coffee, three blocks from her apartment. It was three long hours before her trip would begin. She ordered a vente, two pump, non-fat, white-chocolate mocha and found a small round table in the corner of the room. She thumbed through a copy of the *New York Times*, the paper most interesting today because it helped the time move faster. She checked her watch—6:27 AM.

Would Rick be waiting at the airport, at the lodge, at Huff's cabin, or somewhere else on the ranch? she thought to herself, wanting to envision the moment when she would see him. This would calm her nerves. What will I say? she thought, going over a multitude of scenarios and words. I'm so sorry about your wife. I'm sorry to hear about Sam. No. She checked herself. "Sorry to hear about Samantha." Sarah continued to struggle for the next forty-five minutes, reaching no clear conclusions.

At 7:55 AM, Sarah folded the paper, set it on the counter, and ordered another black coffee to go. On the sidewalk outside, she took the phone from her pocket and typed R-A-C before the name Rachael Field came to the screen. I need to change the last name, she remembered just before pushing Send. Sarah did not expect Rachael to answer. Her sister had vowed not to turn her phone on while on their honeymoon in the Caribbean.

"You've reached the phone of Rachael Strickland. I'm unable to take your call now, but please leave your name and number, and I will get back to you as soon as I am able."

Sarah forgot about her morning briefly, glowing as she thought about the moment when Rachael changed the last name on her message. "Rachael, it's Sarah. I know you're too busy 'getting busy' to answer, but I wanted you to know I'm going to Colorado today, a little place called The Tres Piedras Ranch. I'll fill in the details later. Oh yeah, and ..." Sarah screamed and hung up, laughing to herself as she spun around in a circle, thinking of her message and trying to believe that she was leaving for Colorado in a hour.

Ethyl Schuler answered the knock on her door, "Do you drink coffee, Mrs. Schuler?" she asked, handing her the cup.

~~~~~

A black Lincoln Continental pulled up three minutes before 9:00 AM. Sarah saw it arrive through the window of Ethyl's apartment where the two were drinking coffee together for the first time.

Ethyl saw the car too, "Have a lovely time, dear."

"Thank you, Ethyl. I will see you in a few days."

On the front steps, Sarah stopped briefly, seeing that the driver was standing by the rear door, waiting her arrival. He wore a black chauffeur's uniform, complete with a hat. It was the first time she considered what Rick did for a living.

Bastiaan appeared from the back seat, approaching Sarah and taking her bag. "Good morning, Sarah," he said energetically. "I trust that you had a pleasant night's sleep?"

"I did. Thank you Bastiaan," she replied in the spirit of his greeting. After handing her bag to the driver, he followed Sarah into the rear seat.

"Are you coming to Colorado too?" she asked.

"No Miss ..." he began, then corrected himself. "No, Sarah. I will just escort you to the airport. I'm afraid I have my wife's family in town, so I will not make the trip this time."

Sarah thought she heard him correctly. "You've been to the ranch before?"

"Yes, several times. It's a very beautiful place, isn't it?"

"It is." Sarah began exploring, "How do you know Rick?"

"Ah, yes. Well, that's rather simple; I work for him."

"You work for him, here, in New York?"

"Yes. In the city. I suppose it is more accurate to say that I work for his company. I attended New York University before being hired three years ago."

This surprised Sarah, who had never considered that Rick owned a company, let alone one in New York. She thought about the day they had shared at the ranch and when he had told her he had visited Europe many times. This had not caught her attention in that moment, but now as she thought about it, it seemed curious. There was so much she did not know about him, but she also felt it was unfair to begin quizzing Bastiaan on the subject. She changed their conversation. "Do you and your wife have children?" The children, Sarah learned quickly, were the center of Bastiaan's universe. They had a three-year-old boy, and his wife was due to deliver a little girl in six weeks.

As they spoke, Sarah noted that they had turned onto I-95, crossing into New Jersey. Newark International Airport, she believed, until the Lincoln took the exit onto US-46. "Which airport are we going to?"

"The plane is at Teterboro."

Sarah had never flown from Teterboro. She considered how Bastiaan phrased his answer, "The plane is at Teterboro." She decided the odd combination of Jamaican upbringing and formality that caused him to say it that way. She did not think there was really a plane waiting just for them.

"Did you speak with Rick last night?" he asked.

"No. I thought about calling, but the chances of him being at Huff's cabin must be pretty low. Besides, I'm going to see him today, right?"

"That's true, in a few hours." Bastiaan responded, detecting some nervousness in his guest.

The driver pulled their car into an unassuming parking lot next to a small building. There were less than a dozen cars in the lot. With the engine still running, the driver opened Sarah's door. Stepping outside, she saw she was less than thirty feet from the building's entrance. A sign over the entrance read Charter Jet Service. "I'm taking a chartered flight to Colorado?" she asked Bastiaan as he emerged from the car.

Bastiaan looked at her curiously, seeing the surprise on her face and realizing she knew very little about Rick. He was straightforward, "The airplane is Rick's."

"It's Rick's plane?" Sarah repeated his last words.

"Yes. I assure you it is quite comfortable." His smart answer was delivered with a teasing look.

"Oh, I'm certain of that," she replied. "I just hope it's up to my standards," she joked meekly. Bastiaan offered his signature large, bright smile as he laughed.

"Don't feel you are alone, Sarah. I have never known him to be forthcoming with these types of details."

"The details, yes. I'm learning that very slowly."

He walked her into the lobby, carrying her bag until they reached a small security check with a single guard on each side of the gate.

"This is where I will leave you. You will be met on the other side of the gate by the flight attendant." Sarah glanced to where he was pointing, seeing an older, thin, blond flight attendant lifting her hand in a wave toward them. "It was a pleasure meeting you, Sarah."

"Thank you, Bastiaan. It was very nice meeting you too. I hope we will see each other again sometime."

He had begun walking toward the exit, turning over his shoulder to respond, "I'm sure we will meet again very soon. You have a delightful time in those wild mountains."

Chapter 26

Janet insisted that Mateo fish with Rick in the morning, sensing the hours before Sarah's arrival might be filled with anxiety. Mateo and Janet had stayed up late talking about Rick, Sarah, and of course, Samantha. "He's a grown man, honey," Mateo had replied over his wife's concern.

"You heard what your mom told us, Mateo. He will question himself, and you should be there for him. Besides, even if he doesn't need you, it's not like the two of you get to fish together very often."

"That's a good point," Mateo agreed energetically. "He might need me the rest of the week too."

"Don't push your luck, slick."

~~~~

The morning sun had not yet hit the valley floor when Rick and Mateo entered the river. Their friendship was born from many mornings just like this one, and in these same mountains. Neither one of them had said a word since leaving the lodge. Rick remained quiet until they had passed the last place he had seen Sarah; in her embrace with Greg.

"How about starting at the Duncan pool?" he finally suggested, referencing a deep run of water they both recognized by the name.

"Good." Mateo agreed, turning with Rick and sidestepping down the steep bank. Rick reached the river's edge first, glancing back at Mateo and lifting his chin. Mateo responded, repeating Rick's gesture. Rick would cross the river and take the east bank. They began fishing just before seven in the morning.

For the next four hours, they fished together, exactly as they had in high school, working each section of the river across from one another. Periodically, each one would take the time to watch his friend fishing. Mateo noticed that something was different about Rick today. Normally very patient and methodical in his approach, today he rushed through each section of river. Janet had been right; his mind was clearly grinding through the arrival of Sarah and all that it meant in the context of Samantha.

Rick crossed the river at the top of a large rapid, careful to wade where the water was shallow. "Could you see the spots on that brown from where you were?" Mateo asked as Rick approached along the bank.

"Yeah. Beautiful fish, huh? How long was it?

"I think it went about twenty-five inches, took the wings off a big stone fly." Mateo lifted the fly so Rick could see the damage that the aggressive fish had inflicted. Rick took a good look; the enthusiasm Mateo had expected was absent. "Is there something on your mind, bud?" Mateo asked the obvious question.

"What do you think of me asking Sarah to come here today?"

"I think it's great." Mateo reflected for a moment. "It's time you know? We all feel that way. Janet, my mom, Dad, and everyone." Mateo waited as both men stood staring into the deep water. "Sam would think it was time too. You know that, right?"

"Yeah. I know she would want me to get on with things."

"No. She wouldn't just want you to 'get on with things.' She would want you to start living again."

He didn't look at Mateo, finding the sight of the river easier for this conversation. "I know. I've come a long way, but it's not all that easy." A deep breath settled Rick. "I never thought I would think of anyone else the way I thought of Sam."

"Everyone but you has accepted that ..." Mateo searched fruitlessly for the right word. "... dating will be part of the whole process."

"I know, but it's not going to happen without a lot of consideration."

Mateo decided to lift and change the subject slightly. "So what's so special about this girl? I mean, with your money, I just figured you would buy one of those hot models from Russia."

Rick's eyes came away from the river to find his friend; his broad smile coming as he began laughing, "You're an asshole."

"You're not telling me anything I don't know. So, come on, what's the story with Sarah?"

Rick was serious again. "You'll see, it's hard to describe her, but she makes the world light up." He was energetic in his description, Mateo seeing a joy in his friend that had been absent for years.

"The first time I met her, I had come to the lodge early to grab some coffee. At first, I didn't pay too much attention, expecting to see someone dressed and ready to get on the river. When she stepped out ... well ...it changed everything right there. I couldn't take my eyes off her."

"Beautiful, huh?"

"Gorgeous. God, she is so beautiful. But beyond that, I'm telling you there is something very different about her. It sounds stupid, but I can see that there's energy in her. It's very different. She has a very gentle way about her. It puts me at ease."

Finally, Mateo thought to himself, hearing how Rick described her. It had made no sense that he had asked Sarah to come unless he felt something deep. Mateo was finally hearing what compelled Rick and hearing it in the same tone he remembered the first time he had called after meeting Sam. "So she comes down the stairs, and the next thing you know she's coming back to the ranch?"

"Something like that. We spent some time together during the week."

"I guess she wouldn't be coming back if that didn't go well." He asked a more difficult question, "How did she handle the news about Sam?"

"We didn't exactly get around to that."

Mateo took a long breath. "I guess you have some things to talk about then?"

"I guess. It's not an easy subject. I don't want her to think that's why she's here."

"You know she has my mom's colors?"

"I've heard. Your mom is pretty happy about that isn't she?"

"Oh, yeah. That's all we've been hearing since she found out Sarah was coming back."

It was Rick's turn to change the subject. "Listen, I know Janet wants you back, but I'm going to continue fishing until Sarah gets here. Would you mind bringing her up?"

"Mom and Janet were counting on you for lunch at the cabin."

"I know. Beg out for me if you don't mind? I don't have much of an appetite right now."

Mateo did not offer much resistance, knowing that Rick would be more at ease on the river. "No problem. We'll ride the horses up when she gets here. I'll keep an eye out for you in the river?"

"Thanks." Rick was pointing the end of his fishing rod up river, "I'll get back in on the other side of the red cliffs. I won't go any further than the Deck."

Past the old cabin, the graves, and Cascade Creek, the trail ran along the river before climbing to a small flat area surrounded by century-old pines. It was unique in that it provided the best, unobstructed view of the upper valley. It also sat at the very top of the ranch, before the valley narrowed into the first box canyon. This place was a frequent destination of Maria and Huff's rides. Huff named the place, and Huff first showed the area to Rick and then Mateo.

"No worries. If we don't find you in the river, we'll meet you at the Deck. See you in a few hours."

~~~~~~

Walking north, he had intended to begin fishing after he came down from the red cliffs, but he had begun thinking of Sam, so he just continued wandering up the trail until he reached the old cabin. There he realized how consumed he had been, as the last hour had passed very quickly.

He walked past the Williamses' graves, crossing Cascade Creek where it met the river and continuing until he climbed the incline to reach the Deck. The shade of the old trees offered relief from the midday sun, the air cool and rich with the smell of pine. Rick removed his pack and shoes and stood looking over the valley he had just come through. Pine needles had accumulated over time and covered the ground in a thick mat. They were soft from the recent rains and felt good under his feet, compelling him to lie flat on his back and look up beyond the reaches of the old trees. Wisps of white clouds floated through the sky and the heat of the day added a haze that obscured its true color.

During his walk, he had been thinking about a trip he and Sam had taken to the island of Tilos, Greece, two years before they found out Sam was sick. The home they had rented peered out over the ocean from atop solid limestone cliffs. On the first morning, they followed a steep set of stairs down to their own private bay. At the bottom, there was a small structure, and like the house, it was built from the island's stone. Inside, they found a number of inner tubes and a small rubber raft.

They had decided that launching the raft upside down provided the most comfortable surface for the two of them to enjoy the sun. They drifted aimlessly around their small cove under the heat of the Mediterranean sun. A windless day created a smooth window into the water, each rock lining the bottom seen in exact detail. Sam lay on her stomach, and Rick on his back next to her, letting the ocean's current slowly turn them in circles as they soaked up the sun.

As he studied the sky from the Deck, Rick's mind drifted to that day on Tilos. He was tired, and anxiety over Sarah's arrival kept him awake all night. Drifting off to sleep, his mind confused the day on Tilos with the last day of Samantha's life. "Are you scared?" she had asked him.

"Terrified," he said.

"What scares you the most?" She was persistent because she wanted to get to her point.

Rick did not want to answer, but knew Sam had something on her mind. "The first minute that I know I will never hear your voice again," he said honestly.

"What scares you the most?"

"My biggest fear is that you will never find this again, with someone else." Still asleep under the trees, his dream brought another subject to the conversation on the raft. Rick rolled over and held out the small chain, "Is this to help me?" he asked Sam, seeming to understand its purpose.

"Yes, when you're ready," Sam responded, clutching and folding his fingers into a fist around the object.

~~~~~

Christina Baker had taken Rick's call at 9:00 PM the previous night. "This is Christine," she had answered.

"How come you're not out dancing?" he joked immediately.

Recognizing Rick's voice, she shot back, "I'm still waiting for you to pick me up."

"How are you, Christine?"

"I'm great, Rick. You?" She remembered the last time they spoke. "How was the trip to Europe?"

"I'm good, and the trip was a success … more or less."

Christine wondered why he was calling so late. "Are you in town?"

"No, I'm at the ranch in Colorado."

"Sounds nice—a much better place than here anyway."

"I have a favor to ask."

"Anything. Let me have it."

"I'm sorry about the last-minute notice. Is there any way you can cover a flight down here in the morning?"

Christine thought for a moment. "Sure, I guess. Do you have one of your bigwig clients you want to hustle over fishing?" she jabbed.

When Rick heard Sarah was coming, he began thinking about how fast the whole trip had come together and that it might be a little overwhelming for her. He wanted to make sure that the ride down was as comfortable as possible, bringing him to Christine. "Something like that," he said. "A lady I met down here on my last trip—Sarah. I thought it might be a good idea to have you on the flight."

Christine had known Rick for many years. She had become very concerned after Sam's death, watching as he sank into work to help him forget. It was unhealthy, and she felt better as she observed the dark cloud began to lift in recent months. Still, she was surprised at this. "Sure. Which airport and when?"

"I'll have Bastiaan e-mail you the information in a few minutes." The phone went silent for a moment before he continued, "Thanks, Christine. It's more than I should expect."

"Are you kidding? Anything, all right?"

~~~~~

Christine waved to Bastiaan as he left Sarah on the opposite side of the airport's security screening. Her curiosity had grown since taking Rick's call last night; now she watched intently as Sarah spoke to the guard. She could see that Sarah was exceptionally beautiful, but so too were several other women who wanted time with Rick. She fought the urge to be over-protective.

The guard Sarah was talking with suddenly smiled, laughing as he waved her past the scanner. Christine could see she was friendly. "Hello, I'm Christine," she offered as Sarah reached for the bag that was emerging from the X-ray machine. "May I help you with that?"

"No, thank you. I'm fine. My name is Sarah Field."

"It's nice to meet you, Sarah. I'll be accompanying you on the flight to Durango."

"Thank you," Sarah replied, feeling grateful for the special attention she was receiving.

Christine's hand motioned Sarah toward a set of double glass doors that led out onto the tarmac. "The plane is this way." Just beyond the doors, the whine of the two rear-mounted jet engines came from the Gulfstream G150. Motioning to the jet, Christine directed Sarah, "We're just about ready to go."

Sarah's eyes widened. It was true, she thought in disbelief. A jet was waiting for her. The sudden look on Sarah's face was not lost on Christine. In fact, she had been waiting for just this moment to see how she would react. Christine had wondered if Sarah was from money, if this was expected.

The jet was sleek and perfect at every curve and angle. Sarah felt more like a spectator than a passenger. "It's beautiful," she said, before considering that the plane might be nothing more than a mundane part of Christine's work routine. However, Christine had always felt that this job and the plane were something special, thus understanding the comment perfectly. "I think so too," she replied. Sarah was clearly different from most of the corporate types she usually served. "Wait until you see the inside," she continued, riding the wave of enthusiasm.

The steps led past the cockpit where the pilot was standing. "Hello, Sarah. I'm Bill Jacobs, the pilot. He pointed inside, "Ken Perkins is assisting but, as you can see, he' too busy to say much right now. We'll all have time to catch up at the ranch."

"Everyone is coming to the ranch?"

"Yes. A nice benefit of this job is that Rick has turned me into a fly fisherman."

Sarah engaged Christine in the same conversation, turning to her, "You're coming too, I hope?"

"Yes, it's another working vacation for all of us."

"That's great. I'm so excited to see it again," Sarah responded, genuinely happy that everyone would join in.

"Good," the pilot replied, turning back into the cockpit. "Enjoy the flight; it looks like it should be pretty smooth."

The cabin felt more spacious than Sarah's apartment. Large white leather seats appeared misplaced, more appropriately occupying the living room of some fancy home. The same material covered a small comfortable-looking couch that ran parallel to the cabin. Each seat had its own table, beautifully inlaid with real mahogany. On each sat a foldable LCD screen that could be used for Internet, live TV, or any one of a large selection of movies, Christine explained. Sarah's eyes took everything in; the interior was immaculate. "Was the plane going to Colorado today anyway?" Sarah asked suspiciously.

Christine realized just how much of a surprise this was and explained, "It's going to Colorado for you, Sarah."

As they taxied, Christine performed her preflight duties, making sure the cabin and her passenger were ready to take off. She took the seat next to Sarah before the plane climbed out from Teterboro. Sarah had been very quiet since shortly before liftoff. "Sarah, can I get you some breakfast?"

Sarah seemed to be in a daze at first, slowly coming out of it to answer, "No, thank you."

"Are you okay, dear?"

Sarah shifted, clearly wanting to say something but having trouble starting. Christine took her hand. "What do you have on your mind, honey?"

"Christine, it's just that all this, the plane, and everything, it's a little overwhelming. I shop at Target. The most expensive thing I own is a dress I wore for my sister's wedding. I'm a teacher, a simple teacher, and this is very different from what I've ever known.

Christine now understood the look of concern; it was all so new, and big, and coming at her so fast. She did not know anything about his wealth.

Christine had known Rick for many years, and like most of the others close enough to call him a friend, had been concerned about him since Sam's death. She hoped his first relationship after Sam's death would be healthy. Now, since watching Sarah at the airport, she had come to believe that Sarah might be very good for him. She put her other hand on top of Sarah's and rubbed gently, "Everything you see here, it's not who Rick is. You met him at the ranch?"

"Yes, more than a month ago. I thought he was a fishing guide."

Christine smiled. "It looks like he didn't work too hard to change that perception?"

"Not one bit." Sarah replied as they both found the humor. "This is all so shocking."

"Sarah. He didn't tell you because it's not what matters to him." She then asked the obvious, "You're excited to see Rick because of the man you met?"

"Yes."

"Then don't make it anything more than that. He's asked you down to the ranch because of who he met, not because you're a teacher who has an obsessive shopping habit at Target."

Sarah smiled and laughed, squeezing the hand of someone she now felt might make a wonderful friend.

~~~~~

The newlyweds, Rachael and Andrew Strickland, meandered into the small Caribbean town of St. Croix. It was their first trip into town since arriving at the beach house, rented for their honeymoon. Like the other tourists, Andrew wore knee-length khaki shorts and a loose t- shirt. Rachael wore a light, brightly colored, loose fabric over her bikini. They would find a nice place for lunch and explore the town, hunting for mementos and taking a break from the hours they had already logged on the beach. Both brought their cell phones, breaking a promise they had made to keep them turned off all week. A worker at their cottage had told them that most cell phones would work in town, tempting their commitment to avoid the real world for an entire week.

Outside the restaurant they had chosen for lunch, Rachael listened to her voice mail. There were four messages: the first from Ted, welcoming her to the family one more time. She looked toward Andrew, smiled, and whispered "Your father," before erasing the message. The second message was from one of the bridesmaids. "Holy shit," it started. "I know you're on your honeymoon, but pick up *People* magazine and look at page twenty-seven. Holy shit. Call me." Andrew watched a curious look come over Rachael's face. "Something about *People* magazine," she said, pulling the phone from her ear and looking at the keypad as if there were more information it might provide. She saved the message, moving on to the next.

A loud shriek came from Rachael as the third message played into her ear. "It's Sarah," she screamed without concern for the other tourists sharing the sidewalk. "She's going to Colorado." With that, she took the phone away from her ear, jumping and dancing in a circle, thrilled because she knew how her sister felt.

"Get us a seat," she yelled at Andrew, too excited to sit down and now suspecting there was something to the other message. "I'm going to find the magazine. I'll be back in a minute"

Rachael hurried through town until she came across a small grocery store. Inside she found a rack of outdated U.S. newspapers and a scattering of magazines, but not what she was seeking. She walked another two blocks, searching for any shop that might carry the periodical. Almost passing the small alley, Rachael quickly glanced down the narrow street. A door mounted flush into the perfectly flat, white wall had been propped open by a rack of newspapers. She turned and rushed to the shop, entering it completely out of breath. A female clerk sat behind a small counter and watched as Rachael quickly located the magazines. She scanned them once, then again more carefully, but found nothing. The third time through was even more deliberate but produced the same result. Dejected, Rachael began walking out of the store, lifting her head to a cool breeze produced from a small fan behind the clerk. That is when she saw it; the girl's copy of *People* sat open on the counter. "May I buy that?" she asked breathlessly.

"This?" The girl lifted the tattered magazine.

"Yes, please." Rachael said, her face carrying a look of desperation.

Not wanting to wait or to be denied, Rachael pulled a twenty-dollar bill from her pocket. The young girl studied it and looked back to Rachael before taking the bill and handing the magazine over.

Outside, Rachael stood with her back against the wall, quickly opening to page twenty-seven. At first, she did not recognize Rick, who was wearing a three-piece designer suit instead of being dressed for the river. Page twenty-seven contained the pictures of six men, common in that they were all handsome. At the top of his photo was the number sixteen. Rachael turned two pages back, finding the title of the section, "America's Most Eligible Bachelors." Turning back quickly, she read the caption beneath his photo. It talked briefly about the loss of his wife, apparently indicating enough time had passed that it was acceptable to use him to sell copies of the magazine. It continued, spitting out facts about his age, his company, and finally the reason that separated him from thousands of other attractive men, estimating his net worth to be $230,000,000.

Rachael's jaw dropped, laughing aloud as she thought of Sarah's message and knowing that she had absolutely no idea about any of this.

~~~~~

At 9:10 in the morning, more than an hour after the last employee arrived at work, Greg Watkins stepped out of the elevator with the morning paper and a cup of coffee in hand. The office mood was about to shift, as it did every morning at this time when he made his late entrance. "Good morning, Mr. Watkins," came from the receptionist, with a façade reserved for a man she absolutely detested. He did not reply.

"Your mail, sir," she said customarily, handing him a small stack of letters and a curious manila envelope with no return address. It was interesting, as the address had been handwritten and the postage paid with two rows of stamps. He noticed this too, curiously turning it over and reviewing the envelope as he entered his office. Closing his door, he took a seat at his desk and immediately put the other mail down, inspecting the outside of the envelope and trying to decide what it might be.

Greg Watkins slid the paper opener along the width of the envelope, before slowly placing it on his desk and reaching in to extract the contents. "What the fuck is this?" he mumbled, finding a copy of *People* magazine inside. He reviewed the cover intently, at first seeing nothing, then catching the edge of a small red paper inserted in the pages. He opened to page twenty-seven, studying it until his eyes bulged at the recognition of Rick Wheeler. Greg felt his face become flush—he was already angry before reading a single word.

The entire office heard him yell just ahead of the unmistakable sound of shattering glass. His office door flung open as he charged out. "Two hundred and thirty fucking million dollars," his secretary heard him say as he bullied past her.

Once he was gone, she immediately hurried into his office as the others began gathering outside. The glass covering his custom-built oak desk was shattered, a victim to the stabbing blow of the letter opener. On its way to the glass, it had pierced the small red paper. The secretary removed the opener, then the paper, carefully reconstructing it until she could read the message, "Poor, poor, Sarah."

The secretary and everyone else in the office knew Sarah as well as the story of what their boss had done. She was not sure what this all had to do with Sarah but was certain that someone had finally provided a long overdue lesson to the man they all detested. She turned to the crowd, unable and unwilling to hide her joy, "We need to get a cake."

~~~~~

Nancy tilted her sun hat back, gazing into the warm sun as she thought. The envelope should arrive today, she estimated. It was time for a margarita.

~~~~~

The grasses were still long, but more dry and yellow than they had been weeks earlier. Sarah watched intently as the first field came into site, looking for the three large rocks that she had remembered being so prominent. The fresh smell of pine trees and the grasses now surrounded her, demanding that she again experience the splendor of this place.

The driver was familiar—the same man with a long ponytail. He was friendly; their conversation helping to keep her pulse at a normal rate that the thoughts of Rick could not. The others on the plane, Christine and the two pilots, would arrive after the jet ramped down and was stored properly.

Huff's cabin first appeared with broken flickers of the sun's refection off the old tin roof. Then, as they neared, the old brown logs of the walls revealed themselves. Closer yet, Sarah saw that the yard was filled with people. She immediately recognized Huff and Maria as the car rolled to a stop. Huff's voice came first and was unmistakable, "Sarah, Sarah," he said in a quick repetition, reminding her of her first morning on the ranch.

"Huff," she responded, stepping away from the car and through the small gate. They met with a hug reserved for good friends. "How have you been?"

"Very good, Sarah. I've been very good. It's been another busy summer at the ranch," he replied before quickly yielding to Maria.

"Sarah. You come see me," she insisted. We've been excited since hearing you were coming. It's so nice to see you again." As they hugged, Maria whispered into Sarah's ear, "How have your colors been?" Sarah just nodded. "Come, we're just having lunch now," Maria said, waving Sarah toward the center of the yard and the old picnic table.

Sarah searched for Rick as she walked, glad that the energy of the greetings had distracted her nerves. She did not see him anywhere. A handsome man with dark hair and Maria's skin approached. Sarah recognized him from the pictures. "You must be Mateo."

"Hi, Sarah." he said, taking her hand and shaking it softly. "I've heard a lot about you." He immediately recalled the conversation with Rick, seeing that neither it, nor any other description, would appropriately describe her.

"This is Janet, my wife."

The Colors of Blue

"Sarah, it's nice to meet you." Janet was conscious that Sarah had quickly become the center of attention. Sympathetic to this pressure, she tried to help, "Nothing like being overwhelmed ten seconds out of the car?"

"No, it's fine. I would expect nothing different from this family."

Huff paid the driver, bringing Sarah's bags to the lawn. "We'll get these down to the lodge," he told her.

"Are you hungry, honey?" Maria asked.

Sarah had not eaten all day, but her nerves removed any desire. "No, thank you."

Huff's turn, "How was your trip?"

"It was great. There can't be a more pleasant way to fly," she replied, assuming that they knew about the jet. As she spoke, the two boys drifted over from the edge of the yard, one sitting down next to Mateo's feet and the other hugging his mother's leg. Both of the boys' hair looked as if they had played all day, fallen asleep, and awakened to begin where they had left off.

"These are our boys, George and Mathew."

Sarah instinctively kneeled. "Hello, it's nice to meet you. I'm Sarah."

The youngest, Mathew, stared at Sarah. "Your eyes are very green."

Mathew's opening built confidence in George, "My Papi says you're beautiful on the inside."

Sarah smiled, looking at Huff as she whispered to George, "Tell your Papi I think he's beautiful on the inside, too." Huff returned the smile.

Mathew was not to be outdone. "I think you're beautiful on the outside." A wide grin, missing several teeth, accompanied his words.

"Oh, God," Janet belted. "Can you tell who that kid's father is?" Mateo lifted his eyebrows, giving Mathew thumbs up.

It was George's turn again, "Papi is going to take us down to the river to catch snakes."

Sarah and Janet caught eyes. "I hope I'm not invited on that expedition."

"I'm with you," Janet replied.

Mateo chimed in. "Rick is fishing at the top of the ranch. He's hoping you'll come up to meet him."

"I'd like that," she responded as her heart jumped, wondering exactly how apparent her thrill was to them.

"The horses are saddled; we can go now if you're sure you don't want something to eat?"

Sarah had taken a drink of water, waiting for it to go down before answering, "I'm good. Let's go."

"We're going to have a big dinner at the lodge tonight, after the others get here. Sarah, you tell Rick he'll be in my doghouse if you get there later than 7:00." Maria's face was straight, but Sarah sensed her teasing.

"Don't worry; if he makes us late, I'll let him have it."

"Good," Maria said, taking a step forward, "We girls need to stick together."

~~~~~

Maggie carried Sarah along the same trail they had taken on her last visit, again following Akilah, but this time guided by Mateo. She was already comfortable with Maggie, allowing her to enjoy the splendors of the valley. Mateo was comfortable on his horse too, but not nearly as much of a natural as his father had been.

Like the first time, the horses traveled side-by-side when the trail allowed, providing Mateo and Sarah a chance to get to know one another. Mateo was gentle like his father, his eyes glistening when he spoke about Janet and their children.

The horses climbed toward the top of the red cliffs, passing the spot where she had told Huff about her colors. Dropping down the other side, Sarah turned back to see the rock where she and Huff had watched Rick fishing. During the last month, Sarah had remembered the moment he climbed out of the river and spread his arms into the rain. He had to have been thinking of Samantha; she was certain.

Sarah's colors came easier in this place, perhaps because of the natural splendor, but also because Rick was near. This thought brought her the unmistakable yet indescribable feeling that came when the colors were close. This time, it also made her heart beat faster.

Mateo began looking for Rick where they had left each other earlier in the day. With each turn, he studied the river. Where trees obscured the water, they left the trail to see if they could find him. As they rode and searched, their conversation continued. "He left a book for me," Sarah offered, wondering if Mateo knew anything about the curious compilation of poetry.

Mateo recognized the book almost immediately. "It's blue and looks like it's about a hundred years old?"

"Yes, exactly. Very well used," Sarah said, excited that Mateo might offer something to answer her questions. "There are little notes written on many of the pages?"

Mateo did not look at Sarah. He sat tall on Akilah, somewhat surprised that Rick allowed the book out of his possession. "It was his mother's."

"The notes were hers?"

"Yes. She would read and jot the notes as they came to her. Have you read many of the poems?"

Sarah was not sure she wanted to answer his question. The truth was that in the last month she had read every page several times, already having memorized many of the poems that touched her. More than that, she had read the small notes his mother had scribed, quietly sitting by herself and thinking about their meaning. "I've read every page; I think it's my favorite book."

She remembered one of the notes, reciting it exactly to Mateo. "Life presents only a few precious opportunities to be measured in the mirror, be sure to be proud of what you see."

Again, they rode along in silence, both considering. "I never knew his mother, but from what I gather, he is very much like her. What you just read ... what she wrote, that's Rick." He thought for a second longer, "Yeah, that's him. She must have been a strong lady."

Sarah felt an opportunity, "Why do you think he left the book for me? I mean, it must be so important, and well, we only spent a few days together."

If Mateo had not met Sarah or spoken to Rick about her, he would not know how to answer this question. He had watched his best friend struggle after Samantha's death, getting better with time, yet never looking for anyone to come into his empty world. Before meeting Sarah, Mateo had wondered how his friend could suddenly be so interested in someone after so much time without even a suggestion of looking. Now however, he knew exactly how to answer Sarah's question, "Tell me where you keep the book."

"What do you mean?"

"At home, in New York, where do you keep it?" he clarified.

She was curious, "I keep it in my closet, on a shelf."

"By itself, collecting dust?" he said with a smile.

"No, in a box," she replied, answering only the question he had asked, because she now realized where he was going.

"Just an old box?"

Sarah turned, looking at him as she gave in. "It's a small shoebox. It's light blue. I holds items that remind me of things."

"Oh, special things. Things that you care about?" he persisted mischievously.

"Okay, I see where you are going." She held, letting a moment pass to strengthen her point. "You're a lot like your dad, you know?" Mateo only laughed and grinned.

Mateo got more serious. "Rick would have never left the book with you unless he was sure it would be cared for and appreciated. My point is that he was right, perhaps knowing more about you than you might have thought."

"I'd like to think you're right. As I've read it, it just seems so valuable. I had hoped he knew I would care for it."

Mateo gently pulled Akilah's reins to the left. The horse responded, now following the overgrown suggestion of a trail down toward the river. Maggie followed without the need for Sarah to direct her. "There was something else his mother wrote," she said. "'If you're going to love, be sure to love with every ounce of your heart.'"

The horses carried them over the last drop before flattening out near the river. Mateo thought he understood what Sarah wanted, saying, "I've only ever known him to love one person," he said, now pulling up for Akilah to stop. He swung his right leg down to the ground. Off the horse, Mateo came over to help Sarah off. Holding her hand as she dismounted, he added, "That's exactly how he loved Sam, with every ounce of his heart."

Sarah leaned in and hugged Mateo. "He's lucky to have you as a friend."

"There's a small trail on the other side of that boulder, along the river. About one hundred yards up, the river will bend west. At the turn, there's a small ridge sitting above the river. Rick will be there."

"Mateo."

"Yes."

"I'll be careful with him. I know Samantha is his to bring to me, if it feels right. I am, and I will be, a good friend."

"I know that, Sarah. And he knows that too."

Mateo mounted his horse again, taking Maggie's reins in his right hand. He turned both horses as Sarah started toward the path. "Don't forget—my mother is cooking tonight. Make sure you keep him on time."

"Done," she replied, starting toward the trail.

"Sarah," Mateo yelled, stopping her before she was too far away. "Be exactly who you are. That's all he is hoping."

"Thank you."

~~~~~

Rick woke from his dream, coming back up until he rested on both knees. "The chain," he said aloud, still remembering the dream. Sam had given him the ranch because she knew these mountains helped him with his mother's death. She had hoped they would help him again with her own. He now knew Sam had done something else for him, leaving the chain to help with the most difficult question, one he would face without her. She had hoped that the day would come when there would be someone else in his life. Samantha loved him. She had to let him know that it was okay. More than that, she had to let him know that it was something she wanted and hoped would happen. Nevertheless, Sam also had seen that he was not ready for that conversation while she was alive. She knew that he would not be ready and could not fathom such a thing until the time was right. Therefore, she had given him the chain, and now he understood why.

He opened his pack, finding the plastic bag where he always carried his wallet. Unfolding the leather, his finger slipped deep into one of the slots until it felt the cool gold coiled at the bottom. Pulling it free, it hung straight, catching a thin beam of sunlight. As it swung gently back and forth, it drifted into and out of the light, reflecting on the ring he wore on his left hand.

It did not slip easily from the finger, having occupied the place for so long. Removing it, Rick turned it around and over in his hand, thinking of how Sam knew that someday he would reach this place, somehow providing the answer in the exact moment he asked. He threaded the chain through the ring, bringing it around his neck and clasping it carefully.

~~~~~

The sound was unmistakable, coming from the last incline in the trail before reaching the Deck. Rick turned, listening intently to confirm what he heard. There was a brief silence before he heard the noise again, now certain that someone was just about to reach the Deck. Sarah. It had to be Sarah, he knew. Taking one-step toward the trail, he froze, watching as she came over the crest.

He had been thinking of this exact moment and everything he would say, but it all failed him now. His throat welled and his breath became heavy, leaving it almost impossible to talk or even think straight. He could only watch and wait for everything he had wanted since the very first time he had met her.

As she approached, Sarah's head was down, causing her to miss him standing just yards away. However, as she lifted it, he was there; her eyes closed for a long second as the first color of blue moved through the darkness.

She had run through this moment many times, picturing how they would begin teasing and laughing, as they had before. She would be cautious, holding her feelings back in case he did not want the same thing, waiting carefully to tell him about the colors of blue that had started when they met.

Now, Sarah was stuck too—not a word was possible. Each had a need for the other, and in that still moment, both realized that they had been protecting themselves with walls built in case they never saw the other again. With that fear gone, they were both disarmed and ready.

Rick took the first step, knowing that waiting for the right words to find their way out was futile, at least until she was in his arms. She was ready too, unable to stand still when he started toward her. The distance between them evaporated, Rick lifting Sarah off her feet as they met. They had both waited so long for the same thing, their lips meeting as he turned her in slow circles underneath the old trees.

He lowered their bodies to the needle-covered floor, Sarah's head coming to rest as her dark curls spread over his arm. Pulling away from their kiss, he needed to see the energy behind her beautiful green eyes. However, they were closed, the colors of blue showing her true love for the first time in her life.

As Rick watched Sarah, the lowest branch of one of the great old trees pulled him away. His eyes climbed the tree, limb by limb, until he reached the very top. Now, beyond the trees, he stopped, finding the sky the most striking and enchanting color of blue he had seen in years.

The Colors of Blue.

The Colors of Blue

Authors Note: *The Tres Piedras Ranch is a real place. I have taken some great liberties in my description of Huff's cabin and the lodge, but they too exist, much as they were originally constructed. However, there is no author living or that has ever lived that can articulate the true beauty of this river, the valley and all that surrounds it. I am certain it is the most beautiful place on this earth. I can only hope that I have given the reader some feel of this spectacular place.*

I was shown the ranch for the first time when I was in the fifth grade, growing up in Durango, Colorado. As luck would have it, the owners moved from Denver and our families became true friends. Ann Willard was my mother's good companion and tennis partners and Steve, her son, remains one of my best friends to this day. When I constructed Rick's friend, Mateo, I thought about the many days that Steve and I have spent on the river together and how, just by watching him fish, I can see and understand a true joy.

Several years ago, we were lucky enough to join the Willard's as owners of the Tres Priedras Ranch. Our families and friends have spent countless hours enjoying all aspects of this magnificent place. The times that I have spent here have provided long hours of reflection and allowed me to create the fictional stories of love and loss that touch upon the realities of life.

Encouragement is the most essential nutrient for a writer. For this, I will be forever thankful to Ann Willard and Charleen McCulloch, the two of you have pushed a rough manuscript to completion and publication. Thank you for your kind words! There are many others that I cannot hope to remember in one sitting or contain in this brief space. I thank each of you that have helped by reading, providing your opinions and simply being interested enough to ask about The Colors of Blue.

Most of all, I'd like to thank my wife, Jennifer. She has suffered through the lack of confidence that every first time writer must feel. I sat anxiously in the living room, laid in our bed, and shared time at coffee shops as she drug her way through the disaster of the first manuscript. I watched as she laughed, when I wanted the audience to laugh, and cry when that was my intention for the reader. Finally, she finished as we sat on the front porch at our home in Boulder. She closed the book, turned to me and said, "It's a beautiful story," and I knew she meant it! Because of her, I am on the eve of my first publication. Thank you, Jen.

Finally, thank you if you have reached this last paragraph as it likely means that you have read my story. I sincerely hope that you enjoyed the ride. To see pictures of the ranch, information about me, or to send me a message, please visit the web site www.thecolorsofblue.com. The greatest gift you can give me is to follow the link in the web site and encourage others to read the book. Digital publishing is a grass roots efforts and every reader is part of the community. I hope you will join mine! Thank you!